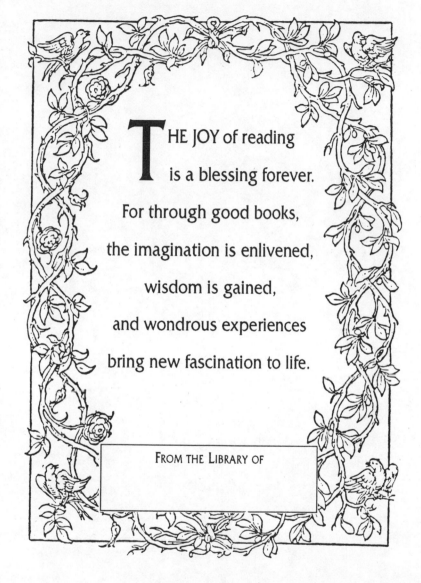

T HE JOY of reading
is a blessing forever.
For through good books,
the imagination is enlivened,
wisdom is gained,
and wondrous experiences
bring new fascination to life.

FROM THE LIBRARY OF

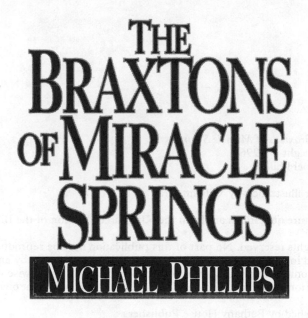

THE BRAXTONS OF MIRACLE SPRINGS

MICHAEL PHILLIPS

BETHANY HOUSE PUBLISHERS
MINNEAPOLIS, MINNESOTA 55438

Published by Bethany House Publishers
A Ministry of Bethany Fellowship, Inc.
11300 Hampshire Avenue South
Minneapolis, Minnesota 55438

Printed in the United States of America.

Library of Congress Cataloging-in-Publication Data

Phillips, Michael R., 1946–
    The Braxtons of Miracle Springs / Michael Phillips.
       p. cm. — (The journals of Corrie & Christopher ; 1)
    ISBN 1–55661–904–9 (cloth; alk. paper)
    ISBN 1–55661–635–X (paperback; alk. paper)
    I. Title. II. Series: Phillips, Michael R., 1946–   Journals of
Corrie & Christopher ; 1.
PS3566.H492B7   1996
813'.54—dc20   96–25227
                                           CIP

To girls and young women everywhere
who, like Corrie,
have committed themselves to truth,
to personal virtue,
and to placing what God wants as preeminent in their lives.
It is my prayer that the Lord Jesus will be your
faithful life-companion,
and that you will, like Corrie, discover character and strength
and the meaning of life within yourself,
and thus will come to know the depths of true womanhood.

CONTENTS

The Hollister Farm

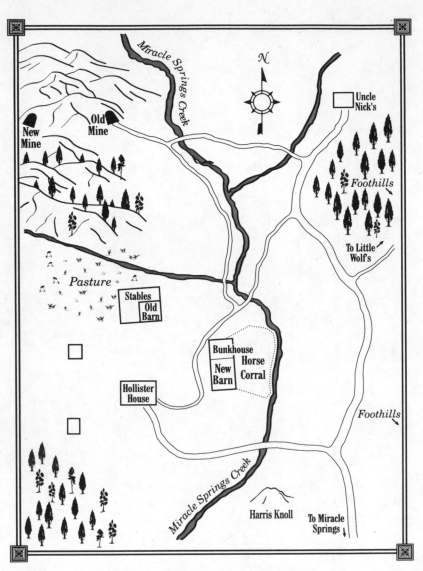

The Hollister Claim

CHAPTER 1

HOW WE WOUND UP IN CALIFORNIA

For so many years I never imagined I would be married at all.

My ma had prepared me for being single—not in so many words, but I came to understand well enough—by letting me know I didn't have as fetching a face as most girls.

When I was older, people told me I was pretty. But when you grow up thinking of yourself as plain, nothing anyone says makes you think much differently.

Ma had packed us up and brought us from New York out to California by wagon train in 1852 to find our uncle Nick Belle, her brother. But Ma caught a fever and died on the way, and my brothers and sisters and I arrived in California alone. I was the oldest, but I was only fifteen at the time.

My name was Corrie Belle Hollister then. The *Corrie* is short for Cornelia.

We found our uncle. But that wasn't all—we found our Pa too, who we thought was dead. Pa's name is Drummond Hollister.

Pa and Uncle Nick had gotten themselves mixed up with some outlaws back East when we kids were pretty young. They'd wound up in jail and then broken out and come west to California in the 1840s to try to get rid of bad men and lawmen and old warrants against them all at once. The gold drew them west too.

But it turned out that they didn't escape their problems at all. Instead, the trouble just followed them west like we did. We hadn't seen either of them or even gotten a letter for years. Ma'd heard that Pa was dead.

11

12

Not only was he not dead, we later found out that he was innocent of most of the terrible things the Catskill Gang—that's what the outlaws they knew called themselves—had done. There had been a robbery and some shootings, but Pa and Uncle Nick didn't kill anyone. When they took off for California, some of the gang thought they had the money from the robbery. So several of them followed Pa and Uncle Nick out West and caused them all kinds of trouble. One such man was Buck Krebbs, who is dead now.

Later, when my brother Zack was riding for the Pony Express in the Utah-Nevada territory,* he ran into another man called Demming who was still following Pa after all these years because he thought Pa had the loot from the Catskill Gang robbery too.

Zack had some adventures of his own with Demming out there in the desert, and by the time he was back home in Miracle Springs, California—that's where we live—the man swore he'd kill Zack *and* Pa, and that he wouldn't stop looking till he found them.

Of course, I had no way of knowing it, but the happiest event of my life, my wedding, would be the very thing that gave Demming the chance to do just that—find Pa and Zack.

We were all in danger, though none of us realized it!

But I am getting ahead of myself. After we got to California and found Pa, the little gold-mining town of Miracle Springs became our home. We had a pretty big gold strike on our claim, Pa married a businesslady in town, a widow by the name of Almeda Parrish, and I started writing newspaper articles for the San Francisco *Alta*.

As I got older, and still figuring I'd never get married, I began to have some adventures of my own. I don't suppose I was always wise in some of the things I did, running around the state—and even the whole country!—pursuing newspaper stories, and getting myself in some scary situations. But the Lord protected me, and I had some pretty exciting experiences that I wrote about as a result.

Because of my writing, I got a little involved in politics. So did Pa. He became mayor of Miracle Springs in 1856, and then later served for a while in the California assembly in Sacramento. Both

*The story of Zack's adventures is told in *Grayfox*, a companion volume to The Journals of Corrie Belle Hollister, published by Bethany House Publishers.

the politics and my writing led me back to the eastern part of the United States during the War between the States in the 1860s when I was in my late twenties. I met President Lincoln before his assassination.

I spent two years in the East, writing articles about the war and working for the Sanitary Commission, and near the end of the war I was shot and wounded, though not from a war battle, outside Richmond, Virginia.

I fell off my horse unconscious. And I would certainly have died if a man hadn't happened along. (Well, he didn't just *happen* along—I don't believe anything just "happens." The Lord sent him to help me.) He found me lying there beside the road, took me back to the ranch where he was foreman, and cared for me until I recovered.

That man's name was Christopher Braxton.

It wasn't too much longer after I was up and out of bed and feeling better before Christopher and I realized we were falling in love with each other. The very thing I thought would never happen to me . . . it did!

Christopher had wanted to be a pastor and had been one too for a short time, although he wasn't anymore. He was such a deep spiritual man who saw God's principles of truth in everything. I had been a Christian for as long as I could remember and had been trying to walk closer to God ever since I was about sixteen. But knowing Christopher helped my faith in God grow more than anything else ever had.

I can't think of anything better for a girl or young lady to say about a man she wants (or hopes!) to marry than that—that he helps you believe and trust in God more than you can by yourself. What greater thing could a man and woman do for each other than that?

I suppose some people would think someone like Christopher would be "too good" to be much fun. All I know is that, now that I know him as I do, I would never even think of marrying a man who wasn't trying with everything in him to be good, to be all God wanted him to be. Christopher is the truest man I have ever known, and I know there are many men in the world like him, even though sometimes you have to wait a long time to find them. I am *so* glad

I waited for Christopher and didn't get married when I was younger to a man named Cal Burton, who came very close to sweeping me off my feet. But that is another story!

Besides, because Christopher is true, he is fun too. And it goes without saying that I think he's handsome—with those light blue eyes and strong shoulders and that wonderful thick brown hair. I love his voice, which is strong and gentle. I love all of him so much!

Some people might say I love Christopher *too* much and therefore don't see his faults. Well, if that's true, I'm not going to worry about it. I know Christopher has just as many faults as anyone else, including me. But I figure when God wants Christopher to take care of any of them, *he'll* let him know better than I ever could.

After I had recovered completely from my wound and the war was over, I returned to Miracle Springs. Christopher followed a while later to ask Pa if he could marry me. That was about a year and a half ago.

Pa was nearly speechless after what Christopher said next. "But I don't want your answer for a year, Mr. Hollister," he said. "I would like to work for you for the next twelve months so that you can find out what kind of a man I am. *After* that time, you will better be able to say whether you think Corrie and I are right for each other and ought to be married. Then you can give me your answer."

Well, Christopher *did* work with Pa for a year, first around the farm, then as a partner digging for gold in our new mine. He lived on our property, in the bunkhouse that was part of our new barn, and he ate his meals with us. Christopher called it an "apprentice-ship engagement." After that, Pa thought even more of him than he had at first. He told Christopher he'd be proud to give him my hand in marriage.

CHAPTER 2

HONEYMOON

I quit being just Corrie Belle Hollister and became Corrie Belle Hollister *Braxton* a week and a half after my thirtieth birthday. Our wedding took place in Miracle Springs on April 3, 1867.

We left that same afternoon for a week's honeymoon in Sacramento.

I don't know what most young women think about right after they're married. I suppose there's lots of things about it that are just too private and personal to talk about to anyone—things you want to keep to yourself and treasure inside.

I had lots of those thoughts. The special feeling of knowing a man loved me, loved every bit of me, and would care for me for the rest of my life. That's a quiet kind of good feeling that makes you warm inside. It made me feel safe all over, inside and out. It was like a whole lot of questions were answered all at once—well, not answered so much as the questions just faded away. I felt protected, too, in a way I never had before. It was a little like when we found Pa. But finding Pa and Uncle Nick after all those years had brought out more questions than answers.

I guess it was also kind of like when Pa married Almeda and Uncle Nick married Aunt Katie, and we had a family again with all the parts in place. But by then I was older and had so many questions about my own future and what God might want me to do in my life and with my writing.

We stayed at a boardinghouse in Sacramento, but even there I felt at home because I was with Christopher. The sense I had had

15

leading up to our marriage—that my heart had found its true home—only got stronger afterward. It felt so right to be together. We had been through so much and had learned really to trust each other. Christopher had become the best friend I'd ever had since Almeda.

I think what was most glorious of all about those first days alone with Christopher was not any of those personal things, but the chance to be with him all the time, twenty-four hours a day. It was so wonderful to be able to talk and share *all the time*, without interruptions—even all night long.

Oh, how we talked!

As much as we'd talked about things before, you'd think we'd have run out of things to say. But that first night we spent together after the wedding, it was as if we hadn't seen each other in five years!

We just talked all night long. I don't think we got more than an hour or two of sleep. It was nothing short of wonderful communicating so deeply and so continuously with someone you loved more than anyone in the world and that you knew loved you just as much.

There's no possible way to describe what a good feeling that was. In fact, since I *can't* describe it, I'm going to let Christopher tell you what *he* thinks!

I don't know why Corrie imagines I can explain our communication any better than she can. This is *her* book, not mine, although she is very kind to include my name on it along with hers. She insists, now that we are married, that we will do everything together. She is Corrie *Braxton* now, she keeps reminding me, no longer Corrie Hollister, and I must confess to a surge of joy and thankfulness at the thought.

Nevertheless, as you well know, it is my Corrie who is the experienced writer, not I. Yes, I have written sermons in years past, when I was in the ministry. (Sometimes I fear the sermonic voice creeps too readily into my daily discourse!) Over the years, moreover, I have been a faithful companion to my journal, as Corrie has been to hers. And yet a writer I am not—far from it. If Corrie asks what I think I shall tell her as honestly as I can. But in the main I shall leave the writing to my very able bride.

Even if I do not espouse writing as a calling, however (and at this point I confess to some confusion over what is my true calling, other than to walk ever onward as a follower of Christ), I do value communication. I have always tried to be honest and forthright in my words and my deeds. I attempted to bring those qualities to my pulpit, and I have tried to bring them to bear in my relationships as well. Therefore my heart resonates with Corrie's when she describes the wonderful feeling of communicating continuously with someone deeply loved.

I thought Corrie and I knew one another quite well before our wedding, and perhaps we did. But during our week together in Sacramento, we seemed to become newly acquainted with one another once more. Each of us discovered so many new things about the other. We talked about everything we had ever experienced, everything we had ever thought, everything we had dreamed of doing in life. We marveled at the way God had prepared us each for the other, even using our individual experiences to enable us to share our hearts and understand one another.

We prayed together as well, ah, what a joy it was to send up to heaven our prayers of thankfulness for the past and anticipation for what lies ahead. Our constant communication was with our heavenly Father as well as with one another.

Can there be anything more vital to the establishment of a strong marriage than such communion—simply *talking* about one's thoughts and feelings and dreams? Can anything be so important as a shared spiritual commitment clearly communicated? Most problems between people, especially husbands and wives, it seems to me, arise because one person is in doubt about what another person is thinking. This leads to misunderstandings and injured sensibilities, and then doubts and suspicions creep in. Surely such problems could be avoided if people simply talked to one another and prayed together more freely, more openly, more graciously.

That, then, seems to be my little sermon for this chapter. I hope you did not mind it too much.

Corrie claims to hang on to my every word when I speak of

matters that are important to me and about which I feel strongly. She insists that she writes down whatever I say. My Corrie, however, is very kind, as well as beautiful and brave and sensible, and she loves me very much. Moreover, as she is the one gifted with the passion for the pen, I will now return it to her. I hope not to intrude again.

No matter what Christopher says, and no matter who does the writing, from now on these will be the journals of *the Braxtons*. The Journals of Corrie Belle Hollister are completed and finished, because never again will I *be* Corrie Belle Hollister. I feel as if both my life and my journals are continuing on and starting over at the same time.

The journals of *the Braxtons* have only just begun—and that is a story that will last the rest of our lives! I am excited to think of all the Lord will do in our years together.

I cried when Christopher finally was able to tell me the whole story about his growing up. You see, he'd lost a mother too, but his story stayed sad whereas mine turned out happy.

Then we both cried and laughed together in our thankfulness to God for how he had saved us for one another and had brought us together.

To think that Christopher had found a wife just lying by the side of the road unconscious, two and a half thousand miles away from her home! If that wasn't God's provision, I don't know what it could be called!

If I had to single out the most meaningful thing about being married, now that I am privileged to call myself a "married lady"— though that sounds so old—I would say it's being able to talk back and forth like that with someone who understands you as completely as anyone is likely to.

Christopher and I promised one another that we would keep talking like we did on our honeymoon—sharing everything and anything we were thinking and feeling and never holding even the tiniest thing back from each other—all the rest of our lives. If two people are communicating, we figured, even if things sometimes come between them, they should also be able to work them out.

CHAPTER 3

UNKNOWN DANGER

In a run-down Sacramento hotel, an evil-looking man set down the newspaper he had been reading and smiled an even more evil-looking grin.

His face was dark and weathered, and a long scar ran from the lower side of his left cheek down over his jawbone onto his neck. The smile was a menacing one, and it made the man look older than he really was because several teeth were missing from his mouth. Those that remained were an ugly yellowish color. The gleam that shone from his eyes could only have been caused by one thing—hate.

How could I be so lucky? the man thought.

This was exactly what he had come to California for, and now he had located them without even having to bribe, threaten, or kill anyone. This was going to be easier than he imagined!

He opened the day's edition of the Sacramento *Bee* once again to the second page where a headline had drawn his attention: HOLLISTER BRAXTON WED IN MIRACLE SPRINGS.

Slowly he read through the article again.

In a ceremony yesterday in the small former mining community of Miracle Springs, former *Alta* reporter Miss Cornelia Belle Hollister was married to Mr. Christopher Braxton of Richmond, Virginia. The bride was given away by her father, Drummond Hollister, former California state assemblyman. Present with Mr. Hollister was his wife, the bride's stepmother, Almeda Parrish

Hollister, the bride's three sisters, Emily Hollister McGee, Rebecca Hollister, and Ruth Hollister, and her two brothers, Zachary Hollister and Thaddeus Hollister. The Reverend Avery Rutledge of Miracle Springs performed the ceremony. The bride wore a blue-lace gown with an embroidered satin belt and carried a white Testament that had belonged to her mother, the late Agatha Belle Hollister. The couple plans to reside in Miracle Springs, which is located in the foothills north of Sacramento.

The man threw the paper down on the floor with a laugh, then rose and left his room for the saloon. This fortuitous news called for a celebration!

CHAPTER 4

OUR FIRST HOME TOGETHER

On our first morning in Sacramento, we came downstairs to breakfast in exuberant spirits, hardly even feeling tired despite how little we had slept.

Then I took Christopher out for a day's tour of California's capital. We hired a buggy and horse and went everywhere. We went inside the new capitol building, and I told Christopher as much as I knew about Pa's time there as state assemblyman. As we rode about the city, I showed him where I'd given speeches for the Sanitary Commission and on behalf of Mr. Lincoln's election.

"You really stood up in front of big crowds of people and gave speeches?" asked Christopher, looking around at the mostly empty park. "And this whole place was full of people?"

"Well, mostly full," I answered.

"There must have been five hundred people listening to you!"

"I didn't say my speeches were any good!" I laughed.

"If people listened, they must have been," rejoined Christopher. "Imagine—my wife . . . a politician and speechmaker! I wish I could have seen it."

The city was growing so fast that much of it was even new to me. I was looking around with eyes even more full of wonder than Christopher! The state continued to grow so fast, and new people poured in almost daily. It wouldn't be much longer before train tracks connected California with the East, and then probably even more people would move west!

By the time afternoon came, we were starting to get real tired.

We decided to postpone the rest of our visit about the city for the next day and went back to the boardinghouse.

When we got back to our room and plopped down in two chairs, we just sat in silence a minute or two, too tired to do anything else. Then I became aware that Christopher was staring at me.

"What?" I said.

"I was just thinking how beautiful you are," he said.

"I am not," I said, laughing.

"I mean it, Corrie—you really are. I know what you've told me, how all your life you thought you weren't. But depth of character has *made* you beautiful, Corrie. It always does. Humility and maturity take over a face and eventually outshine whatever other lacks may once have existed—*if* they existed! You may never see it, Corrie, but you really have become a beautiful woman, as all God's true women do in time."

I couldn't help starting to cry. How fortunate I was for the man God had given me!

"Thank you, Christopher," I said. "You're right; I don't see it. I still see the same Corrie as always when I look in the mirror. But I know you would never say a word that hinted at empty flattery. So I will treasure what you say."

"I mean every word. I love you, Corrie."

"I love you too, Christopher."

The rest of the afternoon and evening we spent reading and writing in our journals—and talking with each other, of course.

We stayed in Sacramento four days, then returned to Miracle Springs.

Just as we had talked all the way down to Sacramento after the wedding, we also talked all the way back home after our honeymoon in the capital was over.

Home!

Everywhere was home now—just wherever the two of us were. But we did need a place to settle in together and to start collecting things of our own.

The subject of Almeda's house in town had come up before the wedding. But the Duncans were still living there, and they didn't have another house to move to. Besides, their rent brought in twenty-five dollars a month for Pa and Almeda.

˙ So in the end Pa and Christopher decided that we could live right there at the property at first—in the bunkhouse Christopher and my brothers had built off the barn.

Tad and Zack were disappointed in one way because they'd enjoyed the independent feeling of staying out there with Christopher. They liked Christopher too, and the three of them had such fun together. But Zack would now get my room in the house, and Tad would have the room the two of them used to share all to himself. So they recovered from their disappointment fairly quickly.

I was excited about the prospect. I'd get to be married and yet stay at home with Pa and Almeda and the family, all at the same time! What could be better than to have the best of both worlds rolled up into one? It didn't bother me one bit not to have a kitchen of my own or even a house of my own. I was so used to sharing and having lots of people around that I wasn't much in the habit of thinking of things as my *own*, anyway. After all, I had a husband to call my own, and that was the greatest part of all! What did I need with a kitchen? Besides, this kitchen had been all mine once— I'd had it practically to myself when we first came to California and found Pa.

So my brothers had moved out of the bunkhouse before the wedding. Christopher and I had begun fixing it up. And that's where we went to live as soon as we returned home from Sacramento. We ate with the rest of the family. Christopher continued to work the mine with Pa and the boys and our old friend Alkali Jones and sometimes Uncle Nick. Life went on pretty much the same as before . . . except that now Christopher and I were married and didn't have to say good night to each other every night.

I suppose a lot of people get married and can't wait to get away from their families. But it was great for Christopher to have a family to call his own after so many years of being alone. My own years in the East during the war had given me plenty of time to get my fill of being on my own, so I was just glad to be close to people I loved.

It was such a happy time!

CHAPTER 5

A VISIT WITH THE RUTLEDGES

During his year in Miracle Springs, Christopher had come to know almost everybody. But as soon as we returned from our honeymoon we wanted to do some visiting around the community.

Christopher had a pastor's heart, even though he was no longer a pastor. He wanted to know everyone, know their problems, know what their families were like, know what the men did, how he could pray for them.

He said that the time would come when we would become more and more occupied with our own lives. Right now we had the time to do some calling and to reach out together. He said that marriage signified a transition point when, after years of thinking mainly about ourselves, it was time for us to look outward and begin sharing life with others—each other first, then other people God might send our way.

"I want us to use every opportunity the Lord gives us to the utmost," he said one day when we were talking about it. "Later on, when we have a family that will keep us more occupied, and when we'll be busy keeping up a home and tending a garden, then we won't be able to spend as much time with people."

So throughout the rest of the spring and summer, usually on Saturday or Sunday, and on some evenings, we'd try to visit someone.

As I said, we both knew most of the people in and around Miracle Springs already, and Christopher had worked for many of the men upon occasion. But it was different now visiting with these people as man and wife. There was a whole new dimension to it. Just as Christopher and I were getting to know each other all over again, so too were we as a couple going through that process with other people, many of whom I'd known half my life.

Now I was a woman rather than the fifteen-year-kid who had wandered into town, orphaned—I thought—and bewildered, with two brothers and two sisters in tow. The sensations were so new and different. Especially the sensation of being *Mrs.* Somebody— *Mrs. Anybody*—for that is surely not something I'd ever expected to be called during all those years!

Everyone seemed glad to see us!

When we'd ride up in the buggy to someone's house, they would greet us and invite us in for tea and something to eat. Overnight it seemed, I wasn't a little girl in anyone's mind, but a grown-up lady. I couldn't help wondering if I'd ever get used to it! Maybe I'd been growing up more during the last few years than I realized. I suppose your personal maturing is not something you can see very clearly through your own eyes as it is happening.

When we called upon Avery and Harriet Rutledge one Saturday morning, Rev. Rutledge was in bed. I thought it strange right off because it was late in the morning, and I knew Rev. Rutledge had always been an early riser.

He got up and came out to visit with us a while along with Harriet and their eight-year-old daughter, Mary. But his face was pale, and you could see he didn't feel very well.

"Avery is still finding himself bothered by last winter's influenza," Harriet explained.

"I don't know what it is with this bout of it," sighed Rev. Rutledge, sinking tiredly into his chair. "It keeps coming back to pester me. I just can't seem to recover completely."

"Then we shall pray for you all the more diligently," said Christopher. "In fact, would you mind if I prayed right now?"

"Certainly not."

"*Father,*" Christopher prayed, "*we do not understand sickness. But we know you are good and love us. We ask that we would allow our infirmities always to draw us closer to you. We all pray now for our dear brother Avery, that your healing and comforting and energy-*

giving hand would be upon him, and that you would restore him to the full vigor of your life within him."

"I appreciate that, Christopher. It is nice to be on the receiving end of prayer, for a change. I am going to enjoy having you around. This is quite a young man you've found for yourself, Corrie," he added, turning to me with what smile he could manage.

"I know that," I said. "I am more grateful to God for him every day!"

"Good. And you just keep thanking God for him, even when he does things to irritate you," rejoined the minister with a glance and smile toward Harriet.

"Surely you never do that to *your* wife," remarked Christopher with a grin.

"Never intentionally. But you know how thickheaded we men can be sometimes."

"Unfortunately, I do," rejoined Christopher seriously, his grin now turning to a knowing nod.

"Those are the times we need patient wives who don't give up on us. I've had one of the best," he said, looking lovingly toward Harriet. "And I know you do too," he added, with another glance and smile toward me. "I've known this young lady for many years, Christopher, and I know of her spiritual fiber probably as well as anyone. So I would say to you, as I did to her—you've found yourself quite a young lady."

"I am more thankful to God than you can imagine," replied Christopher.

"Thank you, Avery," I said, embarrassed but appreciative of his kind words.

"Tell me," the minister went on, "now that you are married and settling in to your new life together, what have you found to be the reaction to your most unusual engagement—if you could call it that—and your decision, Christopher, to work for Corrie's father a year?"

Christopher and I both looked at each other and laughed.

"How do you mean—other people's reactions, or our own?"

"Both."

"Well, speaking for ourselves, if we had it all to do over again,

I don't think we would change a thing. What would you say, Corrie?"

"Just exactly that," I replied. "Christopher is so much a part of the family already, and he and Pa and Almeda are such friends and know each other so well—I can't imagine getting married when all the people involved are still more or less strangers. I agree—I wouldn't change a thing. The longer two people wait, the more they go through together, the better they get to know one another's families . . . the stronger the marriage will be in the end. We're only sorry that Christopher's parents weren't able to be a part of our happiness."

"What about your family, Christopher?"

Christopher and I glanced soberly at one another.

An uncomfortable silence had already begun when Christopher finally answered. "That is a long story, Avery," he said. "I think we'd best save it for another time."

"And what about other people," asked Harriet, trying to bring the conversation back to happier subjects. "How have they reacted?"

Once more Christopher and I looked at each other, and this time we could not help smiling.

"Everybody thought it was the most peculiar thing they'd ever heard of," I said, laughing.

"They thought we were downright crazy would be more accurate!" added Christopher.

Harriet now laughed, too.

"You've got to admit it was a little unusual," she said, "as much as I admired you for it."

"Yes, I know," sighed Christopher. "But the normal and usual ways of doing things don't always lead to the best results. I learned that sad-but-true fact from the church I pastored in Virginia."

"I would say just the opposite is usually the case," added Rev. Rutledge.

"Exactly," rejoined Christopher. "Sometimes you have to do the unusual if you want to make a difference in the world."

"I take it you're such a man," said the minister. "You want to make a difference?"

"You bet I do!"

"How?"

"I want to make a difference in how people think about God and how they live their Christian lives. Surely as a minister you've felt the same thing—"

Rev. Rutledge nodded as Christopher went on.

"—that people are so prone to consider their Christianity just one little aspect of their lives—and perhaps not even the most significant aspect—like a dress shirt they get out and put on once a week, rather than as the dynamic, life-giving, challenging, thought-provoking, obedience-prompting foundation for every breath they breathe twenty-four hours a day."

As Christopher spoke his blue eyes glowed with the passion he felt for his faith. I was reminded all over again why I loved him so much and how thankful I was that the Lord had saved us for one another. To marry a thorough one-hundred-percent Christian like Christopher would have been worth waiting for until I was fifty . . . or even sixty.

"Of course I have felt it," replied Rev. Rutledge. "I've got to confess, however, that early in my ministry I was probably such a one myself."

"I can hardly imagine that of you," said Christopher.

"Thanks in large measure to the challenging honesty of Corrie's father one day at a memorable Christmas dinner," Rev. Rutledge went on, "I was awakened to just the need you speak of."

"I've heard nothing about it."

"Ask Drum to tell you. I've never stopped being thankful to him for it, and we've been fast friends because of it. In the years since, I have indeed experienced that same desire to wake people out of the lethargy I was myself in for a number of years. I suppose it is the fate of the minister to feel that tension. It is clear you still have the heart of a pastor beating within you."

"I do," admitted Christopher. "It is not that I have any future ambitions toward the pulpit, but I do love people and can think of no greater calling than to be involved with them, especially, as I said, in helping them to think of their faith as something more alive and real than many do. I don't miss the preaching, but I do miss the pastoring. That's why I say yes, I want to make a difference in how people think—and why I don't mind doing the unusual once in a while, if it will help."

Christopher paused for a moment

"But more than all that," he went on, "what Corrie and I did in waiting that year, I felt, was the right and wise thing to do. I don't necessarily believe in doing things *just* to be different. Even though I'm still young, I've learned not to rush God. Sometimes it seems that the slower I go, the more I am in his will. I've had to be there to pick up the pieces more times than I have liked for people who have rushed into business moves, marriages, and all manner of things. In my experience, haste usually breeds recklessness. Time is a great counselor."

We continued visiting a while longer. The Rutledges asked us about our plans, and we told them of the living arrangements we'd decided upon.

A brief lull in the conversation came, and Rev. Rutledge gave a little involuntary sigh. He hadn't meant it to be seen, but it was clear he was feeling fatigued from our visit. We stood to excuse ourselves as Harriet glanced toward her ailing husband.

We said our goodbyes to Avery, then Harriet saw us to the door. She put the bravest face on it she could, but as we left, both Christopher and I knew she was concerned.

CHAPTER 6

ANTICIPATION

Almeda and I always had a good time when we worked together in the kitchen. One spring day we were baking bread, and while our hands mixed and kneaded and pounded, we got to laughing and reflecting on the time back in 1853 when she had taken me to San Francisco.

"Oh, I wish I could show Christopher the city," I said, kind of dreamily.

"Why don't you?" said Almeda.

My head shot up. Suddenly it dawned on me that there wasn't any reason I shouldn't.

I mentioned the idea to Christopher the very next time he came down from the mine. He thought a trip to San Francisco sounded like a great idea.

"In fact," he said, "why don't we take the others along with us?"

"Who . . . everyone?" I asked.

"Anyone who wants to go."

"Oh, what fun!" I exclaimed. "Do you really mean it, Christopher?"

"Of course I do."

I was so excited at the prospect! We brought it up at breakfast the very next morning, and before the hour was out, my brothers and sisters and Christopher and I were planning a trip to San Francisco for the first week of May.

Anticipation mounted to such a pitch over the next four weeks that the night before our departure I could hardly sleep. We were all up by morning's light and bustling around getting dressed and packing our bags. Zack had made arrangements for his friend Laughing Waters and her sister, Shell Flower, to meet us in Sacramento and go to San Francisco with us. Zack had met Laughing Waters, whose father was a chief of the Paiute tribe, while he was riding for the Pony Express in the Nevada territory back in 1861. Now she and Shell Flower were living in California. And Zack was so anxious to get to Sacramento that he was up before all the rest of us!

Almeda prepared a big breakfast for our send-off. She and Pa were in lively spirits, joking and laughing. I couldn't tell if they wished they were going or were looking forward to being alone—alone, that is, with our half-sister Ruth, who was now ten, with energy for two or three girls her size.

"You think you can handle this unruly mob, Christopher?" Pa asked as he buttered himself a biscuit.

"I don't know, Drum," laughed Christopher. "Being still a newcomer to the West and a stranger to San Francisco, I intend to let the others lead the way."

"I reckon Corrie and Zack'll keep you outta trouble."

"Time was when Corrie practically lived in San Francisco," put in Almeda, as she poured out a round of coffee into several empty cups.

"I wouldn't say that," I protested. "Although I suppose I did make quite a few trips back and forth."

"City's changing fast, Corrie," added Pa. "California's still growing. People are still coming here even though the gold's slowed up. How long's it been since you was in the city?"

"Hmm," I said, "let me see. It must have been just before I went back East during the war . . . probably sometime in 1863."

"Four years—yep, I'd say you'll likely see plenty you don't recognize."

"Please, can I go too, Ma?" said Ruth in a pleading voice to Almeda.

"I'm sorry, dear—this trip is only for the grown-ups. We'll take you when you're older."

"You and Pa aren't going," objected Ruth, "and you're the only grown-ups. The others are my brothers and sisters. Well," she added looking around, "maybe *Christopher's* a grown-up."

Everyone at the table laughed.

"How does that make you feel, Christopher," asked Pa, "to be thrown in along with me?"

"I suppose in a youngster's eyes, the years between us aren't so many."

"Twenty," added Pa, who was fifty-two at the time. It hardly seemed possible, but Almeda would be fifty next year herself.

"Only nineteen," corrected Christopher. "There's not *that* much difference in our ages, especially to a ten-year-old."

"You're right—you're practically an old man!" laughed Pa.

"It's for the *young* grown-ups, dear," said Almeda to Ruth, still laughing.

Half an hour later we piled all our bags into the wagon. Pa climbed up in front to take us into Miracle Springs. The waves and goodbyes to Ruth and Almeda, standing by the door, continued until we were out of sight.

The southbound train was due to pull out at 8:43. We were all standing on the platform, waiting impatiently at 8:20. A shrill whistle sounded in the distance about 8:32, followed a minute or two later by sight of the big black steam engine rolling slowly into view.

More handshakes and goodbyes followed, this time with Pa.

We all boarded as mail bags were unloaded and loaded and as the engine took on water. By nine o'clock the five of us were seated together—Christopher and myself, Zack, twenty-eight, Becky, twenty-four, and Tad, twenty-two—chugging south toward Sacramento.

Zack would take us all to meet Laughing Waters and Shell Flower this afternoon. They were both living and working in a large school, and we had been invited to join them for dinner. Then they would join us for our outing to the city.

It turned out later that Laughing Waters' sister changed her mind about going. Even though she had been more a part of the white culture than Laughing Waters, she was more than just a little shy about the adventure we had planned. But there was no way Zack would let Laughing Waters stay behind. He had been looking forward to being with her again even more than visiting San Francisco!

We would all spend the night in the same boardinghouse where Christopher and I had gone for our honeymoon, where we had made arrangements by mail a week ago, and tomorrow morning be off for the city.

CHAPTER 7

SAN FRANCISCO

The train ride from Sacramento was certainly faster than the steamer Almeda and I had taken the first time I came to the city at sixteen in 1853, ferrying across the bay in the fog.

As the line of the Central Pacific was being built eastward through the Sierra Nevada mountains, short lines were being extended in other directions too, like the one that ran north through Miracle Springs. Tracks of the California Pacific now followed the Sacramento River southwest to Vallejo at the northernmost tip of San Francisco Bay, so we were able to make most of the journey by rail. From Vallejo, as before, we ferried across to the city. We arrived in San Francisco early in the afternoon.

We hired a buggy to take us straight to a boardinghouse whose advertisement we had seen in the *Alta*. The two rooms we had written to reserve were waiting for us. It was nice to be able to wash our faces and get some of the travel dust off. As soon as we were all settled—Laughing Waters, Becky, and I all shared one room, Christopher, Zack, and Tad another—everyone was itching to get out and see the city.

Zack and I were the only ones who had even been to San Francisco before, and Zack only once with Pa. By the time we got back out to the street, I had been elected tour guide!

"Come on, Corrie—lead the way!" exclaimed Tad. "Show us the city!"

"Where do you want to go?"

"How should we know?" said Christopher. "I'm just an eastern

34

boy. *You're* the one who knows what to see!"

"Should we walk or hire the buggy again?" The cabdriver who had brought us from the train station was still waiting to see if we might need his services again.

"You decide—whatever you think is best."

Everyone stood looking at me, waiting for me to tell them what we would do next. I thought a few minutes.

"All right," I said, "we'll take a buggy out to the Gate where ships come and go from the Pacific. You've got to see that. It's one of my favorite sights in all the city. Maybe we'll even see one come in! Then we'll come back to the wharf and walk along the harbor and back to downtown."

"Wonderful—let's go!" said Christopher, leading the way to the buggy. We all piled into the two wide seats—it was more comfortable now without all our bags—and I told the driver where to go.

As we went, I asked the man to drive us, as much as I could remember, the same way as when Almeda had first shown me the city fourteen years earlier—first up Telegraph Hill, then up and down the hills all across to the beautiful overlook where the Pacific meets the narrow mouth of the bay.

Pa was right, the city *had* grown. There were new houses and buildings everywhere, and more being built wherever you looked. The number of people had increased some four or five times since the first time I had come here.

When we reached the overlook of the Gate, we stopped and got out. Everyone grew quiet at the magnificence of the sight, which no one but me had seen before. It was so awe-inspiring that it took your breath away. Even though we could hear the wind, it produced an eerie silence that blew right through us.

Down below us the blue waves of the ocean crashed against the rugged shoreline, sending white, frothy spray into the air. Stretching away to our left, rocky cliffs were all we could see, just like those across the opening of the bay opposite us. There were wild-looking cliffs over on the other side, with green trees and shrubbery on top of them. We could hear the barking of seals and the shrill cries of white gulls floating so effortlessly on the winds.

What's over there? I found myself wondering as I gazed across the bay toward the land that lay north of San Francisco. *What is that part of California like?*

"This place is truly stunning," said Christopher, interrupting my thoughts. He put his arm over my shoulder. "I never imagined I'd lay eyes on the Pacific, and now here I am standing on the very western edge of the continent."

A few stray bits of fog swirled in and out amongst the cliffs, briefly obstructing our view of portions of the water, then breaking apart again. *What would this part of the coastline be without fog constantly coming and going?* I thought. It was one of the many things that made San Francisco so unique and beautiful.

Along with the ships! We could see two out in the mouth of the bay not far from us—one entering, the other heading out to sea, both trailing a wake of white water behind them. I could especially see in Tad's eyes that he was enthralled with them. The mere sight could not help but give you a sense of adventure and faraway places, and I was sure that's exactly what my youngest brother was thinking.

Zack stooped down, picked up a rock, and gave it a heave over the edge. It fell short of the water, bouncing off the rocks below. Another soon followed, then a third, and before long the competition began between Zack and Tad and Christopher to see who could throw a stone all the way into the ocean.

Becky and Laughing Waters and I walked slowly along the edge of the promontory, talking quietly and enjoying the sights, while behind us the whoops of the men continued. It was going to be good for Becky and me to have this time with Laughing Waters. She had been very shy about meeting us all. Now it would be just us "young people" for a couple of days, and I could already sense that she was starting to relax. She and Becky already seemed to share a quiet, knowing look between them. They were both quiet observers.

The wind was slightly chilly, but I didn't mind. It felt good to have my hair blowing about.

Fifteen or twenty minutes later we all loaded back up into the cab for the ride to the wharf and harbor.

We got out there, Christopher paid the driver, and then we began our long, leisurely climb back toward the center of the city. All varieties of boats and ships, both for fishing and for passengers, were tied up along the wharf, and Tad wanted to look at every one. Christopher, too, was very interested. Becky and Laughing Waters hardly said a word, but they gazed at everything with wide eyes. None of them had ever seen anything like that place.

Seamen and yachtsmen and sailors of many nationalities walked about. We heard several different languages. Suddenly it felt like we were at the very center of the whole world, and that it was all right here in San Francisco.

"Where's the Barbary Coast, Corrie?" asked Zack.

"Up there ahead, along the waterfront," I answered. "Why?"

"I want to see it."

"Oh, Zack, it's a dreadful place. It's shorter to walk around behind it and miss it altogether."

"I just want to see it, that's all."

I glanced at Christopher.

"All right," he said, "but just keep walking."

"And don't talk to any of the people," I added. "I remember being afraid just to be there."

"You were a girl, and younger besides. Nothing will happen."

I didn't say anything more, remembering back to the fright I'd felt at unexpectedly seeing Buck Krebbs come out of one of the saloons near this very place.

We walked quietly past the saloons and run-down hotels of the famous San Francisco waterfront. It didn't seem so fearsome today as when I'd been here with Almeda. Whether it had changed since the early gold-rush days or whether my growing older made it look different, I don't know. Probably it was both. But the people we did see milling about looked none too nice, and I still wouldn't want to walk alone here at night.

Slowly we continued to move back toward the business district. Christopher was especially interested in the architecture of the city's buildings.

"It's so different from what you see back in the East," he remarked as we walked along. "Look at all the protruding windows and the ornate moldings."

The closer to the heart of the city we got, the more Chinese people we saw, many of them dressed in native clothing and wearing their hair in queues. I could tell Laughing Waters was especially intrigued. I wondered if their presence made her feel more like one of us.

It was almost the dinner hour by the time we arrived back at the boardinghouse, and we were all pretty tired. We didn't go anywhere that evening, but instead we visited with several other of the guests in the sitting room in front of a cheery fire. Most were full-time residents, and we asked them lots of questions about the city.

It had been a long day, and by nine we were ready for a good sound night's sleep.

CHAPTER 8

A CONVERSATION ABOUT DINNER

Most of the following day we spent downtown, walking and touring again. I showed everyone the Oriental Hotel where Almeda and I had stayed. We also walked through the Montgomery Building, which had been so new back then.

Since this would be our last night in the city, we determined to make the best of it, so we planned to go out to a fancy restaurant instead of eating at the boardinghouse.

And no trip to San Francisco would be complete without a visit to the *Alta* to see Mr. Kemble, a visit which we made late that morning.

"Well if it isn't my old friend Corrie Hollister!" boomed Mr. Kemble, jumping up from behind his desk as we entered his office.

"Hello, Mr. Kemble," I said, shaking the editor's hand. "And it's Corrie Braxton now—I would like you to meet my husband, Christopher Braxton from Virginia."

"Your husband! That's right—of course! I remember the invitation several months back. Sorry I couldn't make it. Pleased to meet you, Braxton."

"And I you, Mr. Kemble," replied Christopher. "I've heard quite a lot about you."

"I'm not sure I ought to ask you to explain further!" said Mr. Kemble, with a glance and grin in my direction.

"Mr. Kemble," I said, "I'd like you to meet some of my family that are here as well. You may remember them from when you were

39

out in Miracle Springs. This is my sister Becky."

"I'm happy to meet you, young lady. Are you planning to follow your sister's footsteps into journalism?"

"No, sir, I don't think so," answered Becky.

"My brothers, Tad and Zack," I went on.

"You're the young fellow who had some adventures out Nevada way with the Pony Express and the Paiutes, as I recall," said Mr. Kemble as he shook Zack's hand.

I glanced unconsciously at Laughing Waters and saw a look of nervousness on her face. But the conversation went quickly on.

"That's me."

"MacPherson tells me your writing's almost as good as your sister's."

"Thank you, sir," said Zack, more embarrassed I think than he would otherwise have been because of Laughing Waters being there. "But my sister helped me out some."

"And this," I said finally, "is our friend Laughing Waters, whom Zack met when he was in the Utah-Nevada territory. She is the daughter of a Paiute chief."

"Charmed, young lady," said Mr. Kemble, showing no surprise. "Welcome to San Francisco."

"Thank you," said Laughing Waters shyly as she took the hand he offered.

"Well . . . sit down, all of you. I hope your visit is to tell me you've decided to get back in to journalism, Corrie."

"I'm afraid not. I've only been married about a month."

"What do you do, Braxton?"

"I used to be a minister," replied Christopher. "At present I'm working the mine with Corrie's father and brothers."

"Still trying to coax a few more ounces out of those hills, eh?"

"There's still a big vein there," said Tad. "Pa's sure of it. We just have to find it, that's all."

Everybody laughed.

"That's what they all say!" chided Mr. Kemble.

We chatted a while longer, then Christopher asked Mr. Kemble where would be a good place to go for dinner that evening.

"That depends," he said, "on what you want. If you want the best food in San Francisco, in my opinion it's found at Mary Pleasant's place, but then you'd never get in."

"Why not?" I asked.

"It's a boardinghouse. Once her guests are taken care of, she only has two or three tables available for reservations, and they are hard to come by."

"A boardinghouse has the best food in San Francisco?" said Christopher in surprise.

"Not just any boardinghouse. Mammy Pleasant's a well-enough known lady—a colored lady with more spunk than any ten white women, with what you might call a checkered and not altogether savory past. She was housekeeper and cook for Milton Latham, and that's where she made her mark on this city. You know Latham, don't you, Corrie?"

"I know *of* him," I answered. "I've never met him."

"Well, he knows about you, too. I make sure important people read my newspaper. And so does Mammy Pleasant if I know her. She's as feisty a woman as you are yourself, Corrie Hollister."

"Corrie *Braxton*," I corrected him with a smile. "And what do you mean feisty?" I added.

"I mean just that," rejoined Mr. Kemble with a laugh. "Trying to pass yourself off as a man so I'd give you a job, thinking you were worth a man's pay, running off to cover the war right in the middle of the worst fighting this country's ever seen—if that's not feisty, I don't know what you'd call it. You always set out to do what no one would figure you could."

"That's my Corrie!" chimed in Christopher.

"Now stop that, both of you!" I laughed. "I just do what I feel I ought to do, that's all."

"No matter what the odds are against you, and no matter that you're a woman."

"I still don't know what that's got to do with it."

"I know you don't," replied Mr. Kemble, somewhere about halfway between being serious and still trying to kid me in front of my new husband. "And that's what you never understood—things are different between women and men. I'm not arguing with you, understand, Corrie. I've learned to respect you for what you've done, and there's certainly no doubt that you've been an asset to this paper. All I'm saying is that you never let tradition or custom or the practices of the rest of society stand in your way. Mammy Pleasant is just the same way. You and she'd get along pretty well, I think."

"What did she do like Corrie?" asked Becky, following the conversation with keen interest.

"She took Abraham Lincoln seriously, that's what," replied the editor.

At the sound of the dead president's name, a pang went through my heart. I hadn't thought of him in a while, and suddenly I was remembering all the heart-wrenching events of that April of two years before.

"What did she do?" asked Tad.

"Last year, just a year after the war was over, she flaunted her Negro blood by suing the San Francisco streetcar company. They wouldn't let her on the car because she was colored, so she sued them."

"I don't see anything wrong with that," I said.

"Lincoln may have freed the slaves, but there's still a difference between white and black," he replied, "just like there's a difference between men and women."

Before I could reply further, Zack piped up with what had got us started talking about Mrs. Pleasant in the first place.

"What's all this got to do with us finding a place to eat?" he said.

We all laughed.

"I suppose we did diverge a little from the original question, did we not?" said Mr. Kemble. "I was telling you how Mammy Pleasant started her boardinghouse. Like I said, she went to work for Milton Latham. He was a Virginian like you, Braxton—of Mayflower descent, and one of San Francisco's leading bankers. So when he entertained, everyone in the city came. He often gave lavish dinners on Sundays where all the prominent men could be seen. I was even invited myself a time or two."

"I wish I could have seen it," I said.

"Once Mammy Pleasant was in charge," the editor went on, "she served up the guests a remarkable assortment of jellied meats and stuffed birds and all manner of seafoods and pastries. She was instantly hailed as San Francisco's preeminent cook and only several months later opened her own boardinghouse. The place has been so popular that Mrs. Pleasant can pick and choose her boarders from among hundreds clamoring for rooms under her roof."

"And you say she takes in diners in addition to her own boarders?" asked Christopher. I could tell that his, Tad's, and Zack's mouths were watering at everything Mr. Kemble was saying.

"Only a few. I've only been there once myself."

"Don't you know her?" asked Zack. I could tell he liked the sound of Mammy Pleasant's cooking.

"I've met her. I don't think that qualifies me as a close enough friend to ask a favor."

"You said you thought she read your newspaper," I said.

"Yes?" said the editor, drawing out the word questioningly.

"Maybe you could write something about her, or place an advertisement for her boardinghouse in exchange for her allowing you to bring some guests for dinner with her boarders," I suggested.

Suddenly Mr. Kemble's face lit up.

"I've got an even better idea!" he exclaimed. "If everything I've heard about Mammy Pleasant is true, it is sure to work."

"What?" I asked excitedly.

"You all just be back here at five o'clock. If I've been able to arrange it as I'm hopeful of, we'll all go to dinner together—that is, if you don't mind having a crusty old newspaper editor accompany all you young folks."

"We'd be honored to dine with you, Mr. Kemble," said Christopher, shaking the editor's hand. "We'll be back later this afternoon."

CHAPTER 9

SHOPPING IN THE CITY

That afternoon we spent shopping. Everywhere we walked, all the merchandise booths outside many of the shops did their best to lure us inside, and finally, in store after store, we succumbed.

Christopher bought me a lovely handbag, Tad and Zack both bought themselves leather vests, and Christopher bought himself a Western-style hat.

We all laughed until our sides hurt as he was trying it on, looking in the mirror this way and that with now a funny and now a serious expression.

"What do you think, Corrie?" he asked finally, cocking his head playfully to one side, glancing at me while still keeping one eye on himself in the mirror.

"It's perfect!" put in Tad before I had a chance to answer. "Strap a holster to your side and you'll look like a regular gunslinger!"

"No one would ever look at you and take you for a preacher—that much I can say," I answered.

"Not in a hundred years!" added Zack, laughing pretty hard by now at the sight. "But I like Tad's idea about the gun. That's really what you need now."

"Somehow I don't think it would work," said Christopher. "I'd probably shoot myself in the foot just with it hanging there!"

"That is a good idea, though, Tad," Zack added, with a little more seriousness in his tone than I liked. "Maybe I'll get me a new holster and six-gun."

"Zack!" I exclaimed. "Don't joke about something like that!"

"Who's joking? Sheriff Rafferty wears one. I think it looks kinda good."

"He's the sheriff—it's different for him."

Zack said no more, but I could tell he was still thinking.

"What about you, Becky?" I said, trying to divert the conversation away from the subject of guns.

"There was a pretty white blouse with multicolored lace I saw at the store where you got your bag," she replied.

"Why didn't you try it on?"

"I wasn't sure about it. But I have been thinking about it since."

"Let's go back," I suggested. "I want to see what it looks like on you."

"Not back to the women's store!" moaned Tad.

"How about if we men meet you back here in, say, about an hour," suggested Christopher.

"All right," I said, "but you keep them away from any gun shops," I added, trying to make light of the worry I felt inside.

We split up, and the three of us girls turned around and walked back to Powell Street to the Women's Emporium.

Laughing Waters had been mostly quiet that afternoon. It was such a new experience for her—not only being with us, but being in the city, and shopping like this. Not that we were all that used to it either. This was a once in a lifetime adventure for us, too. But for someone like Laughing Waters, who had spent most of her life either in the desert with her people or at a mission school, walking through stores full of expensive clothes and white people was a tremendously unusual experience. I could tell she felt shy and awkward, yet she was enjoying herself at the same time.

I didn't know whether she had any money. I offered to buy her a blouse while Becky was trying hers on, but she didn't want me to.

Laughing Waters was so beautiful, with such dark, mysterious green eyes. And with the way she was dressed—more or less like the rest of us, with her black hair tucked up under a simple hat, no one would immediately recognize her as an Indian. But I knew she was afraid that someone might.

As we talked throughout the three days we were together,

Laughing Waters had told me how nervous she had been about going with us. It was no secret that Indians were not very highly thought of in white society, and I had seen her glancing around from time to time, wondering if passersby were staring at her. But with Christopher, Zack, and Tad close by—all three tall, strong, and confident young men—I didn't feel nervous in the least.

Besides all that, San Francisco was such a mixed pot of nationalities that Laughing Waters blended in with all the rest.

When we met Christopher, Zack, and Tad an hour later, Zack had a package under his arm. It was all wrapped up in brown paper, but I knew well enough what it was.

I could see that Tad was a little quieter than he had been, but no one said anything about it.

I sure wasn't going to bring up the subject of guns again.

CHAPTER 10

WHAT MR. KEMBLE HAD
BEEN UP TO

It had been a wonderful day!

We'd seen so much and gone all over the city and by late afternoon were nearly exhausted.

I didn't know exactly what Mr. Kemble had intended to do when we'd left him earlier in the day, but we were back at his office at five to find out. From the smile on his face that greeted us, I knew he must have been successful at whatever his scheme was.

"Are you ready?" he said enthusiastically.

"Ready," I repeated, "but you still haven't told us where we're going."

"I thought we decided on it earlier—we're going to Mammy Pleasant's place for dinner!"

The three men in our party gave a cheer.

"How did you manage it?" I asked.

"Never mind," interrupted Mr. Kemble. "All I had to say was that Corrie Belle Hollister—excuse me, I mean Corrie Braxton, though I did have to tell her your maiden name so she would know who I was referring to—in any case, all I had to say was that you and your family would be accompanying me, and Mammy Pleasant immediately invited us all to have dinner at her place . . . as her personal guests."

"My wife—the famous newswoman!" said Christopher.

"I am no such thing!" I protested.

"Oh, but you are, Corrie," added Mr. Kemble. "I could never

47

have secured such an invitation just for myself—but the mention of your name, and that was all it took. Shall we be off?" he added, glancing around first at Christopher, then at the others.

We walked back out to the street, where Mr. Kemble hailed a horse-drawn carriage big enough for all seven of us. As we climbed inside, I was thinking there must be more to the story than he had told us—something about his tone as he explained made me suspicious. But I didn't say anything. On the way I found out the rest of the story.

"Actually," Mr. Kemble said as we bounced slowly along in the carriage, "there is one thing I'm going to have to ask you to do in exchange for this dinner, Corrie."

"I thought so!" I said.

"A minor request," smiled Mr. Kemble. "I knew you'd be happy to do it in order to treat your family to the best meal in San Francisco."

"Do I have any choice?" I asked, pretending to be annoyed. I looked over at Christopher and smiled.

"Not really—not if we want Mammy Pleasant to let us in."

"What is it I have to do?"

"The very thing you enjoy more than anything."

I looked questioningly at Mr. Kemble.

"I told Mammy that you were the best woman newspaper writer in all California and maybe in the whole country, for all I know. I told her that you were just like her—not afraid to stand up for what you think is right. So I said that if she'd serve us dinner, you'd write an article about her boardinghouse and the fine table she serves and that I'd print it in the *Alta*. There, you see, nothing to it."

"You want me to write a restaurant column?" I said, laughing.

"Something kind of like that."

"But you've got reporters who do that all the time. I don't know anything about food."

"You know what you like."

"I reckon so, but—"

"And you do have one thing none of my other writers have."

"What's that?"

"The name *Corrie Hollister*. You'll write about Mammy Pleasant's boardinghouse in a way none of my men could. People will read it, too. I haven't had a word from you in so long that just sight of your byline will grab interest."

"Mr. Kemble!"

"On my honor, I mean every word. Mammy Pleasant knows that, too. That's why she agreed to let us come. Just write it like you were writing about your Aunt Katie and her seedlings from Virginia. Mammy Pleasant's an interesting person. But she's never been written about the way *you'll* do it. You have a special way of observing things in situations that most people can't see. And you have a talent for putting what you see onto the printed page in a most unusual way. That's what makes you a good writer, Corrie."

"Are you trying to flatter me, Mr. Kemble?" I asked, smiling again.

"I'm not above such a ploy from time to time."

"If you keep it up, it may just work!" put in Christopher from the other side of me where he was sitting. "I can tell that Corrie's defenses are weakening."

"Exactly what I hoped to accomplish!" rejoined Mr. Kemble. "I've been trying to get Corrie writing again and back on my staff ever since she returned from the East. I have to tell you, Braxton, your coming along when you did has thrown some complications into my plans for your dear wife."

Christopher laughed.

"I meant every word of what I said, Corrie. You are a skilled writer with a unique way of probing into the insides of what you write about. I hope—now that you are married and that you and this fine husband of yours will be settling down together, and after writing this brief piece about Mammy Pleasant's place—as I said, I hope you will reconsider my former offer."

"I will think and pray about it, Mr. Kemble," I answered.

"We will, however, have to give some thought about what to do concerning your byline. Dropping the *Hollister* may lose some readers."

"I will think about that too."

"That is all I ask. In the meantime, if you are uncomfortable with the arrangement about tonight, I'm sure I can—"

"No," I said. "I'll agree to be a restaurant columnist for one evening. After all you've told us about this place, I don't think anyone would forgive me if I made us turn around now!"

CHAPTER 11

A DINNER TO REMEMBER

Mr. Kemble had not exaggerated about the food nor about Mammy Pleasant herself.

The boardinghouse was a big two-story building. I don't know how many rooms it had or how many people there were living under its roof, but the dining room was full and bustling when we walked in about fifteen minutes before six o'clock.

Mammy Pleasant greeted us at the door. She was a stately-looking Negro woman, beautiful, and dressed very expensively.

"I'm happy to meet you, Mrs. Braxton," she said, shaking my hand up and down in hers. "Mr. Kemble speaks so highly of your writing that I am honored for you to do an article about my home. I certainly hope you find the dinner to your satisfaction."

"Thank you," I replied. "I'm sure we will."

She offered her hand to Christopher. He took it, smiled, but said nothing.

Mammy Pleasant showed us to a table at the far end of the dining room. We sat down and presently two young Negro women began to serve us our dinner.

I wasn't sure I liked the atmosphere of the place. It was dark despite the candles on all the tables, and the decor was too gaudy for my taste with red and black flocked wallpaper, big gold light fixtures, and two or three paintings of women on the walls whose expressions I didn't much care for. The sorts of men scattered about at the tables didn't look or sound like the kind you'd want to spend much time with. It wasn't what you'd call a family restau-

51

rant, and I knew from his face that Christopher felt a little uneasy too. But by the time we sensed that perhaps we'd made a mistake, it was too late. The eight or ten tables about the large room had been mostly filled, and people were already being served the famous food we'd been hearing so much about.

Despite the questionable atmosphere, the meal was absolutely delicious.

We were served savory potatoes, pork roast with fruit compote and gravy, yeast rolls, and chard in a fried egg mixture. All the items on the menu were familiar enough, but each one had a distinctive and different taste. It was obvious Mammy Pleasant's chef knew how to prepare things to enhance rather than diminish their natural flavors. The coffee served with the dessert, too, was strong and flavorful without being bitter. It was the best coffee I think I'd ever tasted.

As we ate, we talked lightly amongst ourselves, but I think we all felt a little bit intimidated by the surroundings. All except Mr. Kemble, that is. He spotted several people with whom he was acquainted and walked over to chat. He was having a great time. He'd been trying his best to find a way inside the place again ever since his first visit!

The rest of us, however, did more staring and watching and listening than we did conversing. I suppose we all felt like country folks around all those fancy-dressed city men. Suddenly I realized that Laughing Waters and Becky and I were the only women seated in the room, although there were fancy-dressed women among the servers.

I didn't know what I'd write about in an article. If I stuck to the food like some restaurant columns I'd read, the assignment wouldn't be too hard, because in all honesty it *was* one of the best meals I'd ever eaten. I didn't know if I'd be able to write very much about a dinner, though. How much time could you take describing something you're just going to stab with your fork, chew up, and swallow?

By the time dessert arrived, Christopher had grown more and more quiet. I could tell he was very uncomfortable.

As we began to eat the apple cobbler, he suddenly stood and excused himself, saying he wasn't feeling too well.

"I just need some fresh air, Corrie," he said to me. "I'm sorry. Please, all of you, go on ahead. I'll be back in a minute or two."

Then he turned and left the room by the front door.

I watched him go, knowing there was more to his departure than not feeling well. For Christopher to turn down apple cobbler was unheard of. And he'd been feeling perfectly fine all day.

I tried to make conversation. I'm glad Mr. Kemble didn't seem to notice, but the others knew something was wrong. The editor, however, was too busy relishing the cobbler.

As my eyes followed Christopher, I unconsciously saw him pass someone on his way out the door. I was watching Christopher so intently I paid almost no attention to the man walking into the dining room as he left. It was only later, as I recalled the scene, that I realized there had been a faint hint of recognition even then.

At the moment, however, I turned back to the table and the cobbler on the plate in front of me.

About three minutes later, suddenly the limp conversation at our table was interrupted with the last voice I ever expected to hear. It had been years, but I knew it instantly.

"Corrie Hollister . . . it *is* you!"

I looked up speechless, my face pale. Mr. Kemble was already shaking the newcomer's hand, while I struggled to find my tongue.

"How's it going, O'Flaridy?" he said. "I heard you were back in town."

"Just got back last month."

"Who you working for?"

Robin smiled. "Let's just say I haven't settled down to any of my options yet."

"Still playing all the angles, eh, O'Flaridy?"

Robin laughed. "I keep busy. I've got some sizable irons in the fire that will make me more money in a week than I made writing for you in two years."

"Maybe so, but confidence games can also get you put behind bars."

"It's nothing so shady as that, Kemble."

"I heard about the trouble you got mixed up in down in Nashville."

"I tell you, I'm strictly on the up and up. But I didn't come here to talk to you; I can see *you* anytime—Corrie," he said, sitting down in Christopher's chair and turning toward me, "what brings you to San Francisco . . . and who are these four friends of yours?"

"Uh . . . this is . . . my sister, and my . . . uh, these are my brothers, and our friend Laughing Waters."

"I'm pleased to meet you all," said Robin in his smoothest and most polished tone. "My name is Robert T. O'Flaridy. Your sister and I are old and very close friends." He shook their hands, and I didn't at all like the way his eyes lingered longer than they should have on Becky.

"Robin, there is something . . ." I began, but the moment I hesitated, he turned toward me again and started up himself.

"It is wonderful to see you again, Corrie," he said, more softly, taking my hand in his. "You look very beautiful tonight. Your brothers and sister appear old enough to take care of themselves in the city for one night. I'd like you to spend the evening with me. We'll go dancing, and I'll take you places you never even dreamed existed."

"Robin, I . . . I can't. I—"

"Come now, Corrie. I know you were just a confused kid before. But you're a grown woman now. It won't take long for you to realize that I'm the kind of man you could easily fall in love with. I've loved you for a long time; I've just been waiting for you to—"

That did it! At last I found my tongue.

"Robin O'Flaridy, don't you dare talk to me like that!" I said, pulling my hand out from his.

"Surely you don't deny that you found me interesting and attractive."

"I found you *interesting*, but certainly not attractive!"

Out of the corner of my eye I noticed Mr. Kemble sitting there, silently enjoying the drama. I wished he would step in to help me, but he seemed to be enjoying watching Robin make a fool of himself too much to interfere. Tad and Zack looked nervously at one another.

By now I was furious. Robin had always been presumptuous, but this took the cake!

"You could love me, Corrie, if you only give yourself the chance."

Again he took my hand. Once more I yanked it back, more forcefully this time.

"I have no intention of spending a minute more with you than I have to, Robin O'Flaridy!"

"Then, perhaps your sister—" he added, turning toward Becky with a smile I didn't like, "perhaps she would enjoy a night out in San Francisco with one who knows all the—"

Finally Zack jumped up in defense of his two sisters. If Christopher hadn't come back a minute later when he did, I'm afraid Zack would have clobbered poor Robin right in his face and bloodied his nose all over Mammy Pleasant's carpet!

"Both my sisters will be with me," Zack said, "and neither of them will spend a minute of it alone with the likes of you!"

"Perhaps you should let your sister answer for herself," rejoined Robin, with the trace of bite in his tone, eying Zack with caution, yet hardly able to keep himself from accepting the challenge.

I was so absorbed, I hadn't even noticed Christopher returning from outside and walking toward our table. All at once, Robin became aware of someone standing behind his right shoulder. He glanced around.

"Ah, this must be your chair," he said to Christopher, rising.

Then he turned back to me. "Corrie, you never told me you had an *older* brother."

"This is my *husband!*" I blurted out. If there wasn't smoke coming out my ears, I would be surprised.

Suddenly realizing his error, Robin stepped back so that Christopher could take his seat again. Christopher, however, continued to stand, not sure what to make of what he had seen upon reentering the dining room—a perfect stranger sitting in *his* seat, trying to take *his* wife's hand, and speaking to her in the confidential tones of a lover.

As Zack watched, still on his feet, the two men shook hands, stiffly on Christopher's part, while Robin not-so-subtly excused himself, trying to put the best face on the scene that he could under the circumstances.

"Oh . . . well—how are you doing? O'Flaridy's the name, Robert O'Flaridy."

"Christopher Braxton."

"Corrie and I go way back," he added, already recovering his suave demeanor. "Old newspaper cronies, you know. We haven't seen each other in years. Well . . . nice meeting you all," he added, sweeping his gaze quickly around the silent table. "And it's been wonderful seeing you again, Corrie."

I didn't say a word. I was calming down now that Christopher was back.

Finally Robin turned to Mr. Kemble.

"I'll see *you* later, Kemble," he said, with a significant tone, as if it had been the editor's design to set the whole thing up from the beginning so that he would wind up with egg on his face.

Mr. Kemble nodded, still chuckling over the incident. I certainly didn't think it was funny. Christopher remained silent. Zack, Tad, Becky, and Laughing Waters just sat there, hardly knowing *what* to think.

Robin turned and was gone as quickly as he had appeared, striding across the room to the table where the two men he had come in with were being served the first course of their dinner. I don't know why they were eating here, unless they were staying in the boardinghouse. By then I didn't care to know!

"I'd say it's time for us to leave," said Christopher, still serious.

I was on my feet in a second.

"I'm sorry we must leave so abruptly, Mr. Kemble," Christopher said to the editor. "If you would like to remain, we will be perfectly able to find our way back. We very much appreciate the evening, but I do think I ought to take my wife and her family back to the hotel."

"Yes . . . yes, of course, Braxton," said Mr. Kemble, getting up out of his chair somewhat awkwardly and shaking the hand Christopher had offered him.

"I hope you understand."

"Of course. Perhaps I, uh . . . perhaps I *will* remain a few minutes more and finish my cobbler, perhaps have a glass of port. You're certain you can find your way?"

Christopher nodded.

I thanked Mr. Kemble and told him I would be in touch with him about the article. Then we all made our way out of the room and back outside. I couldn't help glancing again in Robin's direction, but he was looking away and wasn't about to pay the slightest attention to our leaving. I was glad Mammy Pleasant was in another room at the time, so we didn't have to talk to anyone.

In another minute we were out on the street. A thick fog was just rolling in from off the bay, and it felt good to breathe the moist, salty air.

Christopher and I sighed deeply, relieved to be out of the noisy, smoky, boisterous atmosphere. The six of us walked slowly down the street in silence.

Finally Christopher spoke.

"What do you say we walk back to the hotel?" he said. "I think the exercise will help us shake off the dust from that place."

We all agreed. Christopher asked who in the world Robin O'Flaridy was, and as we went I told him the whole story.*

---

*For those of you who may not be familiar with Corrie's first meeting with Robin O'Flaridy, it is found in the two books *Daughter of Grace* and *On the Trail of the Truth*, books two and three in The Journals of Corrie Belle Hollister.

CHAPTER 12

A LONG TALK

It was probably seven-thirty or eight when we arrived back at the boardinghouse where we were staying. Robin O'Flaridy would probably be out on the town for another several hours. But we had had a long day and a good time. Now we were ready to put it behind us and think about going home the next morning. As we climbed the stairs, Christopher lingered behind.

"We need to talk," he whispered to me.

I nodded.

As soon as Tad and Zack were in their room and Becky and Laughing Waters and I in ours, I told the other two girls that Christopher and I were going to go back for a walk.

He was already waiting for me downstairs, and together we stepped back out into the quiet, chilly evening. Christopher let out a long sigh as soon as we were alone. We walked down the street in the opposite direction from which we had just come for several minutes.

"I am sorry," he said at length, "for putting you in that awkward position with O'Flaridy."

"You didn't put me in it," I said.

"Maybe not directly, but indirectly I have to take responsibility for it."

"Why?"

"Because I am your husband, and so I am responsible for you. And then I got up and deserted you just before he came around."

"You didn't desert me."

"Well, I shouldn't have left, and I am sorry. But I just had to get alone for a minute to try to clear my thoughts and ask the Lord what to do."

"You couldn't have known Robin was going to show up."

"It's more than that, Corrie. Don't you see? As the oldest among us, not just between you and me but all six of us, the moment I sensed something amiss in the situation, I should have taken us right out of there. It wasn't the kind of place we should have been. It felt more like a tavern than a restaurant. Surely you felt it?"

"Of course," I nodded. "But it was awkward, being there with Mr. Kemble, and with him so excited about having gotten us an invitation. I don't know what else we could have done, Christopher."

"That's hardly a reason not to do the right thing."

Again he sighed. I could tell he was taking it very seriously and very personally.

"What would Jesus think," he went on after a minute, "if he had walked in, and there we all were, six of his people? Corrie, don't you understand? I had the distinct feeling that the atmosphere of the place was more that of a bordello than a restaurant."

"I know," I said, now sighing myself.

"I have no wish to pass judgment on Mammy Pleasant, or anyone else, for that matter. I just didn't feel comfortable there. I sensed a wrong spirit, and it was all the worse knowing the rest of you were there as well."

"I don't see what else we could have done, Christopher," I repeated.

This time he was quiet a long time. He had his hands clasped by the fingers behind the back of his head, and he was staring up toward the sky as we walked along.

"If we had been alone," Christopher said finally, now dropping his hands and gesturing with them as he spoke, "the moment we walked in I would have turned right around and left and taken us someplace else. But with your editor there, having arranged it all and clearly enthusiastic about the whole affair, I thought perhaps it would turn out all right. As we ate our dinner, however, I felt more and more that I'd done the wrong thing, that I had compromised what I'd known to be right because I was too embarrassed to make a scene."

"I knew you were uncomfortable," I said.

"I didn't want to hurt your editor's feelings or make it difficult for you later on. How can a man like that, without spiritual convictions so far as I know—do you know if he's a Christian?"

I shook my head. "I've never spoken with him about the Lord," I said.

"So how could a man like that understand if we had gotten up and left halfway through dinner, and then if I had later tried to explain that I felt God's Spirit telling me there was an atmosphere of darkness about the place and that I needed to get my wife and her family out of there? He would think I was insane! There's nothing people hate more than a religious fanatic. I don't know, Corrie—how do you take a stand for what you believe when people are bound to misunderstand and misreact? What kind of a witness is *that* for the Lord?"

"Is that why you finally left?" I asked.

"I had to find someplace alone to talk to the Lord about it. I was becoming more and more convicted as the evening went along that we shouldn't be there, and yet I didn't have the backbone to do anything about it for fear of Mr. Kemble's reaction."

Christopher's voice sounded almost despairing. I'd never seen him like this.

"Over and over the verse kept going through my head—*Whoever causes one of these little ones of mine to stumble, it would be better for him that a giant millstone were hung about his neck.* And there were Tad and Becky sitting there, and Laughing Waters especially—don't you see, Corrie? I was the one responsible!"

"Aren't you taking it perhaps *too* seriously?" I suggested.

"That is precisely the reason there is so much unbelief in the world today," Christopher said with anger starting to sound in his voice, "because God's people *don't* take their faith seriously enough in the small, everyday things. They compromise in the little things, settling in to the flow and pattern of the rest of the world, until there's not much left to distinguish the people of God from the people who don't know him. How are people going to know the gospel is true if God's people don't take it seriously enough to *do* it, to stand up and be counted."

I nodded. How could I expect Christopher not to take it so seriously? It was just this passion about his beliefs that made me love him and think so highly of him.

"Please, don't think I'm upset with you or the others. I don't mean to point the finger at anyone else for not taking faith seriously," he continued, "for I am as guilty as anyone. But I want our lives to count for something, Corrie—I want them to count for the spreading of the Gospel. And how else can that happen unless we walk *differently* . . . visibly distinct from the world? Who in that place tonight will have seen the Lord Jesus more clearly as he truly is because we were there?"

"I wondered the same thing when you left," I said, "because I suspected what you were thinking."

"Aren't we supposed to be so distinct from the world that people *see* it in how we behave? I don't mean that we should go around preaching all the time to everyone. There can be just as much hypocrisy in that. We're told to *be* a different kind of people, not by what we say but by how we live. Jesus said we're—"

Suddenly Christopher stopped. He turned his head and glanced over at me.

"I'm sorry," he said. "I guess the preacher in me is bound to come out from time to time. I didn't mean to carry on like that."

"It's all right," I said. "And I didn't mean to imply that we shouldn't take things seriously. I hope you know by now that I am one hundred percent with you on that score. But what's done is done, and we can't go back and undo it now. God is bigger than this one evening."

"You're right," he sighed. "I don't suppose we can so easily stand in the way of his purposes. If God has designs on someone who may have been in that dining room with us tonight—be it Mr. Kemble or Robin O'Flaridy or anyone else—neither you nor I are going to thwart what he might be preparing to do in their lives. God is more sovereign than we usually give him credit for."

"And there is Paul's promise in Romans 8," I added, "that all things will work for good when we give them to God. Even situations like tonight."

"Exactly—how could I forget such a foundational truth? *For-*

give me, Father," he added softly, and I knew he was no longer talking to me.

It was quiet a few seconds.

"You are a good balance for me, Corrie," said Christopher. "I have the tendency to get so passionate that I lose sight of God's sovereignty. I want so desperately to do his will in all things."

"Perhaps we should give what happened over to him," I suggested.

"Yes, you're right. Would you pray, Corrie? I just feel the need to be quiet right now."

I reached out and took Christopher's hand in mine. We walked for several minutes more in silence, quietly calming our spirits.

"Lord Jesus," I prayed after awhile, *"we do now give over all the confusing events of this evening at the boardinghouse into your hands. We ask that you would make everything work out for your good, like Paul said in his letter, in spite of our human weakness. I pray for my husband, Christopher, that you would ease his unrest over this situation, yet at the same time I thank you for his desire to be all yours. We pray for Mr. Kemble. And I pray for Robin too. Forgive me for the anger I felt toward him. We pray that you would do what you purpose in these two men's lives and use us to reveal yourself to them if it is your will.*

"And we thank you for this incident. We pray that it will be a lesson to us. Help us to know what you want me to do about the article I promised Mr. Kemble. We want our lives to count for you, Lord, just like Christopher said; we want people to know you because of how we live. We do not have the ability to make that happen. We are weak and full of faults. But you can make it happen, Lord, and we ask you to do just that. Make our life together as husband and wife count so that people will come to know you."

I stopped.

Christopher added an amen of his own. We turned and began walking back toward the boardinghouse.

Even before the evening was over I had decided that I could not in good conscience write the article about Mammy Pleasant's. How could I recommend a place that was half bordello, half boardinghouse? Both Christopher and I felt so foolish afterward for allowing ourselves to get into such a situation. I would have to tell Mr. Kemble to make whatever excuse for me he could and apologize to him as sincerely as I could. But I simply could not write the article.

CHAPTER 13

NEW TROUBLE FOR PA

We left Laughing Waters in Sacramento at the boarding school
where she and her sister lived. Both of them were teaching orphaned Indian children. We had been talking about a visit to Miracle Springs for them on a holiday.

"I will write," said Zack.

"As will I," returned Laughing Waters.

"And we will look forward to seeing you in Miracle Springs in
the not too distant future," Becky added. She took both of Laughing Waters' hands, held them a moment, and looked deep into her
eyes. There was a new and special friendship budding—the kind
that exists only between sisters in the Lord.

We said our final goodbyes, then made our way straight to the
train station. Zack was especially quiet all the way home. I was
pretty sure I knew the reason why.

The minute we returned from Sacramento, we knew something
was wrong.

Pa and Almeda were sitting at the table in the house talking.
They hadn't even heard us ride up. Their faces wore serious expressions.

They did their best to greet us warmly and asked all about the
trip, but everyone could tell Pa was distracted and troubled.

"What's the matter, Pa?" Zack finally asked, pouring himself a
second cup of coffee.

Pa half looked away, kind of shaking his head in frustration, like
he didn't want to have to tell anyone.

"You might as well tell him, Drummond," said Almeda. "They're all going to have to know sooner or later. And Zack is involved too."

Pa nodded, then turned back in Zack's direction.

"You recollect that varmint you ran into out in the Utah territory when you was with Hawk—the feller that said he rode with the Catskill Gang?"

"Demming?" said Zack, and I could tell there was fear in his voice just from the sound of it.

Pa nodded.

"Course I remember him," said Zack. "He ain't someone I'll ever forget."

"Then when we went back that way last year with Hawk, we heard that he'd got himself drunk and in trouble and thrown in the pokey in Carson City?"

"Yeah, and I was glad enough. I'd just as soon forget I ever heard the name."

"Well, you ain't likely to have the chance to forget him any time soon," said Pa. "Word came to me a while back that he'd busted out. I wasn't gonna say anything—I reckon I figured after all this time he'd have forgot about us. But while you were gone a friend of mine rode up from Auburn, saying there'd been an ornery cuss of a feller prowling around down there, asking about the two of us . . . you and me. The way I figure, it's gotta be him."

"Who is this man you're talking about?" asked Christopher as we all took seats around the table.

"Feller I knew years ago back in New York. He's got it in his head that me and my brother-in-law Nick has some money from the old days he figures he's entitled to."

"But, Pa," I said, "the sheriff at Bridgeville told me the money was all turned in. You remember—I told you all about it."

Pa nodded.

"What was the man's name—?"

"Judd," said Pa.

"Yes. The sheriff said Judd told his son where the money was hid before he died. Then his son recovered the money and took it into Catskill, and they canceled all the rest of the old warrants except for two. Let's see, I forgot the names . . . it was something like—"

"Harris and Hank McFee," Pa answered for me.

"That's them," I said.

"But where does the man named Demming fit in?" asked Christopher.

"As soon as Zack got back from riding with the Express and told me about the feller out there, I had a bad feeling in my gut right off. Everything he said sounded like he was talking about the man Nick and me knew as Jesse Harris. Half the guys we knew back then never used their own names anyhow.

"I kept it to myself, hoping maybe I was wrong and we'd never hear more about it. But from everything Zack said about the man he ran into out there, it was Jesse Harris if it was anybody. He was a mean cuss, and tight with Buck Krebbs too. I think he had a younger brother too, like Zack said Demming did—though the kid never rode with us. But if he and his kid brother came out West shortly after me and Nick did, they wouldn't have had any more way than us of knowing the money's already been long since turned in."

"You really think he'd come after us, Pa?" Zack asked.

"Don't you recollect what he said to you, son—especially after how you got the best of him out there? If I know Harris, or Demming, or whatever his name is, he's likely bent on getting revenge on you as much as holding that knife of his to my throat about the money."

It was silent a minute. I saw Zack gulp a time or two at Pa's words.

If Zack didn't remember, I sure did! I still remember what he said the man named Demming shouted at him: *I won't forget you, Hollister. And you can tell that pa of yours I ain't forgotten him neither. Now it looks like I got a score to settle with the both of you.*

I couldn't help but think of the gun Zack had just bought himself in San Francisco. I said nothing, but it added greatly to the nervousness I felt. I hoped he didn't get it into his head to do anything stupid!

"Did you talk to the sheriff?" asked Tad.

"Rafferty's not likely to head off looking for him when we don't have any more to go on than rumors," said Pa. "He's been talking about retiring—I don't think he's of a mind to go off tracking outlaws these days."

It was Christopher who spoke up next.

"What are you going to do about the man, then, Drum?" he asked.

Pa shrugged his shoulders and let out a long sigh. He looked so tired.

I recognized the expression on Pa's face, and suddenly realized I hadn't seen it for years. It was a look that he used to wear almost constantly, the anxiety over a past that seemed intent on dogging him no matter how decent a life he lived now. I know Pa would say there wasn't anything unfair about it, because he had made some bad choices. But to *me* it didn't seem fair that after all the years Pa had spent being kind and unselfish and doing what he could for other folks, a brief period of his life from so long ago just wouldn't let loose. It just kept coming back to haunt him.

CHAPTER 14

ARE *YOU* WILLING TO BE
THE INSTRUMENT?

While we all sat waiting for Pa to answer Christopher's question, a silence which must have only lasted two or three seconds, it was as if the time since the incidents involving Buck Krebbs had never happened. All the years with Pa being mayor of Miracle Springs, and then being an assemblyman in Sacramento, the years when I had been away in the East—it was as if they had all vanished and here we were again, suddenly facing a danger we hadn't even thought about in all that time.

Yet those years *had* passed.

Pa was over fifty. The rest of us were grown. Almeda's hair was half gray. I was now married. My new husband was sitting here sharing the moment with us. But now here we were facing Pa's past once more.

I knew that was the pain I saw in Pa's face as he sighed again. It wasn't fear for his own life so much as a deep sadness and regret that what he had done so long ago was once again placing the rest of us in danger—especially Zack. When he'd left Ma and us kids so long ago it had been to protect us from the danger following him from trying to help Uncle Nick straighten out his life.

"I don't know, Christopher," he said at length. "Don't reckon there's much I *can* do . . . except pray, then wait to see what comes of it."

Again the room fell silent.

"Then, let's *do* pray," said Christopher after another minute or

68

two, "and ask the Lord for his protection."

Pa nodded his consent, then took another breath, bowed his head, and started to pray aloud without waiting for anybody else.

"Lord, once again I come to you," he said, *"asking you to take care of my family. Just when I think all those days of my own foolishness are gone forever, back it seems to come again. I tell you again, like I have so many times, how sorry I am for not paying more attention to you when I was younger. And now that I've learned a little about walking with you, show me what you want me to do."*

"Keep this new danger from us, Lord Jesus," prayed Almeda.

"I pray for Pa and Zack," I said. *"Keep them safe from this man Demming or Harris or whatever his name is. Show them what to do."*

A few other prayers went round the room. Then it fell silent. We were all feeling things we hadn't felt in years.

Then Pa started praying again. When he spoke, it showed just how much he had changed. The prayer that next came from his lips were not the words of an ordinary man.

"Lord," he said, *"I find myself thinking just now about the words you spoke yourself about praying for our enemies. I've always known you said that, but I don't reckon I ever thought much about it in a personal way before. Hard as it seems to do such a thing, I reckon it's time I found out if my faith in you means much and if I'm willing to obey you in doing a hard thing I probably wouldn't do if left to myself. So right now I'm gonna pray for Jesse Harris, if it's him that is the Demming feller. I used to ride with him, but from the sound of it he's made himself my enemy now. I'm not really sure how to pray for him, Lord. So I guess I'll just say—touch his life somehow. Be God to him, though he ain't much of a God-fearing man. Course I wouldn't have thought I'd be a praying Christian man neither, and if you can get inside my skin and make me new from the inside out, I reckon you can do it with anybody. Do some kind of good work in him beyond what I even know how to pray for. Work your will in his life. Do good for him, whatever that is."*

Again we were all silent. I didn't know about the others, but I felt strange tingles all through me—spiritual tingles, not anything that I actually felt in my body. It was such a huge thing to pray for the good of someone who you knew was trying to kill you. I could hardly take in the thought.

"Do you mind if I share something?" Christopher asked.

Pa nodded, but Christopher knew he meant to go ahead.

"I was praying once," Christopher said, "when I was in seminary, praying for an individual I was having a very difficult time loving—one of my professors, actually, whose manner grated on me. He didn't like me very much and didn't mind that I knew it. I knew I had to pray for him, though I didn't particularly relish the assignment. I was willing enough to pray, but out of duty, not because I really felt any compassion for the man in my heart. I suppose that is a better thing than not to pray at all, but it is still far from the best thing.

"In any event, as I was dutifully saying the words, *Lord I pray for so-and-so . . .* I sensed the Lord beginning to speak to me, telling me that my words were impersonal and detached. It was a good thing to pray for him, but I had not reached the level of Christlike prayer, the kind that is able to move mountains."

"You actually heard the Lord talking to you?" asked Tad.

"I *felt* him saying something like this," answered Christopher. *"You are praying for me to do a work in this man's life. It is well you should pray this, and such it is my desire to do. How willing are you then, my son, to be the one* yourself *through whom I answer your prayer?"*

Christopher was quiet a moment, allowing his words to sink in. We were quiet, too. It was such a new way of thinking about prayer.

"I realized," he went on, "that suddenly my prayers couldn't be mere words anymore. If I was going to take the Lord seriously, everything about the way I prayed would have to change. Praying generally is one thing, but saying to the Lord that he could use me as his instrument of answering my very prayer—that was something entirely more personal. There was no telling what he might require of me if I was willing to pray *that* prayer."

"Are you saying that it's wrong to pray if you don't pray in that way?" I asked.

"Oh no, certainly not. Any kind of prayer for another individual is a good thing that can open doors for the Holy Spirit to work," replied Christopher. "But I believe there come certain times when God desires to explore deeper reaches of willingness within us. At such moments, the act of prayer becomes a more somber act of both sacrifice and possibility."

"Did you pray it?" asked Becky.

Christopher smiled.

"Eventually," he said. "But it was one of the most difficult prayers I ever prayed."

"What happened?" asked Zack.

Christopher's smile deepened. I had come to know the expression that crossed his face and knew there was pain somewhere in the memory.

"It's a long story," he sighed. "Let's just say that the Lord did answer my prayer, both sides of it, but certainly not in ways I would have anticipated."

Again quietness fell.

Christopher had given us a lot to think about. I knew Pa took his words seriously. After a few minutes he got up and walked outside.

CHAPTER 15

A SAD VISIT

A few days after our return to Miracle Springs, Christopher and I went to pay a call on my childhood friend Jennie Shaw—Jennie Woodstock as she was now.

As soon as we rode up, we saw her husband, Tom, going out to one of his fields to work. I know he saw us, but for some reason he didn't acknowledge us. Jenny knew it, too, and felt awkward because of it when she answered the door and saw him walking away in the distance.

She invited us in and we tried to keep up a friendly conversation, but it was difficult because she was so nervous. We could see that something was amiss, and I even felt uncomfortable being so happy. Jennie had had a happy time, too, right after her own marriage, and the reminder of it, with us not that long back from our honeymoon, must have made our visit all the more a strain for her.

"Is something the matter, Jennie?" I finally asked. I couldn't stand pretending there wasn't.

Just the question brought tears to her eyes, and she looked away. She dabbed at her nose and eyes with her handkerchief.

"Oh, Corrie," she said, "it's not good with Tom and me."

"How, Jennie?" I said. "What's wrong?"

Jennie hesitated and glanced down into her lap.

"Why don't I wait outside?" said Christopher, starting to rise and thinking Jennie felt awkward in front of him.

"No, no—please, Mr. Braxton," said Jennie, looking up at him. "It's all right if you stay. It's not you; it's just . . . it's so hard to talk about."

"I understand," replied Christopher. "But really, I'd be happy to leave you alone if you'd feel more comfortable just with Corrie."

"No—no, I think I'd like you to stay. Corrie said you used to be a minister; maybe you can help. I . . . I just don't know what to do, and I've got no one to turn to."

Again she looked away and started to cry. This time the tears began to flow in earnest.

"All right," said Christopher, "I'll stay. But you must call me Christopher, or I'll feel like an old man here with you children!"

Jennie tried to smile politely through her tears, but it was a weak effort. She nodded at Christopher to show she appreciated what he'd said.

Christopher and I sat waiting. It was difficult resisting the urge to want to leave. I knew Jennie needed to talk—and *wanted* to talk. But I couldn't help feeling like we were intruding where we didn't belong. But I had been with Christopher enough by now to know that pastors—or *former* pastors like him—who had a heart of love for people sometimes probed a little to get people to open up about their problems. When somebody was hurting about anything, Christopher could sense it almost immediately, and he wanted to get right in and find out the cause of the hurt to see if there was some way he could help, even just by prayer. I could tell that his heart had gone out to Jennie the instant she had answered our knock on the door.

Finally I got up and sat beside her and gave her my handkerchief.

"I thought it would be so wonderful being married," Jennie began after she had cried softly for a minute. "But it wasn't long before I began to wonder if I'd made a mistake."

I placed my hand on hers, and she clutched at it tightly.

"Oh, Corrie!" exclaimed Jennie, "You don't know how many times in the last two years I've wished I'd had your good sense and not been so anxious to snag myself a husband. That was all I could think of back then. You remember when we used to talk before we were married? I'm embarrassed to say it, but I used to think you were silly for not being, you know, like other girls. You didn't talk about boys and marriage all the time. You had your writing and other things you were interested in. I used to think it was strange—

but now I see you were just waiting for the right time and right man."

Suddenly Jennie seemed to realize what she was doing. She stopped and looked over at me with an embarrassed expression.

"I probably shouldn't be saying all this. I'm sorry—I didn't mean to burden you down with my problems."

"Oh, Jennie," I said. "Your problems aren't burdensome to me in the least. You are my friend. I am interested and want to help."

Christopher spoke up now for the first time.

"We don't want you to tell us any specifics right now, Jennie," he said, "while the wounds are so fresh. It's best not to confide hurtful things about someone else when you are upset, when your perspective is clouded. It's been my experience that often people say things under such circumstances that they wish they could retrieve later."

Jennie nodded.

"Corrie and I both want you to know that we will do whatever we can. It is enough right now that you have shared your hurt with us. We want to extend to you all that we can be as friends and listeners. We will pray for you. You can know that you are not alone in this. I would encourage you to pray as well. God will hear you. He loves both you and Tom and wants only the best for you."

Christopher stood up.

"I think I'll mosey out to the field and see what Tom's up to. Maybe I can strike up a conversation."

Jennie looked doubtful, but she didn't protest. She and I continued to talk quietly between ourselves, both of us sharing the adjustments we'd had to make to married life, while Christopher left the house.

CHAPTER 16

FENCEPOSTS AND RAILS

Christopher walked outside, glanced around, spotted Tom in the distance, and headed over the uneven terrain toward him.

The two had, of course, met and had seen one another any number of times in the almost year and a half since Christopher had come to Miracle Springs, but there had never been any kind of camaraderie between them. Tom Woodstock was not a sensitive or a talkative man, and I doubted strongly whether he had any interest whatever in spiritual things. I don't know what I had to base that statement on except that I had never once seen him in church and that his personality was kind of sharp and rough.

I had never really understood what Jennie saw in Tom, but then sometimes girls can be attracted to young men for the strangest of reasons, often having nothing whatever to do with what kind of person these men are inside. I suppose that some girls deceive themselves into thinking a man is of worthy character in order to justify the emotions they feel for good looks or brawn or something else like that. I couldn't imagine any other reason why Jennie would have fallen in love with someone like Tom Woodstock. And maybe some girls figure they'll be able to tame a rough man—change him to be what they hope he'll be, all the while overlooking what he really is.

Tom was struggling to attach a long six-inch split rail to the top of two fence posts that stuck out of the ground from two holes he had dug for them. But the rail was heavy, and he was having difficulty keeping the loose end where he had perched it on top of the post while he tried to wire-wrap the other end long enough to steady it. Already it had fallen twice, and frustration was beginning to set in, aggravated by the knowledge that his wife was inside talking to her friend and her cheerful do-gooder of a husband—probably about *him*, if he knew Jennie!

As Christopher approached, Tom did not look up or greet him in any way.

Christopher, who had installed miles of fences in his time, saw immediately what the problem was as he drew closer. He broke into a run, reaching the loose end of the rail just as it was about to wobble to the edge of the post and crash down to the ground for a third time.

"Hey, Tom," he cried, "looks like you could use a hand!"

He latched onto it and held it steady while Tom completed the temporary fastening of his end.

"Toss me the wire, and I'll tie this one down," said Christopher.

Nonchalantly, and still without saying a word, Tom threw over the wound bale of wire, which landed with a thud at Christopher's feet. Still holding the end of the rail in place with his left hand, he stooped down, retrieved the bale, and in thirty seconds had tightly bound the rail to the post with several strong diagonal strands.

"Got some cutters?" he asked, relaxing his hold now long enough to roll up his two sleeves.

Two seconds later the tool landed at his feet. Christopher picked it up, snapped the wire in two, twisted the two ends to hold the rail in place, then faced Tom.

"What were you going to do, run a piece of doweling through the two posts?" Christopher asked.

"Yep, figured that's what I'd do," answered Tom, speaking for the first time.

"Got your brace and auger bit out here?" asked Christopher. "If you'd like, I'll get started boring a hole in this end."

"Yeah, right over here."

Christopher walked over, Tom handed him the bit, and the next moment Christopher was circling his hand around and around on the handle while the bit chewed into the wood. In three or four minutes the tip of the bit protruded out the other end of the post and a little pile of the hole's former contents lay at Christopher's feet.

"There, that ought to do it," he said, twisting the bit back out backward. "I'll go ahead and get the second hole drilled on your side if you want to pound in your dowel."

Christopher and Tom traded ends, went about their respective jobs, and in another ten minutes the rail was solidly in place. Tom sawed off the excess dowel while Christopher unwrapped the wires that had held up the two ends temporarily. Then they stood back to admire the result.

"Thanks, Braxton," said Tom. "That sure made an easier time of it."

"How many more of those you got to do?"

"I don't know," shrugged Tom. "About a dozen."

"Could you use some help?"

"Naw. Me and Jennie's a little short right now, I couldn't afford to—"

"I wasn't asking you for a job, Tom," laughed Christopher. "I was just asking if you could use some help—neighbor to neighbor. Believe me, I won't ask for a cent, and wouldn't take one if you offered it to me."

Tom shrugged again.

Just then Christopher saw Jennie and me emerging from the house.

"Ah, looks like our wives are done with their visit," he said, slowly moving in my direction. "You going to be working on the fence this afternoon?"

"I reckon so," shrugged Tom.

"Let me ask it another way, then. If I were to show up here to help you, would you run me off?"

"No, I don't reckon I'd do that," said Tom with a reluctant up-turn of his lips into something that could have passed for a weak smile.

"Good," said Christopher. "Then I'll be back in two or three hours and we'll finish up your fence."

He ran back to the house, then jumped up into the buggy beside me. I could tell he was itching to tell me about it, which he did as we rode home.

CHAPTER 17

MOLES AND DARK
PASSAGEWAYS

It was probably a week later when I got up a little before Christopher one morning. I came out of the bunkhouse and saw Pa standing alone behind the house.

I went slowly in that direction. He was standing, staring out at the grass that grew between the house and the edge of the woods. I walked up and slipped my hand through his arm and stood at his side.

Neither of us said anything for another minute or two. I knew Pa would tell me what he was thinking when he was ready.

"See them mole mounds there, Corrie?" he said at length.

I nodded, looked out where three or four fresh piles of black dirt sat in the middle of the grass.

"I been fighting them moles ever since we came out here, trying to keep their holes from making a horse stumble and break his leg. Just when you think they've disappeared for good, up pops a new, fresh bunch of mounds."

"Are those new ones, Pa?" I asked.

"Yep. New this morning. I ain't seen evidence of moles right out there in six months or so. Then all of a sudden there they are again."

He sighed.

"It's just like that rascal Harris," Pa went on. "Him turning back up's just like a mole mound popping up from out of nowhere just when you think your problems are behind you."

"A little worse than a mole, Pa," I said. "He sounds to me like a bad man."

"He's an ornery varmint—I reckon you're right there. But the moles reminded me of him anyhow. Standing here looking at them mounds puts me in a mind of how our lives are sometimes. You can put on a front for folks and make them think you're a nice enough feller. But down deep where no one sees, I reckon we all got our dark passageways and tunnels where our own black critters crawl about and live—just like our property here's got moles running around it down outta sight. Just because we don't see them for months at a time, they're there all right. They got their burrows and tunnels all over out there."

He swept his hand out across the yard in the direction of the woods.

"That's just like us. We got our hidden places no one sees . . . till, all of a sudden, something like this deal with Harris comes along and up pops a black, ugly pile of dirt from inside for all the world to see."

I couldn't help smiling.

"Sounds like some of the articles I used to write, Pa," I said.

"Well, maybe you helped me to learn to see a mite deeper into things, Corrie Belle," Pa replied. "I reckon your writing did me good that way, whatever it did for anybody else."

"I didn't know that, Pa," I said.

"I read ever' word you ever wrote, Corrie."

"I knew that. But I'm your daughter. You had to read it."

"I read it 'cause I wanted to, 'cause it was good writing. I'm telling you the truth—it helped me, too. I figured if my Corrie could see things the way you did, well then I oughta see if I couldn't try to see things like that, too."

"You don't know how pleased that makes me, Pa," I said. "That makes everything I wrote worth it ten times over."

"It's the truth. I was mighty proud of you. Still am."

"Thank you, Pa," I said softly. I was about to cry! What a wonderful thing for a father to say to his daughter.

"And since Zack came back from his winter with Hawk, why, he won't stop talking about hidden things and how they tie into our lives. Anyhow," Pa went on, "what I'm seeing right now is that sometimes we're none too pretty to look at, which is how I been feeling this last week—full of dark things out of the past, with black dirt popping up out of me all over the place."

Again he sighed. We stood there quietly for some time. *What an openhearted man he'd allowed himself to become,* I thought to myself.

"Well," he said after a while with a determined sigh, "I reckon I'm finally ready to do it."

"Do what, Pa?"

"Pray that prayer Christopher told us about," he replied. "Come on, let's go inside. Everybody's probably there by now. This is something we all gotta be part of together."

CHAPTER 18

WILLING PRAYER

Pa and I turned and walked back toward the house. The others were all just gathering for breakfast. Pa said he'd like to talk to everyone. We went into the big room, sat down, and waited.

"I been thinking hard about what Christopher told us the other day," Pa began after a few minutes, "about how to pray for things." He drew in a long breath.

"I reckon I'm ready to do it," he went on. "I mean, I think God's telling me to do it. He's been asking me the same thing he asked Christopher—if I was willing to be the person he might want to use to answer my own prayer. Seemed a mite cockeyed a thing to me at first—praying for somebody who's out to put a bullet in your head, then telling God that instead of hiding from the feller you'll let him answer the prayer through you! How could he even do such a thing? I been trying to make sense out of it for a week, but I can't.

"Then it came to me how all God's ways of doing things are a mite cockeyed from man's way of looking at them. Anyhow, it ain't so much a matter of whether I can *make sense* of it, but just whether or not I'm willing to *do* it.

"So I figure if my praying's gonna do much good, I gotta be willing. But I'd really like the rest of you to pray with me. It's a fearsome thing when a man like Harris is involved. I'm sure Zack'd say the same thing. Harris is a bad apple. This is a new thing for me, and I ain't sure I'd be able to pray it by myself."

"It would be our honor to pray with you, Drum," said Christopher, rising and walking to Pa's side. He laid a hand on Pa's shoulder, his own father-in-law, and closed his eyes. Almeda was immediately at Pa's other side, and the rest of us gathered around him, too.

"*Well, Lord,*" Pa prayed, "*here I am coming before you again. I want to pray for Harris like I did last week. But this time, Lord, I just want to tell you that I'm ready for you to use me to answer that prayer, that is, if there's some way you can use me, or if you want to. I can't think of anything I could do that'd help you in any way. What could I do that you couldn't do better yourself—especially since the man wants to see me dead? But if there's something you can and want to do, then, like I say, I'm willing to be the tool you use.*"

He sighed deeply, and I knew the words I'd just heard had not been uttered without a cost to Pa deep inside him. I knew he'd struggled for a week over this, facing the extent of his own willingness. I could not help but be reminded of Jesus' prayer in the garden. I knew this was Pa's own way of saying to the Lord, "Not my will, but yours, be done."

"*I can't say that there ain't a part of me that's scared to pray it,*" Pa went on, still talking to God. "*I know it may be that it'll cost me my life, 'cause sometimes that's what it takes to get through to some men. But if you want me to give my life for another man, I don't reckon it's more than you did yourself. You gave your life for me and all the rest of us, including Jesse Harris. My life's yours anyway now, to do with what you want. I don't reckon my faith's worth much if I'm not willing to follow you and do what you did.*

"*So I pray you'd do your best for Jesse. Like I said before, I pray that you'll be God to him, and however you want to use me to do that is all right by me.*"

Whispered amens sounded from two or three of us.

Almeda was crying softly. So was I. We both loved Pa so much. But we also knew what Pa's prayer could mean. Sometimes God *did* use people's *lives*.

Everyone admired Pa for what he'd done. But my heart was heavy, too. I couldn't help being afraid.

"The Lord will honor your obedience, Drum," said Christopher softly. "You are an example to us all."

CHAPTER 19

A DISHEARTENING PROPOSITION

Christopher and Pa, Tad and Zack were still working the mine every day. They'd bored and picked and dynamited their way halfway through the mountain, but so far they had only found small amounts of gold.

Alkali Jones was around most days, too, and usually ate lunch with us and sometimes supper, but it seemed to me he was getting too weak to do too much of the actual work.

Alkali had *always* looked old to me. But it had been more than fifteen years since I'd first laid eyes on him, and I didn't know any other word to describe him now than *ancient*. I hesitate to use the word *feeble* to describe a man we all loved so dearly. But he did walk more slowly than before, and every once in a while I was afraid his tired old knees were going to give out altogether.

Ever since the men had found the lode of quartz the previous October, their hopes had run high. But through the winter, and then with the wedding and our two trips away, enthusiasm gradually slowed. The hard work and aching muscles just weren't getting them anywhere, and it wasn't hard to see that discouragement was setting in.

Finally one day at supper Pa said what they had probably all been thinking to themselves.

"I think it's time we shut down the mine," he said matter-offactly before stabbing a hunk of potato with his fork and popping it into his mouth.

The room was silent a moment as Pa chewed away, paying no attention to everyone's surprise.

A few heads turned this way and that, then gradually every eye settled on Pa.

"What are you all staring at me for?" he said after swallowing the bite.

"You can't be serious, Drummond?" said Almeda.

"Course I'm serious. We ain't finding nothing."

"But . . . but I hear you all talking every day about all the gold there still is to find and how well you're doing."

"It's all talk, Almeda. We're just trying to keep each other working, that's all. But we haven't found a thing in months. And today that big wide run of quartz we thought was going to lead us to gold shrunk down to less than an inch wide. We been following it into the mountain since October and it's been getting smaller ever since. I reckon it's time to face the fact that it's leading nowhere—our mine's finally played out."

Again it was quiet, the only sound the clink of forks against the plates.

"Pa's right, Almeda," said Zack at length. "I didn't want to say anything. I'm willing to work as long as Pa is. But we haven't set eyes on any nugget as big as a fingernail since last summer."

Tad nodded. I looked at Christopher.

"I don't know what I can add," he said. "I'm such a newcomer to all this, I didn't know whether this was normal or not. But in all honesty I haven't really seen much gold."

Again it was quiet. Even though Pa and Zack and Tad had all been thinking the same thing, just to talk about shutting down the mine was such a major change to contemplate. Almeda and Becky and I were astonished, because it took us so by surprise. That mine had, in a sense, been the center of our lives for fifteen years, even longer for Pa and Uncle Nick. I could hardly imagine what impact it would have on all of us for the mine *not* to be operating.

"What . . . what would you *do*, Drummond?" asked Almeda.

"I don't know. I reckon there's plenty of things I could keep busy with."

"Politics again?"

"I doubt it. But you never know. It's these young fellers here

I'm thinking mostly about. We can't all just keep working up there forever without finding anything. Our bank account's thinning out, Almeda—you know that as well as I do. Before long we might have to think about selling off some of the land if there isn't a change of some kind. Christopher here's got his own life and family to think about. Zack'll likely be thinking along those lines here soon enough. And Tad . . . I don't know—it just don't seem fair to keep them working away here for me when maybe it's high time they was getting on with their own plans."

"We're not worried about ourselves, Pa," interjected Zack. "As long as there's any more gold at all and as long as you say, we're behind you."

"Thanks, son. But all that's not to mention," Pa went on, turning back toward Almeda, "that I made these fellers all a bargain, and so I figure I owe them all some return on their investment of time and work, though it ain't as much as we figured a year ago. If Corrie's man here had known it was going to turn out like this, he might not have agreed to my proposal. I've held him up with whatever he plans to do with himself as it is. Maybe it ain't fair of me to hold him up any longer."

He glanced over at Christopher with an expression that looked like he felt he'd let Christopher down.

"You don't owe me a cent, Drum," said Christopher. "You made it clear enough when we began this partnership that we might not find anything. It was a risk we all took. Besides, I feel I've been more than amply paid with room and board all this time."

This time the silence around the table lasted more than five minutes. Pretty soon everyone was through eating.

I felt a lump rising in my throat. It was all so sad! I had the feeling I might one day look back on this evening as the beginning of the breakup of the Hollister homestead. The talk sounded like the partnership they'd all made last year was coming to an end.

Oh, but I loved it here with everyone together! I didn't want us to all start going our separate ways. Yet what else would it lead to if they shut down the mine?

Pa was right; we were all grown-up adults. We couldn't stay this way forever, with us all living in one big family.

Pretty soon Tad would get a job somewhere, maybe move away from Miracle Springs.

Zack would probably go back to the horse business with Little Wolf and his father, and probably be marrying Laughing Waters before long. Then *he'd* be gone too.

And what about Christopher and me? What would *we* do?

My heart began to sink within me with all these thoughts and fears and uncertainties.

My reflections were cut short by the last thing I expected to hear at a sad time like this—laughter.

"Hee, hee, hee," sounded the cackle of Alkali Jones' high-pitched voice. "You're all talkin' like a parcel o' lily-livered old geese. Ain't *no* more gold gonna be found round hereabouts without a dang sight more work 'n when we first came. Hee, hee, hee. What ye expect, Drum, fer the blame stuff t' appear down at yer feet like it did when I first sloshed through this here Miracle creek? I ever tell ye about the size o' the first nugget I took outta here? Why the blame thing was as big as—"

"Yep you have, Alkali—a time or two," interrupted Pa, with a wink in Tad's direction.

"Hee, hee, hee . . . couldn't recollect if ye knew about that or not. But if ye can remember that fer back, surely ye ain't fergot that when we found that blame quartz last year, there was *two* lines of it leadin' into the dang hill."

Nobody said anything for a minute, and a few more glances went back and forth around the table.

"Yeah," said Pa slowly. "But that other wasn't no bigger than my little finger."

"Hee, hee, hee—an' I told ye *that* was the one ye oughta foller."

"The other was six inches wide, Alkali—more quartz than I'd ever seen compacted in one vein like that."

"The look o' things don't always tell ye all there is t' know, Drum. I tell ye—ye went the wrong direction. Hee, hee, hee."

"Well, I'll think about what you say, Alkali," said Pa. "Maybe we'll poke around tomorrow and see if we can find that little finger-vein you're talking about."

I could tell by the tone of his voice that Pa wasn't convinced in the slightest and that nothing Mr. Jones said had changed his mind.

CHAPTER 20

UNCERTAINTY

Nothing changed much for the next several days. Christopher and Pa and the boys went up to the mine the following morning just the same as they always did, though not quite so early.

Pa was a little quieter than normal for the rest of the week. The others, and Almeda and I too, were kind of watching him to see what he was going to decide about the mine. Knowing Pa, he realized it too, and that only increased the pressure on him to make a final decision. When he told us about shutting down the mine, his words were *almost* like those of a decision, but they weren't quite final. Then everything Alkali Jones said had muddied the water about what to do. And when Pa said nothing more, the future was left up in the air, and nobody knew quite what to think or what Pa expected.

Everybody, I suppose, had their own reasons not to talk about it openly, because what Pa had said couldn't help but cast doubt onto everyone's future. Even Christopher and I didn't talk about it right at first, and we usually talked about *everything*.

Two days after Pa's surprise announcement about shutting down the mine, Zack left for the afternoon to Little Wolf's, and Christopher went over to Tom Woodstock's again to help him finish up the fence they had been working on together. That left just Tad and Pa at the mine—Mr. Jones wasn't feeling too well and left early too—and when the two of them came down about four o'clock, it was clear enough they were through for the day, even though they usually worked till six or seven.

87

It was already obvious that everyone was thinking of a change. Meals gradually grew quieter. Zack began to spend more time with Little Wolf again. Two mornings later Tad rode into town, and we later found out he'd gone to see Mr. Simms about getting his old job at the livery stable back. Mr. Jones—I don't know why, sensing maybe that Pa hadn't taken kindly to his idea—didn't come around for several days.

I didn't like what was going on, but I was afraid to say anything. I don't know what I would have said anyway. Pa was right. If they weren't finding gold, then what was the use of pounding away on rocks for eight, ten, or twelve hours a day month after month?

When Christopher gradually grew quieter and quieter, I began to be even more concerned. It wasn't like him. He had always been so open and communicative; now for several days he hardly spoke whenever we were alone, and when he did speak it was only about the most superficial things.

Finally I just had to ask him what was wrong.

"Christopher," I said one evening after we had retired to our little home in the bunkhouse, "why are you being so quiet? What's wrong? Have I done something to make you upset?"

"Oh no, Corrie," he replied, looking at me with a pained expression. "It's nothing about *you*."

"What, then?"

"It's just . . . I've had a lot on my mind."

"But what—what about? Why can't you tell me?"

"I didn't want to bother you with it."

"It's worse *not* being bothered with it," I said. "What else can I think but that it has something to do with me . . . with us."

"Oh, but it doesn't at all—that is, not directly."

"Oh, Christopher, you're just making it worse by being so vague. You've got me really worried. I've never seen you like this."

He sighed, and I could tell I had only succeeded in adding to whatever the cause was of the burden he was feeling. We were quiet a minute.

"I'm sorry, Corrie," he said finally. "The last thing in the world I want is for you to think I'm upset with you. I really am sorry."

"Thank you," I said softly. "But when a man gets quiet, that's the first thing a woman thinks. I don't know—somehow you can't help it."

"I suppose you're right," he sighed again. "But on my side of it, when a man is uncertain about a decision, wondering about the future, asking the Lord what to do in a given situation—sometimes that uncertainty brings with it an introspection and quiet that you just can't help, either."

"Why can't you just share what you're thinking?"

"Sometimes it isn't that easy."

"For most men, maybe, but you've always been different. You always talk to me about what's on your mind."

"It isn't that I'm trying not to talk about this; it's that I just can't—not yet. I just have to sort and pray something through on my own. I don't know how to explain it other than that, Corrie. Even for the most open and expressive of men, there are times when a sense of quiet comes over you that you just can't help. I don't say it's right or good or that it ought to be that way, only that sometimes you can't do anything else."

I didn't say anything for a moment.

"But don't you see how hard that makes it on a wife like me?" I asked at length.

"Yes," Christopher nodded. "And I truly mean it when I say that I am very sorry."

Again it was silent for a minute or two.

"Can't you tell me *anything* about what you're thinking?" I finally asked.

"I'm thinking about what your father said a few days ago—you must realize that."

"About closing the mine?"

Christopher nodded.

"What about it? I don't see why that would cause such a melancholy to come over you. You're not finding any gold anyway, even you said that."

"It's not about the gold," replied Christopher with just a touch of exasperation in his voice that I could even think such a thing.

"What, then?"

"Don't you see?" Again I felt the exasperation.

"I guess I don't."

"If we quit working the mine, then where does that leave us, Corrie?"

"What do you mean? It doesn't leave us anywhere. It leaves us right here. What do you think, that Pa will ask us to leave?"

I suppose there might have been a little exasperation in my tone by this time, too.

"Of course not."

"They love having us here."

"I know that. What I'm saying is where does it leave us as far as the future is concerned? What will I do?"

"I don't know—work like you did before the mine partnership? You're a hard worker. You'll find something."

"It was different then. I'd just come here, and I needed something to occupy my time and earn a few honest dollars. It's all changed now."

"How?"

"Corrie, how can you even ask such a thing? We're married now. That changes everything. What do you think, that I'm going to be satisfied supporting a family doing an odd job here and an odd job there, living forever in the back end of a barn?"

"What's wrong with this?" I asked. "I think it's romantic."

"It is. I think it's romantic, too. I love it here. But, don't you see, it can't last forever. Someday we will have to think of the future, of what I am going to do with my life, of what kind of a life I am going to provide for you and our family. When your father said what he did the other night, suddenly that *someday* crashed in upon me and I realized that maybe I needed to think about that future now."

At last I saw what had so burdened Christopher down. Of course it would have made him anxious. How could I have been so insensitive to what he was going through?

"Christopher, I'm sorry," I said. "I think I'm beginning to understand."

"Don't worry about it. You didn't do anything wrong."

"Still, I'm sorry."

"Apology accepted. Thanks. What about mine?"

"Your what?"

"My apology," smiled Christopher, and it *was* good to see him smile.

"Your apology accepted, too," I said, returning his smile.

He stretched his arm around me and pulled me closer to him where we had been sitting together on the bench. I snuggled in close, and we sat contentedly like that for five or ten minutes without saying anything more.

"It's different for you," said Christopher at length. "This is your family. You have been here most of your life. As much as I love your family, and as much as they have accepted me and I know they love me, I'm still not as much a part as you are."

"Of course you are, Christopher. You and I are one now."

"On one level. But can't you see that to accept that fully is difficult for one like me, one who hasn't known *family* like this in the past? I don't want to be beholden to your father beyond what is proper. I appreciate all he's done. But you heard him—the mine is now draining him financially, and there is no denying we contribute to that. If the mine's not going to produce, then I have to begin carrying my fair share as the head of *our* family."

"I see what you mean."

"There we are again at the question of our future. We can't just stay here indefinitely when to do so might eventually mean that your father would have to sell some of his land."

"But you'll get a job, and then you'll begin paying for our share of the expenses. And the Supply Company's still doing well."

"True. But there we are again at what I'm going to do with my life. Odd jobs or working for Almeda at the Mine and Freight are just not a permanent solution. I'm willing to work at anything the Lord gives me. You know that. At the same time, I want my life to count for something in people's lives."

"Your life *will* count, Christopher. You could clean out horse stalls every day and your life would count, just because of the man you are."

"I know," he sighed. "Of course you're right. But I'm concerned for what kind of life I'll be providing for you, too."

"I will be just as happy married to a stable hand as to the President of the United States—just so long as it's *you*. I don't care where we live or how much we have. We can live in a cottage somewhere, or the back of a barn, or even in a huge mansion. It is you and me that make it a home, Christopher."

"I know," he smiled. "I suppose that's another difference between men and women. Most women can be happy under any circumstances, as long as they have a man who loves them and does his best to take care of them. For a man, however, there are so many other factors that contribute to his sense of worth. A man *has* to try to build a meaningful life for himself and his family. It's just the way we are. As much as I love it here right now, I could not feel worthwhile as a man if I did not try eventually to provide better for you."

"I understand," I said. "Just so long as you know that all I want is to be with you."

"I think I realize that."

Again silence fell. It was late, and all we could hear in the warm early summer's darkness outside was the sound of crickets in branches of the oaks. Everyone else in the big house was sound asleep by now. It was probably between eleven and midnight.

"Do you see why I've been so quiet, what I mean when I say I have a lot on my mind?" Christopher asked finally.

I nodded.

"I've been talking to the Lord about all of this too—even though I haven't been talking to you about it as much as maybe I should have," he added with a smile. "But so far there just haven't been any answers."

"There will be," I said. "I have confidence in your ability to hear the Lord when he speaks."

"I've been trying to listen. But if he's speaking, his voice is awfully soft."

"He'll show you what to do when the time comes."

"Would you pray with me?"

"Of course."

We quieted ourselves as we sat there close together. I was so thankful that we'd talked. Just getting it out in the open helped me feel so much better. But I knew that simply talking wouldn't help Christopher through the predicament of uncertainty. He needed to know what to *do*.

"Father," said Christopher softly, *"we come to you in some per-*

plexity concerning the future. But you are our Father, and our concerns are really no concerns at all once we lay them in your hands. So I do that at this moment—I lay my uncertainties and anxieties and questions and concerns in your hands. Take care of us, Lord. Do with us what you will. And show me what you would have me do. Until that time, let me honor you by serving those around me with the loving heart of a friend and the willing hands of a servant. Thank you for caring for us, Lord. Amen."

What was there for me to add that would not have been mere words? Christopher had prayed what there was to pray.

Quietly, therefore, all I added was a soft amen of my own.

CHAPTER 21

CHRISTOPHER AND ALKALI JONES

Immediately when Christopher came into the house one evening a day or two later, we all knew he had big news.

He'd been gone most of the afternoon. He'd told me he was going into town, but when he wasn't back by suppertime I was beginning . . . not to worry exactly because I knew I had nothing to be anxious about, but to wonder what he'd been up to for so long.

We were all sitting at the supper table with his empty plate vacant when we heard his horse ride up. Then a few minutes later, when he burst through the door.

"Where have you been?" I asked.

"From that big smile on his face, I'd say he's been up to no good," said Pa with a grin of his own. It was so good to see them both smiling at the same time again.

Christopher took off his hat, hung it on the peg, then walked over slowly to the table and sat down, everybody watching him, waiting for him to say something.

"Well, are you gonna tell us or aren't you?" said Zack finally. "The rest may be able to sit there like cats has got their tongues, but I want to know what's up."

Christopher threw back his head and laughed, then began dishing food onto his plate from the bowls as I handed them to him.

"I spent the afternoon with Alkali Jones," he said.

"Alkali—nothing's wrong, is there?" asked Pa. Mr. Jones had hardly been around all week.

"Nothing at all. Quite the contrary, in fact," answered Christopher, taking a bite of roast beef. "If you'll all just go back to your suppers and let me get a little food into this hungry stomach of mine, I'll tell you all about it."

We all began eating again, and gradually Christopher filled us in on his visit with Mr. Jones.

"A couple of weeks ago," he began, "Alkali began to be on my mind. We'd been working close together up at the mine one afternoon. We had talked some, but it wasn't that particularly—nothing either of us said. It was just that I began to see him in a new light, began to see him as a *person* just like me."

He paused and thought for a moment, then smiled.

"You know how it is sometimes," he went on. "You're acquainted with someone for years, but all the while they remain impersonal to your eyes. You never see *inside* them. Then all of a sudden, one day you look and behold them in a new way, see expressions on their face that pierce your heart, maybe see a vulnerability or a loneliness in their eyes. You find yourself amazed that you didn't see them this way before."

As he spoke, Christopher looked around at the rest of us. There were a few nodding heads, and it was clear we knew exactly what he was talking about. We'd all had exactly that same experience with people we'd known. Almeda especially was listening intently. She loved Christopher so much. Sometimes when he spoke like this, she would start crying, just from being so happy that I had a sensitive, caring man as my husband.

"Every time this happens to me," Christopher continued, "I find new places opening up in my heart for the person God is suddenly revealing to me. What else can you say but that all at once you *love* that person . . . maybe, for the first time, a little bit like Christ himself loves him.

"Well, that's how I felt toward Alkali. I had always thought he was an interesting old character. But now I just suddenly found that I *loved* him in a new and deeper way than before.

"When a love like that blossoms in your heart, it changes everything about how you relate and interact. When you love someone, you can't ignore them or behave impersonally to them. You immediately want to reach out and help and find ways to go out of your way for them.

"That's what I wanted to do for Alkali. For the next couple of days I couldn't find enough to do for the dear man! I was nearly obsessed with trying to find ways . . . just to love him as Jesus would if *he* had been working alongside him. Of course I had to keep what I felt mostly inside, or else he'd have thought I was doting on him. I didn't want him thinking I thought he couldn't hold up his end of the work."

Christopher paused and took a few bites while we all waited for him to continue.

"Then that evening came when you, Drum, spoke about the future of the mine, and Alkali said we ought to try in a different direction. And ever since . . . well, it's no secret that we've all been wondering within ourselves what the future does hold."

He paused, and a few nods went around the table.

"Anyway, since then Alkali hasn't been around much. In fact, there were three or four days when we didn't lay eyes on him at all, and I began to wonder what the future held for him, too—not in relation to the mine, but in relation to God.

"As I lay in bed two nights ago, I found myself praying for him again. As I did, the thought struck me that he was an old man. I felt the Lord might be speaking to me, telling me that perhaps Alkali didn't have that much time left.

" 'Is that why you opened my eyes to him, Lord?' I asked.

"But I didn't sense any answer coming, only that he was my brother and that I was to continue to love him.

"Then yesterday—you remember, Drum," said Christopher, glancing toward Pa, "Alkali showed up again to work, and we were all up at the mine. But then about midway through the morning he said he wasn't feeling well. Then Nick kidded him and even tried to coax one of his stories out of him, but he couldn't even get a chuckle out of him. Not too long after that, Alkali went home for the rest of the day."

Pa nodded, a deep look of concern now on his face. The supper had by now grown cold, and nobody was thinking about food by this time.

"He was coughing pretty bad, too," said Tad.

"Yeah, now that we're talking about it," added Zack, "he did look more than a mite paler since we'd seen him last. I noticed that he seemed more tuckered out than usual."

"I noticed, too," said Christopher. "And as I was praying for him last night, I realized that those are the kinds of things you just can't ignore unless you want to wake up one day and find out that you waited too long . . . and by then it's too late. That's when I decided—right when I was praying—that today I was going to go see him and talk about some important things with him."

Christopher paused and took a deep breath, suddenly conscious, I think, of how long he'd been talking and wondering if we were getting bored with it.

Becky got up to get the coffee. A glance around the table was all Christopher needed to make him continue. Every one of us loved Alkali Jones, too, and we were anxious to know what had gone on between them.

"So I went to see him out at his cabin this afternoon, and that's where I've been ever since."

"How'd it go?" asked Pa.

"What happened?" asked Almeda almost at the same instant.

Christopher laughed.

"He invited me in, surprised to see me. He'd been lying down and was only half dressed. The place was a mess—"

"Always is," put in Pa.

"The sweet old man!" said Almeda, and I could tell the emotion of Christopher's story had gripped her.

"He offered me a chair, the only one in the room I could see, and he sat down on the edge of his bunk. It was cold in there, and I noticed there wasn't a fire in his stove. The day was warm enough, but you know how the cabin sits in the shade. So I asked if he'd like me to build him one. He said he'd be much obliged. He'd have done it himself, he said, but he was just too bushed, and he'd been in bed most of the day. I asked if he'd had anything to eat. He said he hadn't."

"Oh, but why didn't he—" began Almeda, but then stopped and turned away, her eyes filling with tears. She put a handkerchief to her face and was silent.

"He had some wood, so I built a good fire, and while it was

warming the place up, I went outside and chopped up a good supply from his logs into smaller pieces and brought enough inside to last him a couple of weeks or so. He followed me out—he didn't have any shoes on, just socks—and we chatted while I chopped up the wood. Then we went back inside, and I put together a pot of what I could find from what he had into a soup and set it on the warming stove. We chatted some more, but I wanted to get some food into him before getting down to the business of why I had come.

"People can't concentrate too well about serious things when they're hungry. That's one thing I have always noticed about Jesus in the Gospels—that he was always intensely practical about food.

"Anyway, after an hour or so, after we'd shared a couple bowls of my watery soup, and walked around a little outside together, and when the cabin was warm and comfortable, Alkali and I sat down again, me in the chair, he on the edge of his bunk, and I finally got around to the reason why I felt God had prompted me to come visit him."

CHAPTER 22

A DISARMINGLY DIRECT QUESTION

Since Christopher was there and I wasn't, I'm going to let him tell you about the rest of his conversation with Mr. Jones in his own words.

––––––

"Alkali," I said as he and I sat there, "tell me about the condition of your spiritual life."

He just sat there, staring at me with a bewildered expression for a few seconds, not knowing what to think.

"I ain't sure there's anything much to tell," he said finally. Then he laughed. You know how he laughs?

(Here I can't help intruding, because now *we* all laughed as we listened to Christopher.

"Hee, hee, hee!" laughed Tad, and it was a pretty good imitation.)

"I ain't even sure I got what you call a spiritual life," Alkali added.

"Everyone's got both a physical life and a spiritual life, Alkali. Including you. It's just that some people's spiritual side is mostly asleep, so all they're aware of is the physical."

"I reckon that's likely to be me," he said.

"Then, let me ask you something," I said. "Have you ever had any kind of personal spiritual experience?"

"How do ye mean?"

99

"Have you ever had an experience of salvation?"

"Ye mean at one o' them there revivalist meetin's—gone up t' the front cryin' and wailin'-like, an' fallin' down on yer knees?"

"I don't necessarily mean that," I said.

"Good thing," he replied, "'cause I ain't never done nothin' like that, that's fer sure. Not sure I want to, neither."

"No, I meant something more personal than that. It might not have had anything to do with a church service at all."

"Ye got me a mite confused there, Braxton. Ye talkin' about religion that ain't got t' do with church? Next thing I know, ye'll be tellin' me it ain't got t' do with heaven neither."

I couldn't help chuckling. "Actually, Alkali, that's true," I said. "If the Bible can be trusted, being a Christian doesn't have much to do with heaven. It's about how we live here and now."

"Ye don't gotta be religious t' git t' heaven?"

"Not according to what Jesus said. All he spoke of was what we *do*, how we *live*—whether that spiritual part of us is awake and making a difference in how we live . . . *right now*."

"Not sure I ever heard o' such kind o' religion."

"I'm not talking about religion at all, Alkali, but about God and you . . . and whether the two of you've ever had dealings together."

He just looked at me without saying a word, so I went on.

"Have you ever felt like God was talking to you?" I said. "Have you ever prayed when you were by yourself? Have you ever thought about whether God was up there or not and wondered what he might think about *you*, Alkali Jones?"

"I reckon I prayed a time or two."

"Did God ever answer your prayers?"

"Guess not that I could tell. Reckon he coulda, but I just didn't know it."

"You've never felt that God was talking personally to you?"

"Didn't figure he talked personally t' folks nowadays. Figured that was fer Moses and them long-time-ago fellers."

"He speaks today, too," I said, "though in different ways. You ever wondered about whether God was up there or not?"

"Sure, ain't ever'body?"

"I think so. You ever wondered what he thinks about *you?*"

That one caught him off guard, and he had to ponder it a while.

"I ain't sure," he said finally. "I ain't exactly thought about it jist like yer sayin'. Though when a body does somethin' wrong, ye can't help wonderin' if the Lord's gonna strike ye down."

"You think that's what God's like, waiting to strike folks down when they do things wrong?"

"I reckon. Ain't it?"

"Not if what the Bible says is true."

"Huh . . . what about hell an' all that there brimstone stuff?"

"That's in the Bible, all right, but not when God's character is being described. The Bible says that God is loving and kind and good. Jesus says he's our Father, not some great monster who's waiting to pounce on us when we do something wrong."

"But I know he don't like it when folks does bad."

"Of course he doesn't. But not because he's waiting to punish them, but because he knows they'll be happier if they're good. Punishing people isn't the first thing on his mind."

"So, what is?"

"God wants to *love* his creatures. That's what he wants to do more than anything. He made us, after all, for no other reason than that."

"Than what?"

"To love him and to be loved by him. But if we keep the spiritual part of us asleep, there's no way he *can* show us that he loves us."

"Well, how does a body wake it up?" he asked.

"That's the personal experience of salvation I asked you about before. You've heard about being born again, haven't you?"

"I reckon I heard about it. Don't reckon I know much what it is, though."

"It's nothing more than waking up that part of you that's asleep, that spiritual part of you that God put inside every man and woman. When he made us, he put a little piece of himself way down inside us. The trouble is, most folks don't know he put it there. When most folks think of *life*, they think all it means is being physically alive. They don't realize there's an even more important part of life waiting down inside them to be awakened—be brought into life, just like being born."

"Never heard nothin' about all that."

"Most people haven't."

"Why don't God just wake it up? Why does he put it inside folks, sleepin' like that? Don't seem t' make much sense. Seems like God'd know better'n that."

I couldn't help laughing. It makes me chuckle again just to tell about it. Alkali was so honest about it that he took me off guard.

"I'm not exactly sure, Alkali," I answered him, "but I think it's because he doesn't want to do the waking up himself. He wants to give us a share in the waking-up process. He wants us to wake *ourselves* up."

Alkali didn't say anything for a minute or two, and I could tell he was thinking hard about everything I'd said. I just waited. Finally he spoke up again.

"All this time," he said, "I been around plenty of folks that was religious enough. Even ol' Drum got religion hisself after his family come and after he got hisself hitched. There ain't no mistakin' that he's been a different feller since then. The whole town sees it and respects him fer it. So maybe that's what yer sayin' about wakin' up that religious side o' ye. An' I reckon, watching 'em all like that, I'd have t' say it looked kinda nice t' me, but no one ever told me how to get in on it myself."

"I've seen you plenty of times in church," I said. "What do you think when you sit there listening to talk of spiritual things?"

"Yeah, I been in church plenty o' times, and the Rev. is pretty good. I mostly like what he says, but I still always kinda thought o' myself as a visitor."

"Why do you go, then?"

"Don't know. T' see folks, I reckon. Guess I figured ye was supposed to go t' church. Don't get me wrong, I like what I seen happ'nin' in Drum and Nick, though at first I weren't none too sure. I always hoped when the time came for me t' pass over t' the other side, I'd be right with the Lord and that he'd have favor on an ol' coot like me. But I wasn't never too sure."

"Would you like to be?" I asked.

"Like to be what?'

"Sure that you are right with the Lord."

"You bet I would. But I didn't know if ye could be sure o' them kinds o' things, and I reckon I was always a mite embarrassed to ask Drum."

"Well, you *can* be sure of them, Alkali," I said. "And it's not just a matter of the Lord's having favor on you when you pass over to the other side, like you say. The same thing that will help you there will also wake up the sleeping spiritual side of you now so that you can know what it is to live completely . . . right now."

"So how can a feller be sure?"

"By saying to your spiritual side, that little piece of God that's inside of you: *Wake up!* It's what Jesus called being born again. It's so simple to do that it only takes a minute. After that, life begins all over again, with both your physical *and* your spiritual halves awake.

"Would you like me to help you wake up your spiritual side, like your friend Drum has done?"

"I'd be obliged to ye, young Braxton. Ye just tell me what t' do an' I'll do it."

CHAPTER 23

WAKING UP THE OTHER HALF

As Christopher spoke, I could not help glancing over out of the corner of my eye at Pa where he sat listening. His eyes were glistening and wet as we heard Christopher talk about his conversation with his old and dear friend. But I'll let Christopher continue on with the story.

"All right, Alkali," I went on. "How do you feel about talking to God?"

"Ye mean prayin'?"

"Doesn't matter what you call it. Do you think you can talk to God?"

"Don't rightly know. . . . I reckon."

"Some men can't. It takes a strong man, with guts and courage. It's not the kind of thing a weakling can do."

"I reckon I oughta be able t' give it a try. But why's a feller gotta talk t' God t' wake that place in him up?"

"Because you need God's help to do it. Only God can wake it up, but he can't wake it up without your asking him to. You can't be born again all by yourself. You need God's help, but you have to ask him for it."

"Wasn't you gonna tell me what t' do?"

"All right, just say to God—"

"I gotta close my eyes?"

"Doesn't matter."

"I thought ye had t' close yer eyes when ye was prayin'."

"You just have to talk to God. Imagine that he's sitting right here in this room with us. Would you close your eyes to talk to him?"

"Don't reckon. But he ain't in the room."

"Of course he is. We just can't see him, that's all."

"You're sayin' I should pray with my eyes *open?*" asked Alkali. It was such an incredible thought to him that God was right beside him and not way off in the sky somewhere.

(We all smiled at the thought of Mr. Jones trying to imagine God coming and sitting down in his messy little cabin. He had spun so many tall tales in his life, but I think he'd finally met his match in what Christopher was now telling him.

And everything Christopher was saying was true, unlike some of Mr. Jones' most outlandish stories!)

"It doesn't make any difference one way or another," I went on. "Let's just begin talking to him, and you can do whatever you feel like. How's that?"

"Fair enough," said Alkali. "Ye're gonna tell me what t' say?"

I nodded. "Now just tell him that you would like his help in waking up the spiritual side of you that's been asleep."

He looked at me, eyes wide. There was no fear in his expression, just a childlike, innocent bewilderment. It was all so new to him.

"What do I call him?" he asked after a moment.

"You can call him *God*, or *Lord*, if you like. People pray to him using many of his names. What he mostly wants us to call him is *Father*, because that's what he is to us. That's what Jesus called him and what he told his disciples to call him."

"So now I just say it to him, huh?"

I nodded.

"How?"

"In your own words—however it comes out."

"All right, then, here goes. God . . . er, uh . . . *Father*," he said, stumbling some at first, "I reckon it'd be good . . . uh, fer this other side of me t' get woke up. Braxton here says I can't . . . uh, do it without yer helpin' me, an' so I'm askin' ye t' do whatever it is ye do t' wake old men like me up when they ain't been in the habit o' thinkin' too much about religious things."

"Good, Alkali," I said to him, "that's just exactly right. God is listening, and he's heard everything you've said. He's very pleased. I'm sure he's smiling right now, just like a proud father would be when his little son is first learning to walk."

"Ye really think so?"

"Of course he's pleased. That's what you're doing—you're just like a little boy, reaching up for your father's hand to learn how to walk on your *spiritual* legs. Now, tell him you want to be one of his children. Tell him that you want to be part of his family and that you want to be born again so that you can be his son forever."

"God," he said, "ever'thing Braxton said is right. I reckon I'd like t' be born again so I can be in yer family along with Drum an' his family an' the Rev. an' Braxton here an' all the rest of 'em. I don't know exactly what t' do, but I'd like t' be yer son, that is, if you'd have me."

"That's excellent, Alkali!" I said. "Now, just tell your heavenly Father that you're giving yourself to him so that he can be in charge of your life from now on."

"God, I'm givin' myself t' you, like he says."

By now it was all I could do to keep the tears from gushing out my eyes, but I forced myself to remain calm.

———

As the rest of us listened to Christopher tell it, I think we all felt exactly the same way! I don't think there was a dry eye in the house.

Christopher stopped and looked around at all of us. I didn't know whether to laugh or cry. Pa was looking down, just kind of shaking his head.

"I . . . I just never realized," Pa said. "I figured if Alkali wanted to know more, he'd ask. I didn't want to push it on him."

"It's sometimes very difficult to tell what someone is thinking," said Christopher. "Especially about spiritual things."

"I just figured he was coming along with the rest of us," said Pa. "I'm happy for him, and I'm indebted to you, Christopher, for leading the way for him like you done. I just can't help wondering if I should have done more earlier."

"Put it out of your head, Drum," replied Christopher with an encouraging tone. "The Lord makes use of many factors in a person's life to bring them to a point of readiness to say, *Wake up!* to their spiritual being. Your life has been a tremendous influence upon Alkali all through the years. He would not have been so eager to respond to the things I had to say had it not been for you."

"I reckon you're right."

"Another thing to remember, Drummond," added Almeda, "is that oftentimes the Father will use someone other than those closest to us when that moment of decision actually comes. You and Agatha gave Corrie, for instance, all her early training and instruction, and you set her values and attitudes in a godly direction. Yet there came a time in her life when he chose to use me in a more direct way as well. And he brought Hawk along in Zack's life just at the right time. Such it is with Alkali and you and now Christopher. God makes use of us all, in distinctive ways, to carry out his purposes."

"You're both right," said Pa. "I just hope I didn't overlook Alkali and maybe take him for granted."

"You didn't," said Christopher. "He considers you his best friend. He's been watching you all these years, seeing the changes. Your life affected him in a thousand ways, whether you ever talked to him directly about God or not. I truly believe, Drum, that you are the chief reason for what happened today."

"And the Lord wasn't overlooking him all this time," said Almeda. "That's why he turned Christopher's prayers toward Alkali once the time was ripe to harvest the seed you had been silently sowing through the years."

"Well, I want to know what happened next," I finally said to Christopher. "Did you and Mr. Jones talk any more?"

Christopher laughed. "Did we ever! He was full of questions and just as eager to listen to what I had to say as a little child. It was wonderful."

"Then, on with it!" boomed Pa. "We want to hear every word."

Christopher drew in a deep breath, then continued on.

CHAPTER 24

MAKING SPIRITUAL LEGS STRONG

"Very good, Alkali," I said. "You've done it. Congratulations."
I reached out my hand to his and shook it. "Welcome to God's family!"

"That's all there is t' the thing?' he said, surprised to find it over with so quickly.

"That's all."

"I don't feel no different."

"That doesn't matter," I said. "You asked God to wake up your spiritual life. That's what he was waiting for. It *is* awake now. You *have* been born again. You *are* his son, and he *is* your Father."

"I feel like just the same tired ol' man."

"That's the physical part you feel, and it *hasn't* changed. It's only the spiritual part that has changed. While the physical part of you is still the same old man, the spiritual part is like a newborn baby, just barely awake. That's why you don't feel it yet."

"Reckon what ye say makes some sense."

"The spiritual place down inside you doesn't know much about living yet. You and the Lord working together have wakened it up. Now it needs to be taught how to *live*, just like your physical side had to learn how to live when you were a baby."

"Will I feel it down there someday?"

"Sure, once it learns how to walk. Spiritual muscles are just like physical muscles—you've got to make them strong by exercising them. You've got to teach your spiritual legs how to walk."

"How in tarnation does a body do that?"

"Practice . . . exercise—the same way a child's physical legs get strong."

"Practice what?"

"Using your spiritual muscles."

"How's that?"

"Practice walking like God wants his sons and daughters to walk."

"Huh?"

"Behaving like God wants his people to behave. Talking like God wants his people to talk. Doing what God wants his people to do. Thinking like God wants his people to think."

"How does a body know all that stuff God wants?"

"I imagine you know quite a bit already, Alkali. You told me yourself that you've listened to Rev. Rutledge many times. So now I'm going to ask you—what do *you* think God wants his sons and daughters to do? How do you think he wants them to behave?"

A surprised look came over the old man's face.

"Uh . . . I reckon he wants them t' be good . . . t' be nice t' other folks, I reckon," he answered.

"Certainly," I said. "That's right at the top of the list. What else?"

"Uh . . . t' pray?"

"That's very important as well. You must talk to your Father if you want to know what he wants you to do."

"Ye mean . . . jist talk t' him, like we done a minute ago?"

"Yep—just like he's your Father."

"What do ye say?"

"Tell him what you're thinking and feeling, what you're wondering about. *Father*, you might say, *what do you want me to do?*"

"Ye make everything sound too blame simple, Braxton!"

I laughed. "It *is* simple, Alkali," I said. "Not always easy, but simple enough."

He just sat there, sort of shaking his head.

"All right," I went on, "besides being nice to people and praying, is there anything else you can think of that God would want his people to do?"

"Well . . . don't know—being good seems likely t' cover it."

"I think you're probably right. So how does a person be what you call good?"

"I don't know . . . puttin' other folks ahead o' himself, I reckon."

"That's exactly it. Putting other people first. Just simple unselfishness. If you do those few things—be nice, be good, put other people first, and then, like I said, talk to your Father and try to listen to what he says and do whatever he tells you—then your spiritual legs will get the exercise they need to grow strong."

"That's all?"

"That's not *all*, but that's where it starts."

"How do ye find out what else he wants ye t' do?"

"First of all, when you and he are talking together, you can ask him to speak to you."

"How's he do that?"

"In your heart, in your mind. He puts thoughts there. You can ask him to help you hear him, and he'll do it. Then it's important to do whatever you think he might be telling you to do. Your legs will grow stronger, too, by listening to Rev. Rutledge and putting into practice everything you learn from him and by always trying to do whatever you think Jesus would do in any situation.

"That's how your spiritual legs get strong, Alkali—*by doing what Jesus would do*. That's what being a Christian is—following Jesus. Doing what he would do, thinking like he would think, treating people like he would treat them, being a son to your heavenly Father just like he showed us how to do."

The cabin got quiet. Finally it seemed he was out of questions.

We sat for several minutes, and this time it was silent for quite a long time. I saw Alkali shiver slightly and realized the fire in his stove had burned low. I got up and put a few more logs onto it and stirred up the coals. When I sat back down I could see that he was thinking hard about what we had been discussing. I waited.

"Blamed if it ain't completely different than anything I done heard about afore," he finally said. "Ye ain't said a word, Braxton, about what a body believes or don't believe. Ye ain't talked about heaven an' hell or that thing I heard about called santeeficashun—whatever in tarnation that is—and all the other kind o' highfalutin stuff religious folks is always jawin' about. You just make it all down t' earth so's a body can git a grip on it with his teeth."

"Does your friend Drum go in for the up-in-the-clouds kind of religious words and jargon you're talking about?"

"No, don't reckon he does. No, Drum ain't no highfalutin kind o' feller. He's like you—practical about it."

"The kind of religion that doesn't mind some dirt under the fingernails and sweat on the shirt?"

"That's it—hee, hee, hee! Dirty, sweaty kind o' religion. Hee, hee, hee!"

(We all laughed to hear Christopher tell it, trying to imitate Mr. Jones' cackling laugh. But Christopher couldn't do it as well as Tad.)

"That's Christianity, Alkali. It's not for people who want to keep their hands clean. Practical—you bet it's practical! It's the most practical creed you can live by, the most down-to-earth religion there is. That's the kind of man Jesus was too—dirt in the fingernails, sweat on the shirt . . . a real man's kind of man. That's why we're supposed to try to live like he did."

"I always figured him fer—if ye'll pardon me sayin' it—fer kinda a limp-wristed womanly sort o' feller."

"Many people make that mistake, Alkali. But if you read through the Gospels, you'll find something altogether different.

"Let me ask you a question. If someone you didn't know was to come along and tell you to come with him, and he looked to you like a weakling, would you follow him?"

"Ain't likely," he answered.

"What about your friend Drum," I said. "Is he a weakling?"

(I glanced over at Pa, but not so much as a muscle of his face twitched. He was too caught up in Christopher's account even to react to the question one way or the other.)

"Not fer a second," said Alkali.

"And that's why you like to be around him?"

"Ye're right there."

"Why do you think the rest of the community thinks so highly of him—because he's weak?"

Alkali snorted. "Drum ain't weak!"

"Exactly! And that's just the way Jesus was. Why else do you think those big burly fishermen left everything to go with him?

Would they have done that for a weakling?"

"Don't reckon so."

"They followed him. Huge crowds followed him. Women followed him, men followed him, rich people followed him, poor people followed him. He was a man's man. He knew how to fish, and those nets could be as heavy as the big rocks we pull out of our mine, Alkali. He worked with his hands. By trade he was a carpenter—no doubt had to lug around big boards. He walked long distances. When he took a whip in his hands, everyone scattered in fear. This man Jesus was a strong man who made folks stand up and listen."

It got quiet again, and Alkali and I sat in silence for a long time. I think finally poor Alkali had taken in about all the new information for one day he could handle.

Well, that's about it. I think I've recounted nearly the whole conversation.

We all kind of shuffled around on our chairs. All the supper things were still on the table. Nobody'd touched anything in an hour. I shivered now, too. Our fire had almost gone out just like Mr. Jones'.

"I just have one question," said Pa, chuckling even as he thought of it.

"What's that?" said Christopher.

"Back when you were first telling us about Alkali praying and him wondering about whether to look or not . . . did Alkali have his eyes open or shut?"

Christopher smiled at the memory.

"He kept them open," he replied, "staring down at the floor the whole time."

Again we became silent around the table.

The magnitude of what Christopher had been telling us struck us all over again.

What a wonderful thing it was!

None of us could believe it . . . though of course we did believe it! I think every one of us wanted to run right over to Mr. Jones' cabin right then and give him a big hug, but of course it was way past dark by now and much too late.

"God bless the dear, dear man!" said Almeda after some time had passed.

The words were scarcely out of her mouth when Ruth bounded rambunctiously through the door from having dinner with her three cousins—Erich, twelve, Joan, nine, and Jeffrey, six.

"Hey, Ruthie!" said Pa, getting out of his chair and scooping her up into a great big bear hug. "Your Uncle Nick at home?"

"Yes, Pa."

"How'd you like to do something for me?"

"Sure, Pa."

"Would you run back up to your aunt and uncle's and tell them we gotta see them as soon as they can get down here?"

"Why, Pa?"

"You tell them we got some big news they're going to want to hear."

Pa put her down on the floor, and she was off again with even more energy than she had made her arrival with.

Gradually the house quieted once more.

"Well, Christopher, I gotta say it again," said Pa, "I am deeply in your debt for what you've done. I want you to know how much it means to me. I see how what Almeda said a while ago is true— I couldn't have helped ol' Alkali see it all so clear as you've done."

There wasn't anything more perfect to be said. We had always loved Mr. Jones so much. He was like one of the family.

Now he truly *was* one of the family!

CHAPTER 25

IDLE GOSSIP

The morning after Christopher's talk with Mr. Jones, the old prospector showed up at breakfast bright-eyed and smiling. He didn't say anything about what had happened and neither did anyone else. But it was obvious he was happy about it and pleased with himself. He might have even tried to comb his hair, but I couldn't quite tell, and I didn't want to ask. If he had, the attempt wasn't too successful, which was hardly a surprise because I doubt it had been combed since he was a boy!

Mr. Jones was eager and ready to get to the mine, though he was coughing quite a bit and didn't seem altogether well enough to work. But after what had happened, Pa wasn't about to say anything about shutting down the mine. So everything went on as usual, and gradually we all fell back into our old ways.

The men resumed work at the mine pretty much like before. I think the change in Alkali Jones had more to do with it than anything, because Pa still hadn't made any more of a firm decision about the future. They didn't find any more gold, however, and I couldn't help wondering how long the mining would last.

Summer came, and the weather got hot.

I visited Jennie Woodstock another time or two. Things hadn't gotten any better between her and Tom that I could see.

Christopher had done his best to strike up some kind of relationship with Tom, but without much success. Tom had seemed genuinely appreciative of Christopher's help with the fence work, but afterward he hadn't seemed any more inclined to talk or establish a friendship. Some people are receptive to spiritual things, some are just uninterested, and still others seem to resent them. I was gradually getting the idea that Tom was the last kind. I think he resented Christopher, even though Christopher never said anything about the Lord at all, just because he knew where Christopher stood in his faith.

Christopher and I continued to visit other people, in addition to Jennie and Tom. We also took long rides on horseback in the late afternoons and warm evenings, exploring places even I'd never been before.

Several days a week I rode in to town to help Almeda at the Hollister Supply Company. Back when we first met Almeda, this was her business, the Parrish Mine and Freight. But after she married Pa and the business gradually changed from supplying miners to supplying farmers and townspeople, she and Pa decided to change the name. Half the time, though, we still called it the Mine and Freight.

It was a little funny, because now that I was married, Almeda insisted on paying me a wage along with the other workers. I objected at first, but eventually I had no choice but to give in.

"It's only fair, then," I said finally, "if you pay me to work for you, that Christopher and I pay you and Pa something in return for letting us live in the bunkhouse."

"That's between Christopher and your father," laughed Almeda. "As long as I'm running the Mine and Freight, you're working for *me*, and *I'm* going to pay you—and accept nothing in return except good honest work."

"All right," I laughed, "you win!"

One day when I was in town and business was slow and there wasn't much to do, I took an hour off and walked about and went into some shops. I happened to be in the Mercantile, away from the counter and with my back to the door looking at some fabric, when Mrs. Sinclair and Mrs. Gilly walked in. That they had no idea I was anywhere within sight or hearing was soon more than obvious.

" . . . how they can all stay there together when the children are grown and well past marrying age is beyond me," Mrs. Gilly was saying as they walked in and the door shut behind them. "It's just unnatural."

At first I paid little attention, having no idea who they were talking about, until the town's most energetic gossip spoke up in reply.

"I certainly would not have wanted mine to stay at home. I was glad to get my own four girls married off as soon as possible."

"Let their husbands have the trouble, I always say."

"They've always been a bit of a strange bunch, to my way of thinking," Mrs. Sinclair went on, "ever since the Parrish woman took on that Hollister clan and tried to reform that father of theirs."

My face reddened, and my ears perked up, and immediately I wished I could find a hole to crawl into. Better yet, a mole tunnel like Pa had talked about, so that I could burrow right out of that shop!

The lady at the counter, Mrs. Tarrant, wasn't someone I knew very well, and she had been occupied when I came in. So she didn't know I was in the shop and so did nothing to alert the two gossips. I had no choice but to stand there listening, out of sight, and look for a chance to make my getaway without being seen.

" . . . and that young Becky," Mrs. Gilly went on, lowering her voice now that they were inside. "Why she isn't married yet I can't imagine."

" . . . pretty enough, but . . . must be something they aren't saying. . . ."

I was doing my best not to listen, to block their busybodying voices out of my ears, but it was impossible. Especially when a moment later I heard my *own* name mentioned!

"What about Corrie and that husband of hers?"

"He doesn't seem in too big a hurry to carry his own load, just staying there mooching off the folks."

" . . . don't know what to think."

I was furious! But now I had to stay calm to hear whatever else they might say.

" . . . thought it was a good match at first, despite the man's peculiar views about courtship and marriage."

" . . . an unusual one. . . ."

" . . . can't help but wonder, what with them living right there with her parents—and in the barn, from what I hear!"

" . . . can't mean it!"

"That's what I hear."

" . . . well I never. . . ."

" . . . don't know whether to believe it. Whoever heard of such a thing!"

" . . . and that Drummond Hollister . . . promising future in Sacramento . . . turning his back on it and returning to mining. . . ."

" . . . at his age. . . ."

" . . . and a played-out mine at that!"

" . . . goes to show, some men never change. . . ."

" . . . got the gold fever again . . . probably be running off and leaving his family again just like he did when he was in the East. . . ."

"There always was something strange about the whole clan . . . when the children first came down . . . father wouldn't even claim them."

"What about Almeda Parrish? Acting like a man . . ."

" . . . wearing pants and running a freight company . . ."

" . . . how I hear it . . ."

At that point Mrs. Tarrant greeted the two women and asked if they needed help. They thanked her but said they just wanted to look about, then continued on with the real purpose behind their shopping trip—catching up with one another on all the town gossip!

" . . . and that Jennie Woodstock—she wanted that husband so bad, you'd think she'd at least work a little harder to keep him. . . ."

" . . . seems like a nice enough young man. . . ."

" . . . well, do you know what I hear?"

I couldn't stand another word! By this time I didn't care if they saw me or not—I had to get out of there!

I put down the bolt of fabric and walked to the front of the store, along the aisle next to the window, opened the door quickly, and hurried outside, taking in several big lungfuls of air to calm myself. Then I half-ran across the street and back to the Supply Company.

I didn't know whether to be hurt or angry, and I must confess to probably more of the latter than was good.

I was distracted most of the afternoon, but by the time I got home and told Christopher, I was ready to laugh about it with him.

It was a hot evening, much too warm to cook and eat inside. We invited Uncle Nick and Aunt Katie and the cousins down for a barbecue. Pa cooked up a side of beef over the fire pit, and we ate together and talked outside between the house and the bunkhouse, sitting on makeshift benches and chairs from the house.

I recounted what I'd heard, without telling the names of the gossipers and of course without mentioning a word about what they'd said about Becky. By the time I was done, everyone was laughing hard.

"Mrs. Sinclair and Mrs. Gilly, eh?" said Uncle Nick.

"I didn't say who it was."

"You don't have to, Corrie!" laughed Aunt Katie. "Everyone knows how this community keeps up on its news . . . and it's *not* from the newspapers!"

Again there was laughter.

"But why us?" said Zack. "Of all the people they could talk about . . . why *us?*"

"Anyone who tries to do something a little different than everyone else is an immediate magnet for the interest of such types," said Almeda.

"We're not *different*," remarked Tad.

"Probably more than it seems to us," laughed Almeda.

"Different from the likes of them two ol' biddies, that's for sure," laughed Uncle Nick.

"Now, be nice, Nick," chided Almeda.

"Aw, you're right—but people who go about spreading hearsay about other people get my goat."

"Don't they know that families are *supposed* to stay together?" said Christopher. "Why, who was in the ark?—Noah and his sons and their wives and families."

"And Noah was six hundred years old at the time!" added Almeda. "That's a *really* long time to keep a family together."

"Why, the Hollister clan is doing no more than Noah's family did!" added Christopher. "I think it's the most natural thing in the world."

"It is sad," said Aunt Katie, "that families break up, and children go their own way all too soon—and wind up too far away to visit home." Her voice began to tremble as she realized she was describing herself, so many miles away from her Virginia birthplace. Uncle Nick moved over behind her and put his hands on her shoulders. She smiled up at him and patted one of his strong, rough hands.

"Or fathers leaving when they shouldn't," remarked Pa with a tone more serious than the rest, obviously thinking of his own past.

"Noah's sons remained with him in a single though extended family unit for years," added Christopher, "maybe even hundreds of years after they were grown and married. One of his sons was ninety-eight at the time of the flood, and who knows how long they remained together afterward, because Noah lived for another three hundred fifty years."

"So—there you have it, Tad," said Almeda triumphantly. "If we *are* different from most families because we're all still here together—all except for Emily anyway—and because Drummond and I like having you here with us, we're only different because we're doing what Noah did!"

"Well, then, that sets my mind at ease," laughed Tad. "Though I'm not sure I'll stay here with you quite as long as Noah's sons did. By the time *I'm* ninety-eight, I plan on moving on to some other things!"

CHAPTER 26

WAYLAID

The jail in Auburn wasn't the worst he had seen. But it was a jail, and that made it bad enough.

"Hey, deputy," he called out, "when's lunch?"

"Shut up, you!" replied a voice from the other end of the small wood and brick building. "Lunch is when it comes, and you're lucky to get any at all."

"When's the sheriff gettin' back? I gotta get outta this hole."

No reply came. A moment later booted footsteps sauntered toward the three bare cells, two of which were empty and the third of which contained the troublemaker who had shot up half the town the night before. The deputy stopped a yard or two in front of the occupied cell and stared at his prisoner with considerably less fear than he would have had the bars not stood between them.

"You ain't going *nowhere* anytime soon," he said in the haughty tone of one who enjoyed lording his position over another.

"I want to talk to the sheriff. I gotta get outta here—got business t' tend to."

"Business! Ha, ha, ha," laughed the deputy. "What kind of business could the likes of *you* possibly have?"

"My *own* business, that's what kind!" the prisoner shot back.

"You tell me your business, and I'll see what I can do," baited the deputy, who had not the slightest intention of doing anything.

"Let's just say I got business in the gold country."

"Don't you know the gold's all gone?"

"My business ain't got to do with gold, but lead," said the pris-

120

oner, the hint of a grin revealing not as many teeth as it should have.

"Well, the sheriff ain't gonna be back for a few days," rejoined the deputy, tiring of the pointless banter, "so you just get used to your new quarters. 'Sides, he said you might be our guest here for a coupla months."

"Months! On what charge?"

"That's what comes of losing your head over a poker game and shooting up a saloon. Unless you can pay the three hundred dollars in damages, you might as well get used to that cell of yours. Ha, ha!"

"I ain't gettin' used to nothing. I gotta get north, I tell ya."

"Well, you're a blamed fool if you think you're gonna talk me out of the key to that door. And you're even a bigger fool if you think you're gonna bust out."

The deputy turned to walk back to the office.

CHAPTER 27

THROUGH NEW EYES

In May Mr. Henderson died.

None of us had known him too well. An elderly widower, he was one of the many newcomers to Miracle Springs during the years of growth after the gold rush. He'd arrived shortly after I left for the East during the war, come from New York alone to spend his last days in the booming new state of California. How or why he wound up in Miracle Springs I didn't know. But he did wind up here, and from what everyone said he had loved every minute of his last few years.

People said he was wealthy, though he didn't look it or act it. Books, he said, had always been his passion, and his collection of three or four thousand titles was one of the few things of value he had crated up and brought with him through Panama by ship. The town gossips had had a wonderful time speculating about what was in all those boxes he arrived with!

No one knew if he had any relatives, but the whole town found out soon enough right after he died. Mr. Henderson had left almost everything he owned to the town of Miracle Springs—especially his books!

The books of theology, about two or three hundred of them, went to Rev. Rutledge. All the rest went to the town for the establishment of the Miracle Springs Library, along with five thousand dollars to build a new wing on our small town hall to house the books. If any money was left over, which Pa said there surely would be, it was to be placed in a fund for the purchasing of additional volumes.

122

Miracle Springs was all abuzz when the news came out. No-body'd even ever thought about a library, and now we would have the nicest one north of Sacramento.

"I doubt the church cost us more than a couple hundred in ma-terials," Pa said when we were talking about it after the church ser-vice where Rev. Rutledge had made the surprise announcement. "If all the men chip in and do the work, why, I can't imagine there'd be less than four and a half thousand left over!"

"It will no doubt be the finest library in northern California outside of San Francisco and Sacramento," Almeda had remarked. "Quite a thing for a little place like Miracle Springs."

"I can't wait to see the books!" I said.

"Nor can I!" added Christopher, his mouth watering at the thought of it.

A ground breaking was scheduled to coincide with the July fourth celebration.

Pa and Rev. Rutledge and some of the other men got together and made plans. The annual town picnic was moved up from early fall so it could all happen together.

They would break the ground, we'd have a picnic feast and fireworks, and construction on the new library wing would begin the following week.

It was too bad it took a death to do it, but the news about what Mr. Henderson had done sent an excitement through the whole community. Nobody talked about anything else, it seemed, for weeks.

"It makes you realize, though," Christopher reflected when we were alone together one evening in June, "how easy it is to take people for granted. Every day I pray that the Lord will open my eyes to those around me. Yet here was this man living among us that, now that he is gone, we realize we hardly knew."

"I know," I said. "Just think what kind of a man he must have been to love books so. Yet now it is too late to find out. It's sad in a way."

"We won't be able to know him more personally. But it may not be altogether too late."

"What do you mean?" I said.

"I find it intriguing how much you can learn about an individual by the kinds of books he or she reads," said Christopher. "I'm already anticipating the chance to pore through the Henderson treasure trove—not just for the books and the authors themselves, as much as I will love that, but also to learn more about our loving benefactor."

July fourth came and everyone was in high spirits.

Rev. Rutledge had pretty much recovered from his spring illness and, while moving more slowly than he used to, presided over the events with a great smile on his face. Who could have appreciated the formation of a library more than a minister or a teacher? He and Christopher and Mrs. Nilson the schoolteacher could hardly wait to see the library completed so as to get all the rest of the books out and onto the shelves that would be their new homes. Rev. Rutledge, of course, had already seen most of them because Mr. Henderson had named him executor of his estate.

"Just like old times, isn't it, Drum?" Rev. Rutledge called out to my father as we all arrived. "Who'd have thought we'd still be raising buildings together after all this time?"

"I doubt they'll let either you or me up on the roof like we were on the new church back in '53," rejoined Pa with a laugh. "We're getting too old for that kind of thing!"

"Well, I'm at least going to pound as many nails as I can," said the aging minister. "For me, a library will be *almost* as good as a church."

"Amen to that!" added Christopher, jumping out of the wagon and then helping me down.

Everyone who came brought a shovel from home. As wagons rolled in you could hear the clunking and clattering of shovels bouncing around in back. By the time everything was ready, there must have been three or four hundred shovels!

We got the tables all set up with the food spread out first, then everyone moved to the south side of the town hall where the new wing was planned. Rev. Rutledge gave a short speech, then everyone crowded in with all their shovels. I don't think there was an inch of ground that wasn't about to be broken into.

Rev. Rutledge gave the signal, and with hundreds of shouts and hollers everyone dug into the ground to try to scoop up a piece of the dry earth to turn over.

The ground was hard and hot, but that didn't stop the shouts and the enthusiastic digging. Then followed a great cheer from everyone, and we stood back to look at what we had done.

All of us working together had barely managed to scoop two or three inches off the top. But the ground had been broken and the brown grass and weeds scraped off—the new library begun!

We all retired to the tables for our Fourth of July feast. All the women had outdone themselves—there were almost as many full plates and platters as there had been shovels!

After we were through eating, I excused myself, walked to the wagon, got my sketchbook, and began walking up the slope east of the church building.

"Hey, where you going?" Christopher called out, running after me.

"For a little walk," I answered.

"Want some company?" he said as he reached my side.

"If you don't mind, Christopher, let me have ten minutes to myself. Then come up and join me, and I'll show you why."

"Ten minutes, then," he said, leaning down to kiss me, "but not a minute more!"

I continued on up the hill, then took my seat on a familiar rock and began my drawing.

It had been my tradition, every year at the town picnic since the very first one when I was only sixteen, to climb up this hill overlooking the town and draw a sketch of what I saw. I now had more than ten of those sketches, and every year you could see how Miracle Springs was changing and growing.

Now I drew in a long breath and gazed out over the scene with contentment and satisfaction. How it had changed since Zack, Emily, Becky, Tad, and I had arrived here with Mr. Dixon, young and bewildered, not knowing a soul and having no idea what was going to become of us.

Not only had the town changed. So had all the people.

Most of all, I thought, how I had myself grown and changed! I could hardly believe it—*I was a married woman!*

Would I ever get used to the thought?

Looking out over the town like this always reminded me of so many things that had happened over the years. I suppose that was one of the reasons I kept doing it—I liked to rekindle the memories. I never wanted to forget a thing I had experienced in my life, good or bad. Everything goes in to contribute to the people we are—a character stew, Zack said his friend Hawk had called it—and I didn't want to forget what the Lord had put into mine.

I laughed to myself as I heard one of Alkali Jones' high *"hee, hee, hee"* laughs! It might not have been quite as energetic as it once was, but he sure had been happy lately since giving his heart to the Lord. When they weren't talking about the new library, folks in town were talking about that.

I took out a pencil and began to sketch the town and its surroundings, beginning with the church as I always did. Not really so much had changed since last year. There were no new buildings, nothing that would appear on my paper. The biggest change was within *me*. I wondered if those kinds of things made a difference in the way a person drew.

The ten minutes passed quickly. Before I knew it, I glanced up, and there was Christopher striding toward me with a smile on his face.

"I told you—ten minutes!" he said. "What have you been up to?"

He knelt beside me and looked at my paper, then I flipped back the pages and showed him all the rest, starting with the one where down at the bottom, in my sixteen-year-old hand, were the words: *Church Dedication, Miracle Springs, 1853*.

Christopher gazed and pondered each one in order, nodding and smiling occasionally.

"This is wonderful, Corrie," he said at length, after he had gone through them all. "It's a whole visual history of Miracle Springs."

"They're only sketches," I said.

"But don't you see? They capture a moment of time that will never come back, and all together . . . what a story they tell!"

Suddenly his eyes shot open wide.

"I have just had the greatest idea!" he exclaimed.

"What?"

"What would you think," said Christopher excitedly, "of making frames for each one of these and then displaying them on a wall in the new library? I can see it now—*A History of Miracle Springs*

As Seen Through the Eyes of Corrie Belle Hollister."

I laughed.

"I might agree," I said, "as long as there is one small change made."

"What's that?"

"As seen through the eyes of Corrie Hollister *Braxton!*" I said. Now Christopher laughed.

"I don't suppose I'm thoroughly accustomed to the change yet, either!"

I put aside my sketch pad and we talked for five or ten minutes more. Then suddenly it came to me how today's scene was most different from all those that had come before. Whether it would be suitable to hang in the new library, I suppose Christopher would have to decide. But my yearly drawings were first of all for me, not anyone else, and so I would draw it as I saw it.

"Sit here, Christopher, right on my rock," I said, getting up and taking my sketch pad with me further up the hill about fifteen or twenty feet. "Just gaze out over the town like I was and tell me what you see."

Christopher did exactly as I'd said while I sat down and resumed my drawing. As he spoke, with his back turned to me, I did my best to reflect what *Christopher* saw.

Thirty minutes later I was done.

I got up and brought it down to show Christopher. I handed him the pad to inspect my work. There was the town spread out in the background. And in the foreground, on my rock with his back turned, sat Christopher himself. It was a drawing of *him* looking down upon the picnic scene below.

"I finally realized what is new about the town this year," I said. "It's that *you are now in the picture* . . . and I am learning to see through your eyes as well as my own."

CHAPTER 28

A CONVERSATION WITH BECKY

As much as both Christopher and I loved being on Pa and Almeda's property as part of the Hollister/Braxton community, we were conscious of the need to be *ourselves* in the midst of it.

Especially since I knew that Christopher was trying to figure out what we ought to do with our lives if Pa *did* decide to shut down the mine, we were more aware than before that we were a separate family from the others. I suppose that is part of learning what it means to be married—realizing that a *new* family has begun, that suddenly you are the husband or wife rather than the child.

For us the realization was more gradual than for some young people like Mike and Emily, because we were still living as part of Pa and Almeda's larger family. Yet we wanted to learn how to be a family of our own too.

Through the summer we began to eat a few of our meals alone together in the bunkhouse. There was no kitchen, or even space for one, but we fixed up the corner of the large space into a sitting room with a table and a small sideboard for dishes. Then we brought meals once or twice a week out to the bunkhouse in a warm cast-iron pot. I cooked a few simple things on the top of our stove, and of course I could boil water for tea and coffee.

Every once in a while, too, we'd invite some of the others out to "our house" to have supper with us. We had Tad and Zack and Becky, even Pa and Almeda by themselves once, and it was fun to be able to be the hostess and to serve them at *our* little table.

128

Becky came over to have dinner with us after church one Sunday in early August. Christopher and I were particularly playful and happy that day. The three of us took a ride together, then came back and ate in our little bunkhouse.

Gradually Becky grew quieter and quieter. I didn't know why at first. But when Christopher went outside for a minute and almost immediately tears came into my sister's eyes, I soon found out.

"Becky dear—what is it?" I asked, reaching out my hand across the little table and placing it on hers.

"Oh, Corrie," she said, "seeing you and Christopher together, so happy, talking and smiling and having so much fun—I can hardly stand it. I'm just so afraid it's never going to happen to me, that I'm never going to get married." By the time she was through saying that, she was sobbing long, stored-up cries.

I got up and went around to the other side of the table, sat down beside her, held her, and let her cry as long as she needed to.

"How did you feel, Corrie," she asked, "when you were my age and didn't know if anyone would ever love you enough to marry you?"

Suddenly it was all so clear, and I couldn't help feeling bad for the effect that the happy day Christopher and I had enjoyed had had on her.

"Oh, Becky," I said, "I'm so sorry we've made it difficult for you!" I put my arm around her and gave her a hug.

"*You* didn't make it hard," said Becky through her sniffles.

"I am still sorry we weren't more sensitive to what you were feeling. And I should have been, because I have had plenty of those same thoughts myself."

"So how did you keep it from making you depressed?"

"I suppose I got it into my head early in my life that I wouldn't marry," I answered. "That isn't to say that I didn't struggle with it, but I learned to accept it."

As we sat, I thought how different it had been for my younger sister. Everyone had just assumed Becky would marry. If *anyone* would marry in our family it would be *her*, not me. She had always been prettier than me. She was lively and fun and gay, and from the time Becky was fifteen boys were taking an interest in her. She had had plenty of young men callers, but no one that she'd ever been serious about. Now here she was almost twenty-five, with no serious suitor in sight. I hadn't even realized how anxious Becky had been growing over it as the years passed.

"Accepting it—that's the hard part," said Becky.

"Becky, I *am* sorry," I said. "I realize now that it must have been difficult for you with Christopher and I being so close all the time and so happy together. It has been, hasn't it?"

Becky nodded, her eyes still wet.

"I always thought I would be married by now," she said.

"I guess I hadn't stopped to think what it was like for you."

"It was different with you, Corrie. Like you said, you didn't expect to be married. Sometimes I didn't even think you wanted to get married."

"I struggled with it too," I said, "though probably not so much as you."

"I've dreamed about being married and having a husband and family ever since I can remember," Becky said. "You had your writing and travel, but there's nothing else I've ever wanted but a home and family of my own. And now—"

She stopped and glanced away, eyes filling again.

"Now . . . now it's hard trying to accept the fact that it may never happen."

"Oh, Becky, you're still young to be saying that."

"I'll be twenty-five in a couple of months, Corrie. I've got no prospects. There really never have been any serious prospects."

"I was twenty-seven before Christopher and I met. He was thirty."

"It was different with the two of you—surely you must see that. Neither of you are like most young men and women."

"Only in that I wasn't looking for a husband," I said. "But if God brought us together at twenty-seven and thirty, surely twenty-four isn't so old that you should despair."

"I suppose you're right," Becky sighed. "But it still seems more and more hopeless all the time. Oh, my heart yearns to find a man for me like Christopher is for you, but there aren't very many around."

I couldn't argue with her. The Lord had indeed been good to me.

"You are fortunate, Corrie."

"I know. You're right, and I am very thankful to the Lord," I said.

"What makes it all the more difficult is that I don't want to go through life lamenting the fact that I'm not married. If this is my lot in life, I want to make the best of it."

"You make it sound so horrid not to marry."

"That's how it seems to me, Corrie."

"I don't consider my life horrid up till last April," I said. "I *enjoyed* my life before Christopher came along."

"But like I said, you are different."

"I don't think I'm *that* different, Becky. Besides, there are worse things in life than not being married."

"Like what?"

"Like being married to someone it wasn't God's will for you to marry," I answered.

Becky was silent a moment, contemplating what I'd said.

"When Emily married it wasn't so bad because I was still so young," she said at length. "But when Christopher came, even though I said nothing to you, I admit that I had to battle feelings of jealousy, wondering why it was you instead of me who had a man that loved you. It didn't seem fair. You had never sought it or wanted it, yet you had the most wonderful, godly man in the world. And I have desired it and prayed for it, yet I've never met a man of Christopher's caliber in my life. I tried to pray for you, and truly I wanted you to be happy. Yet just being around the two of you hurt so deeply."

"I'm so sorry, Becky."

"There's nothing for you to be sorry about, Corrie. You didn't do anything wrong. It was my own attitude that wasn't right. Eventually I took it to God, and he has helped me. But it remains difficult because those feelings of wanting to be married are still there."

"Has the Lord given you any peace at all about it?" I asked.

She thought a few moments.

"One good thing that has come of it, I suppose," answered

Becky, "is that at least I now know what kind of man to pray for. If I had never known Christopher, some other man might have come along who wasn't half the man of God he is, and I might have married him when possibly the Lord had someone better waiting for me—my *own* Christopher Braxton."

"Just like *my* Cal Burton," I suggested.

Becky smiled. "He was a dashing, good-looking man, Corrie. You can hardly be blamed for being taken in."

"You know, I just realized as I spoke Cal's name," I said, "that they both have the same initials—C. B."

"Like yours," added Becky, "Corrie Belle."

I laughed.

"That, too! But what I was thinking was how similar the false can sometimes be from the true—just like fool's gold and real gold. At first glance they can look just alike. With people too, the false can mimic the true. If you're not careful, you can be taken in."

I stopped and shuddered involuntarily.

"What is it, Corrie?" asked Becky in alarm. "I've never seen such a look on your face before."

"It just suddenly dawned on me how close I may actually have come to marrying Cal without even realizing it at the time. If I had been anxious to marry, as many girls my age would have been, just think of the miserable life I could have made for myself. Worst of all—I'd have never met Christopher!"

Again I trembled and tried to shake the thought away. "Come on, Becky," I said, "let's take a walk. I have something I want to say to you."

We rose and went outside, then linked arms and walked slowly away from the bunkhouse toward the stream and up in the direction of the mine.

CHAPTER 29

THE LORD IS A FAITHFUL LIFE-COMPANION

"You know," I said after we had walked a ways in silence, "that I struggled with all this too, don't you? We have talked about it several times."

Becky nodded.

"Just because I thought I probably never would marry doesn't mean I didn't want to or didn't think about marriage just like any girl. I've thought and cried and prayed, too. I went through stages of desperately wanting to be married and other times of not wanting to at all. One time I even thought about being a nun, like the sisters I stayed with back East. So when I say what I am about to say, you mustn't think I say it only because none of this mattered to me. I have felt some of the same things you are feeling, Becky."

Becky nodded as I spoke.

"There was a time," I went on, "back when I revisited our old home in Bridgeville, that I saw some things in a new light. It was as if I relived the first fifteen years of my life all over again."

I stopped, remembering again the moments I had experienced under the old oak tree.

"Go on, Corrie," Becky urged.

"I realized that life could be wonderful, not because I might someday marry but because I had the Lord himself to be with me no matter what happened—forever. That's when I first began to feel free to call God Father in a way I never could before."

The memory of telling Becky about it brought back so many

133

feelings that I felt my eyes starting to fill with tears. We were both quiet a few minutes.

"I'm glad you told me that, Corrie," said Becky. We were quiet again and walked in silence for a while. Finally I reached over to lay a hand on her shoulder.

"Can you trust me enough," I went on, "to accept what I might say to you as from someone who has felt what you are feeling, even though, as you say, maybe we were different in many ways too?"

She turned to me with big eyes.

"I'll try," she said softly.

"As I listen to you, Becky, and from everything I know about you as my dear, dear sister, I sense a heart that really desires what God wants, even though at times it is difficult and your soul wants something for itself—like to be married. Is that how you feel?"

Becky nodded.

"Sometimes those feelings struggle against one another," I went on. "I have known that struggle. But I have come to believe there is a special place in God's heart for young women who have the opportunity to learn to trust him in ways that those who marry young never experience. These feelings you are now having, the ones I encountered when I was in the East—those are not feelings Emily will ever be able to share with us. Some of us marry. Some don't. That is in no one's hands but the Lord's alone. What is most important is how we respond to the Lord as he makes his will for each one of us known. Do we begin to feel an underlying resentment that blames God that we are not married? Or, even though it is hard, do we learn to trust God? Do we learn to say to him, like Mary, *I am the Lord's handmaiden, be it unto me according to your word*?"

Becky said nothing, and we continued walking slowly alongside the stream. She seemed to be thinking seriously about what I was saying.

"That is a difficult thing for a young woman to say," I added. "It is never easy to relinquish something we dearly want. And yet I think those very words of Jesus' mother are often the door into deeper intimacy with God."

"But *why* wouldn't God want me to be married?" Becky

blurted out finally. "Does he want me to be miserable and lonely all my life?"

"Oh, Becky, of course not!" I cried as her tears began again. I wrapped my arms around her, patting her slim shoulders, waiting for the weeping to subside.

Presently she pulled away, gave her head a little shake, and pulled up the edge of her skirt to wipe her eyes. Then we continued to walk, passing the mine—quiet this Sunday afternoon—and continuing along the path into the woods.

Lord, what would you have me say now? I prayed silently.

It was probably five minutes before either of us spoke again.

"What do you think, Becky," I asked finally, "is it more important to do God's will than to be married?"

Becky nodded.

"Jennie thought it was more important to be married than to do God's will, and now look how miserable *she* is. You talk about being lonely, but your temporary loneliness is nothing compared to the garden of weeds she has planted for herself and now has to watch sprout."

Becky took in my words without replying.

"Maybe you will never marry, Becky," I added. "I don't know what the Lord has planned for you. But if that should be the case, the only way to really come to terms with it is in thankfulness to God."

"It's hard to be thankful for that."

"That may be. But do you know why you truly *can* be thankful?"

"Why?"

"Because the Lord has something even more wonderful planned for those of his Father's daughters who don't marry."

"What could that be?"

"His own intimate companionship. He has chosen such a woman for *himself*, to walk with him as his *own* bride. And Jesus, more than any mortal man that ever walked the earth, is a faithful and loving life-companion."

The Lord had shown me this truth when I was in the East and wrestling with this very thing Becky was now facing inside herself. But I could tell it was new for her to take in.

"You should have seen the joy the Sisters of John Seventeen had," I added. "It was so wonderful to be part of it—it was that joy that made me consider joining them."

We walked a distance longer as she mulled over my words in her mind.

"If you can only try to take a long-range, lifelong perspective," I said after a bit, "it may be that you will look back with huge thankfulness that the Lord kept you single for a long while, protecting you from the heartache that might have resulted from a wrong or hasty marriage.

"Believe me, there is a lot of heartache over at the Woodstock home these days! And just think how awful it would have been had I married Cal!

"It really could be that the Lord has chosen you to walk with him and him alone, and that really could be a great blessing. On the other hand, maybe he wants to nurture you for several more years, preparing you and preparing your future husband so that a much stronger marriage can result.

"What is another five or ten years, if it means you are that much more mature spiritually and emotionally by then? What are a few more years of singleness if they mean the prayerful and thankful wait enables God to bless you with a man who is close to God— and loving and understanding to his wife?

"Wouldn't you rather wait until age forty, if that meant having a happy marriage to a mature man, than marry too soon and then discover your husband was not as kind and loving as you thought, like Jennie has sadly discovered? Speaking for myself, I would sooner have waited another ten or even *twenty* years for Christopher!"

Becky sighed. I think she knew I was right, but the words *ten* and *twenty* sounded so long to her right then. Twenty more years would almost be her whole life all over again! To her ears, I might as well have said *forever*.

"As I look at it, Becky, I think a happy late-life marriage that would endure into old age would be far better than an early marriage that is full of conflict and pain. After my visits with Jennie, frankly, I do not see your situation as so awful. I know it may seem lonely at times. But I happen to think that possibly the Lord might

have just the sort of man you desire picked out for you, but that
he is waiting for the right time in order that your marriage will be
founded on maturity rather than immaturity."

"I hope you're right."

"Do you trust him enough to say, *'Lord, if I spend my life single,
I will thank you . . . if I marry at forty I will thank you . . . if I marry
at sixty I will thank you . . . I trust you, Lord . . . be it unto me according to your word'?*"

By now we had gone about to the end of the path. We stopped
and slowly turned around and began walking back the way we had
come.

"I don't know, Corrie," sighed Becky at length, "sometimes I
think that there just aren't men like Christopher for girls like me.
Maybe you found the only one."

"I don't believe that for a minute, Becky," I replied. "Good,
godly, gracious men do exist for young Christian women who are
willing to seek and pray for them, then put the timing into the
Lord's hands and not try to hurry him along in his work. They may
be few and far between. But the Lord is fashioning men who want
nothing but his will. They are worth waiting for. Even worth waiting twenty or thirty years for!"

"You didn't have to wait thirty years, Corrie."

"Perhaps not. But I was willing to."

"Being willing isn't the same as doing it."

"Maybe it was because I was willing that I didn't have to."

"You mean if I am willing, maybe I won't have to wait thirty
years either?"

"Perhaps not. But then once you *are* truly willing, such a question would never occur to you."

CHAPTER 30

CHRISTOPHER'S WISDOM

We were nearly back to the house now.

"Let me ask if you're willing to do something a little more immediate than wait thirty years," I said. "Would you be willing for us to go inside and ask Christopher about this?"

"Oh, I'd be too embarrassed, Corrie!"

"He is a wise man."

"I know that, but . . ."

"I'm certain he could shed more light on it for you than I've been able to."

"Maybe, but you are my sister. You understand these kinds of things. It'll be hard to talk to a man about it—especially your husband."

"Christopher's not only my husband, Becky. He's your brother now, too. Just talk to him like you would me."

We went inside the bunkhouse. Christopher was sitting in his chair reading. He glanced up with a smile. I could tell he noticed Becky's tear-stained face and my serious expression, but all he said was, "Have a nice walk?"

"Very nice," I replied. "We would like to talk to you about something."

"Of course. Have a seat."

Becky and I sat down on the only other two wooden chairs we had in the room. I briefly recounted the gist of my conversation with Becky, and eventually Becky repeated her most pressing questions for Christopher, too.

138

"It's just so hard," she concluded, "to understand why God would want me not to be married and why he hasn't answered my prayers about it."

The small bunkhouse fell silent. Christopher always collected himself before saying anything. I knew he was inwardly praying for the right words.

"The questions you raise are good ones," he finally said, "and very difficult to answer. You've voiced some things I know many people wonder about. You can't imagine how many times I heard similar questions when I was pastoring. That experience was one of the things that helped me be so patient myself in waiting for Corrie."

He paused. "So you say you have prayed about this, Becky?"

"Oh yes," she answered, "for years."

"But you think God hasn't answered you?"

Her voice quavered, fresh tears not far away. "I'm not married. So I assume he hasn't answered me."

Christopher paused another long moment and then answered with great gentleness, "But what if his answer is no? What if his answer is that he has something else planned for you that is just as good, or *better*—but that you can't see as better yet?"

Becky shrugged. "Something better than marriage?"

Christopher nodded.

"I don't know," she said after a bit.

"Let me ask you something else, Becky," he said. "I want you to give me a straight, honest answer—agreed?"

"I'll try."

"All right—does it seem to you as if I probably don't know how you feel, that I probably haven't faced the kind of heartache you are going through, that probably all of my prayers *are* answered?"

Becky squirmed a little in her chair.

"I suppose maybe so," she said with an uncomfortable smile.

"I thought perhaps that might be the case," Christopher said. "That is often how it is—after someone has grown and has developed a certain level of spiritual maturity, which is perhaps how I seem in your eyes, it can be easy to assume that person has led an easy life, when in fact it may have been severe hardship that has led to that maturity over the years. Let me tell you something,

Becky—I have had a very difficult and painful life. Perhaps one day I shall be able to tell you about it. Meeting your dear sister has truly been the most joyful thing that has ever happened to me—the *only* really happy thing . . . outside of knowing God, I mean."

When he said that, it was my turn for tears. What a privilege—and a responsibility—to be that to another person!

"I have come to be very, very thankful to God for my past," Christopher went on, "but it was a gratefulness I had to learn. One's first response to hardship is to complain, and I am no different from anyone else. I have had to learn how to pray in difficult circumstances, too. I have had to struggle with thinking the Lord hasn't heard me. I have had to face the answer of no many times when I wanted the Lord to say yes.

"And through all those experiences I have learned some deep truths that I have come to depend on for my daily existence as much as I depend upon air to breathe and water to drink. May I tell you what they are?"

"Yes," Becky nodded.

"The first truth I have learned to depend on," Christopher said, "is that I *know* God is good. I know that God is *always* good and is good in *all* things, whether I see it or understand it or not. That must remain our foundation stone in life—yours and mine and Corrie's and everyone who calls himself a child of God—when we don't see answers.

"God is good. We must hang onto that, even if sometimes there aren't answers we can see. Perhaps sometimes that in itself is the answer: *God is good!*"

Christopher paused, and Becky nodded. She seemed very intent on what he was saying.

"I know also that God operates on a longer timetable than we do. Imagine—he waited four thousand years to send Jesus after man had sinned. God's purposes are never rushed. How much less will he be hurried in the small matters of our lives?

"Another truth I have learned to depend on is this: Besides being good, I know God is trustworthy. Therefore, I think our responsibility is to trust him even when we see nothing and where his timetable is lengthier than we would like.

"Does he hear our prayers? We see no answer . . . but we trust him anyway.

"Is life hard? Often, yes . . . but we trust that God is good.

"Will we see answers to all of our prayers before we die? Perhaps not . . . but God is still good and to be trusted, and we cannot hurry his purposes.

"Would you like to be married and don't understand why God might have other plans for you? Yes . . . but he is good and you can trust him to do his *very best* for you. Do you see the perspective I am trying to get across?"

Becky nodded slowly. "I think so."

"We can pray our prayers, trust him to hear, trust him to respond as he knows is best—which will always be best, because he is good—and then rest in that . . . trusting him.

"I suppose in short I would simply ask—do we believe God can be trusted above our own desire at times to see quick answers to our prayers?"

"And do you always believe that?" she asked. "Is it always so easy for you? It isn't for me."

Christopher met her eyes and sighed deeply. "Oh, Becky, if only you knew. No, it's a daily struggle for me, too, as it surely is for all growing Christians. I have to say over and over, 'Yes, I do believe that—God help my unbelief.'

"Do you remember that story in the New Testament?" he asked. "Help my unbelief—I love the dear father of the demon-possessed boy who replied to Jesus with those words. What an example for us all!

"We cannot help but struggle with these things, Becky. We always will, because we are temporal human beings. There is a portion of us—the part that wants to do good—which believes. There is another portion—the part that *doesn't* want to do good—which we might say is ruled by *un*belief. And the two will always be in constant tension as we work at learning to listen and act upon faith rather than unbelief. But learning is a lifelong process.

"I can tell you that Corrie struggles with such things as well. But even as we struggle, we remind ourselves that God's purposes—his eternal purposes and his very specific and personal purposes for us—generally take longer than we in our shortsightedness are comfortable with. Then we try to return to the fact that we can trust him."

He sighed once more, deeply, then leaned back against his chair. "But I am preaching again, when you came to me for brotherly counsel." He leaned forward again. "It may be that my answer will seem cheap to you. After all, I am married, so how can I possibly know what it is like for you? But I just ask you to remember that Corrie and I were unmarried when we were your age and planned to remain that way."

"I'll try to keep that in mind."

"It is obvious that most people do marry," he said. "Yet being single is truly not the end of the world. It is only the end of the world if you let it be. I think it all boils down to whether you trust God or not."

We all sat silent for a very long minute, then Christopher surprised us all with a very blunt question.

"Do you want to be close to God, Becky?" he asked her.

"Yes . . . yes, of course," she replied.

"If you had to tell me the deepest desire of your heart—would it be to be married or to be close to the Lord for the rest of your life? I'm not saying you can't do both. I only ask which is the *deepest* desire? Which do you want most?"

"I suppose to be close to God?"

"Are you just saying that? Or do you really mean it?"

Becky thought in silence a minute.

"No, I think I really do want to be God's daughter more than anything and to be close to him . . . even though sometimes it is hard."

"All right, then. Do you trust him?"

"I think so."

"Do you trust him to do what is best for you?"

Becky nodded.

"What if—just maybe—he knows that the way to answer that prayer—*Lord, bring me closer to you*—is for you to remain single?"

Becky sat staring into her lap but said nothing.

"I do not say this is the case," Christopher added, "but it *might* be. You say that sometimes it seems you receive no answers to your prayers, but that you desire to come closer to God. What if being single *is* the answer? What if God has things for you to learn un-married that you could not learn if you were married?"

Again he waited. I know this was a hard thing to put so straight to her, but I knew Christopher felt Becky was sure to continue be-ing miserable if she didn't see what was really at stake in her life— God's plan for *her*.

"If singleness is God's will for you," he went on, "and I do not say one way or the other, only that *if* it is—then you owe him deep and loving thanks . . . for by it he will be doing his very best for you. And whatever his ultimate plan for you is, it is obvious that it is his will that you are single *now*. So thank him, treasure this time—make the most of it!

"Again the question is: Do you trust him?

"Just think, Becky—your remaining unmarried may be the best tool for the Master to use to mold your character into Christlike-ness for eternity.

"On the other hand," Christopher now went on after a brief pause, "maybe you *will* marry some day. If so, let me offer some perspectives.

"For one thing, marriage is difficult. It is not all happiness and bliss. Tom and Jennie are having a tough time of it. Corrie and I will inevitably face misunderstandings and disputes.

"Because of this, there are those couples who are not able to weather it. I could cite you many examples from my pastoring days. I witnessed a few marriages break up. I saw many others in which the partners lived together in emptiness and pain. Even among married Christians there is separation and heartbreak and broken lives.

"And then, finally, there are a lot of unworthy and immature young men out there for a woman to marry who will make married life far more miserable than is single life. I become downright an-gry when I see some of the awful things my fellow males do and say to their wives. It's terrible and yet all too common."

By now Christopher was leaning far forward, his elbows on his knees, a tender fire in his blue eyes.

"My advice, then, would be this: Stay single, and rejoice in be-ing single for as long as God chooses to keep you that way! It is not only all right to be unmarried. It is something you can learn to see as a great blessing! It may be that your singleness will protect you from an unpleasant marriage situation.

"On the other hand, marriage may be in your future. But don't settle for an immature man without spiritual character and fiber just because you want so badly to be married. God is in the business of making men of God. Give him time to make one for you!"

The bunkhouse fell quiet, and Christopher let his last words settle deeply into Becky's consciousness.

"But what should I spend my time doing?" Becky asked at length. "Sometimes I cannot help being lonely for someone."

"How well I know!" replied Christopher. "Yet there are so many ways to make use of this time. Maybe the opportunity will come for you to visit Emily or Laughing Waters. Read to your heart's content. Relish the opportunity to be a help to others. Do things that young married women miss out on. If this single time is for a season, you don't want to look back when it is ended and feel that you wasted the time that was given you."

"I suppose you are right," she said hesitantly. "There is a lot someone like me can do that Jennie and Corrie and Almeda and Aunt Katie and Emily aren't able to do."

"Exactly. I would emphasize to you again, Becky," he added softly at length. "The Lord has you right where he wants you. If it is his will for you to find a worthy young man some day, then that man will have found a gem, too.

"If that is *not* his will, then the Lord is preserving the precious jewel for himself alone. That jewel is you!"

When Christopher stopped, I knew from the tone of his voice that he was through. Becky's head was bent, and she was softly weeping.

I knew this had all been very difficult for Becky to listen to. Christopher had a way of probing straight into the heart of things. He had done it with me, and I saw him doing it constantly with himself. I had learned to trust his wisdom and silently prayed that Becky would be able to as well.

I reached over to put a hand on Becky's shoulder, loving her, feeling how much she hurt, and yet deeply grateful to God for giving me a man of such wisdom.

A minute later Christopher rose and left the bunkhouse, leaving the two of us alone.

CHAPTER 31

A CONVERSATION ABOUT
GOD'S LEADING

The next day I called on Jennie again.

"How is she doing?" Christopher asked me that evening.

"Nothing too much has changed," I answered, "but I think she appreciates having a friend who cares."

"What did the two of you do?"

"We picked several quarts of berries and then made jam and a cobbler out of them. She was in a gay mood and wanted the cobbler to be just right for Tom. Then he came through the kitchen and made a comment about a splotch of flour on her face. He was no more out of sight than she burst into tears. I told her she had taken his comment wrong and that he had meant nothing by it, but she was sure he was criticizing her."

"What did you say then?"

"I tried to help her laugh at herself, without a whole lot of success, and then we finished the cobbler. Oh, but it is sad Christopher," I sighed. "Do you know what she told me?"

"What?"

"She said, 'But, Corrie, I don't even love him anymore.' Then she started to cry. And they haven't even been married two years. How can feelings change so fast?"

"Probably because the marriage was a mistake to begin with," replied Christopher. "If the foundation is faulty, it's unlikely you're going to be able to build a strong and durable structure on top of it."

145

"But I've heard you say that any two people can make a marriage work. Why would you then say it was a mistake?"

"Any two people *can* make it work. That doesn't mean there aren't some matches that are more suitable than others. There's also the matter of the Lord's will. The fact that any two people can make it work doesn't mean the Lord doesn't select certain people to be together and not others. Once we make a decision, whether with the Lord's leading or outside of it, we're stuck with our decision, come what may. Of course Jennie and Tom can make their marriage work—they have to make it work. That is not to say the marriage might have not been God's will."

"Is that what you mean by a mistake?"

"That . . . and timing. Sometimes the match is right but the timing is wrong. People get in a hurry. They put their immediate feelings ahead of the attempt to find out what God's will might be in the matter. That can lead to equally serious consequences."

"Why are people so anxious to marry?"

"People get in a hurry. They put their immediate feelings ahead of the attempt to find out what God's will might be in the matter."

"But don't you think most people think they *are* doing what God wants when they make that decision?"

"Convincing yourself you're in God's will to validate doing what you *want* to do anyway is not the same thing as being in God's will, independent of what you want."

"Hmm . . . I hadn't thought that we might convince ourselves we're in God's will when we're really not. How do we know the difference?"

"It's an easy enough thing to talk yourself into believing that you're in God's will. Anyone can do that. It's another matter to be experienced enough in listening to God's voice that you are able to set your own will and feelings aside so as to listen and be able to discern what is his leading. That's not something very many people are well-practiced at."

"Why not?"

"Because it's difficult, for one thing," laughed Christopher. "God's voice can be very, very soft—and if there is the slightest noise being made by our *own* emotions and inclinations, they will drown him out, and we will hear only our own wishes speaking to us."

"I know that feeling," I laughed.

"The main reason people aren't well-practiced at it," Christopher added, "is simply because they don't want God's will near as much as they like to think they do. They want their own will. They try to convince themselves it is God's will they want, but in many cases that is just a little game they are playing with themselves."

"That is a pretty harsh thing to say, isn't it?"

"Maybe," sighed Christopher. "You have to remember, I did much of my spiritual maturing as a pastor. Unfortunately, that is a role in which it is possible to grow cynical about people's motives very quickly."

"How *does* a person know what God wants them to do, then?" I asked. "Someone like Jennie, who isn't as experienced at listening to his voice as someone else."

Christopher thought a moment.

"Probably the first thing," he said, "is to listen to the voice of God through the advice of mature people who know you and love you. In Jennie's case, I seriously doubt the Shaws were in favor of her marriage to Tom."

"No, they weren't."

"If a person doesn't take the good advice of people more mature than he himself, people whom God has placed there to help, it is doubtful God will speak in other ways."

"You're surely not saying you should *always* do what people tell you?"

"Of course not, only that God frequently makes his will known through others—especially to young people. Learning to discern and heed the wisdom that is around you is one of the first signs of maturity—and one of the most important ways to walk close to the Lord."

"I know that Jennie wasn't about to listen to anybody once she set her mind on marrying Tom," I said.

"Then, no wonder she's having trouble knowing what to do now," he said. "You asked how an inexperienced person knows what God wants them to do? I would say we must obey those things we are shown, then we will be shown more. As we obey, more light will be given. But the opposite is true, too. If we don't obey what we are shown and what we know to be right, even the little light we do have will eventually go out. God won't force his leading on people who aren't listening."

As Christopher and I talked further, I realized it was no wonder Jennie had gotten herself into such a pickle. I couldn't remember ever once in her whole life when I'd heard her so much as mention a desire to do what God wanted.

"By the way, what was your answer?" said Christopher after a minute.

"My answer—to what?"

"To what Jennie said about not loving Tom anymore?"

"I told her that it didn't matter, in fact, it had nothing to do with anything. I said, 'You made a promise, Jennie. Marriage isn't necessarily based on love. It's based on promises made and promises kept.' "

"Good girl! That's exactly right. I couldn't have said it better myself."

I put my arm around Christopher, and he took me in the two of his.

"That won't happen to us, will it?" I said softly, with my head against his chest.

"What, that we don't love each other anymore? Absolutely not." He paused briefly, then added, "But the love will fade from time to time. It can't be helped."

"We know that," I added with a smile. "We've already experienced it."

"But the *promises* will never fade, and they are the glue that will always hold us together."

CHAPTER 32

WHO MAKES THE DECISIONS?

The following Sunday, as if reading my mind, Rev. Rutledge got up to preach and announced that his topic would be "Who Makes the Decisions in Your Life?"

"I would like to speak to you this morning," he began, "about a very personal aspect of faith. It is, in fact, one of the most important aspects of all, yet one in which many who call themselves Christians lack in experience. If you happen to be one of those, I hope these few words of instruction may help you get started down what I think is a very exciting road of discovery with your heavenly Father.

"You've all heard, I'm certain," Rev. Rutledge said, now smiling just slightly, "phrases that begin 'There are two kinds of people in the world. . . .' "

He paused while a few nods went round the church.

"Well, I am going to give you another one to think about this morning. But when I greet you afterward at the door, I'm not going to ask you which side of the fence you happen to find yourself—"

"Amen!" called out Uncle Nick from the second row, and everyone laughed, including Rev. Rutledge.

"Although I may ask *you*, Nick Belle!" he shot back good-naturedly, still laughing with the rest.

"However," the minister went on after the chuckling had subsided, "I earnestly hope that each one of you will ask *yourself* where you stand . . . and whether any sort of change might be necessary in your own personal life.

"So, here is my statement: There are two kinds of Christians in the world—those who make a habit of asking God what he wants them to do and then do it . . . and those who simply do what seems best in their own eyes."

He paused, this time for several long seconds, to allow his words to sink in.

"In other words," he added, "those for whom God directs the decision-making process and those who direct it themselves, who give God's view of the events of their lives very little thought.

"Now, don't make the mistake of thinking that I'm speaking of Christians and non-Christians. Remember, my statement was that there are two kinds of *Christians* in the world. . . . You see, it's easy enough to believe in all the Christian ideas, which I am certain all of us here this morning do, and yet still not *do* very much practically about it. That's one of the unfortunate things about Christianity. It is entirely possible to believe all its doctrines accurately and yet never once in all your life actually ask the question, *'Lord what do you want me to do?'*

"That is why I say that there are two kinds of Christians in the world. There are those who make a frequent habit of saying, *'Lord, what would you have me do here . . . what is your will for me there . . . what would you have me say . . . fill me with your thoughts.'* And, on the other hand, there are those to whom it may never even occur to ask such questions.

"Where does the direction for life originate, from within yourself or from Another? Are you your own master, or have you chosen to occupy the position of a child looking to your *Father* to direct and orchestrate what comes and how you respond to it? Are you your *own* master . . . or are you God's *child?*"

He glanced about momentarily.

"An even more important query might be," he added, "Which do you *want* to be? The question I would present you with this morning reduces to this: *Who makes the decisions in your life?*"

Rev. Rutledge paused, then coughed two or three times to clear his throat. I glanced over at Harriet. She was looking at her husband with endearing love mingled with concern.

"There is a passage in the Old Testament I find fascinating in light of this question," Rev. Rutledge went on. "Let me read it to you. It is found in the very last verse of the book of Judges . . . let me see. . . ."

He flipped through the pages of his Bible until he had located the passage.

"Here it is— *'In those days,'* he read, *'there was no king in Israel: every man did that which was right in his own eyes.'* "

Again he paused.

"Ponder the implications of those words, my friends," he said at length.

"How were decisions made? 'Every man did what was right in his own eyes.'

"How are decisions made in your life . . . or in mine? Do we not generally do exactly this—act and think on the basis of what is right in our own eyes, *what seems best to us to do?*

"Now note—it does not say that the Israelites 'sinned' in everything they did. There is no judgment placed on *what* they did at all. This passage of scripture is not a statement on *what* the people did. It is a statement about *how* they did it, about *how* decisions were arrived at. It is about the *method* rather than the result.

"Likewise, I am challenging you to reflect upon the method by which *your* life functions. In no way would I suggest that you or anyone else is doing wrong or sinning. For years I myself stood on the side of the fence where I would have to have answered the two-kinds-of-people question by saying that I was most definitely one who had never asked, *'Lord, what would you have me do.'* It was not until I came here and had been among you for a time that such things began to occur to me, and I began to realize that despite the accuracy of my beliefs there was much missing in the practicality of my faith. But I was not a bad man, not a dreadfully wicked sinner. I simply recognize now that the *method by which I ran my life* was flawed. I did what was right in my own eyes.

"Note further—I did what was *right* in my own eyes, not what was *wrong* in my own eyes. I did not do willful wrong at all. I lived, as far as I was able, what we call *a Christian life.* But, you see, it was all according to how I *myself* regulated my actions and determined what that right was. I never asked *God's* opinion in the matter.

"Neither do I say that any one of you is doing wrong. I speak of *how* you do what you do—who determines what is the *right* that you do? Where does your life's momentum come from?

"As I said, for years I did what appeared right in my eyes. Why? For the very same reason that such was said of the Israelites of old—I had no king."

The minister paused a long time to let his words sink in.

"We are meant to have a king," he said after a while.

"We are not meant to be our own masters. We are not meant to do what is right in our *own* eyes, even if our own eyes are very skilled at distinguishing right from wrong and then doing what really is right.

"It may not be the *what* of our lives that is out of balance because we may be living very upstanding, moral, virtuous, even selfless lives. It is entirely possible to live selflessly and still have it said of us that we are doing what is right in our own eyes.

"It is the *how* that is out of kilter. The *method* is wrong. We are determining *what* to do in the *wrong* way.

"The Israelites of old were given a king because they failed to make God their king. They were given a king because they could not see the truth that Jesus later came to teach mankind—that God is our Father.

"God is our Father," he repeated, "and we were meant to live as his children."

Rev. Rutledge stopped and wiped his pale forehead. I could tell he was tired, for he had been preaching energetically.

"I don't suppose ten minutes is a very long sermon," he sighed with a smile as he pulled his watch from his vest pocket and glanced down at it. "But I think I have about said what needs to be said about this extremely important topic. I doubt you will hold it against me if we dismiss a little earlier than usual.

"I would ask you to do one thing, however," he added. "This afternoon, will every one of you say to the Lord in the quietness of your room or barn or meadow or walking path, *'Lord, if there are ways in which you want to be more my Father than you have been till now, please reveal them to me.'*

"Say that," he added, smiling again, "and the Lord himself will finish this sermon in the private sanctuaries of your own hearts. Let us pray together."

He bowed his head and closed his eyes, as did everyone in the church.

"Our Father in heaven," Rev. Rutledge prayed, *"we ask you to be more our Father now than ever before. Be our Lord, be our Master, be our King. Give us hearts and minds, give us hands and feet, give us a will, give us feelings that all turn to you to ask, 'What would you have us think, feel, and do?' Make of us a people who look to you for our decisions. Make of us a church and community of believers that is different. Let it be said by all those who observe us, 'Those people do not do what is right in their own eyes. They do what their Father tells them.' We ask that you would show us what you want of us, our Lord and our King. Amen."*

CHAPTER 33

THE FALL

You never know when something is about to happen that will change the direction of your life. It can even seem a little thing at first, like a storm that gathers as a tiny speck on the horizon. You hardly pay it any attention, but then it comes closer and closer until pretty soon the whole sky is black and threatening.

When Christopher went to see Mr. Jones earlier in the summer and came back with the report that he seemed so weak and tired, of course we were excited that he'd given his heart to God, but we were concerned too. It was obvious that he was getting older and that his health wasn't as good as it once had been.

For several weeks after that, Almeda, Becky, and I made sure we always made extra of whatever we were fixing. If he didn't happen to be eating with us and if one of the men wasn't free, then one of us took a meal down to his cabin every afternoon, with enough for that night and the next day. For those weeks we did all his cooking, and we three women did what we could to help tidy up his place, although I don't suppose there was much hope of making it too orderly after all those years of him living alone like he had.

Pa tried everything he could to persuade Mr. Jones to leave the cabin for a while and come stay with us. We had plenty of extra rooms, he insisted, especially with Christopher and me out in the new bunkhouse.

"Dad-blamed if he ain't a stubborn ol' cuss!" Pa exclaimed in frustration one afternoon after returning from a visit and leaving a portion of that night's stew. "He's as ornery as one of his own mules!"

But Mr. Jones wouldn't hear of leaving his place. He said he didn't want to put us to all that trouble.

"I told him he'd be making it easier on the women, having him right there instead of having to take his supper down to him every day. That almost did the trick. He doesn't cotton to the notion of folks having to nursemaid him—even his best friends."

"What did he say to it?" asked Almeda.

"He thought about it some, but then he said he was feeling a lot better and wouldn't be needing our cooking much longer anyway, though he did tell me to tell you how obliged to you all he was."

Almeda smiled. She'd always had a special place in her heart for Alkali Jones. So had we all.

"*Is* he better, Drummond?" she asked after a moment.

Pa sighed. "Yep, I'd have to say so," he nodded, "a little, anyway. But Alkali ain't no spring chicken any more. He's slowed more'n a step or two, that's for sure."

He stopped and sighed again. Then he stood up from the table where he'd been sitting and turned away as if trying to find something to do. "I don't know . . . I just don't know," he muttered to himself.

Pa and Almeda were older than the rest of us. They knew the signs and had seen them. We all just thought Alkali wasn't feeling well for a while and would get better like people usually do.

We kept taking him his meals, and by and by through the summer he did start feeling better and before long was coming up most days to the mine. We were glad to see him more like his old self again, and whenever he did come, he ate with us and that made it easier. Pa still tried every day to convince him to stay the night with us. He figured if he could just get Mr. Jones to sleep one night in one of our beds under our roof, then he wouldn't mind the idea so much and would stay longer.

But it didn't work. Mr. Jones insisted on returning every evening to his own cabin.

One day in August, all the men were up working at the mine. We women were in the kitchen, plucking a couple of chickens for that night's supper when all of a sudden the door burst open with such a crash it sounded like it had broken off its hinges. We all jumped and turned to see Christopher running into the room.

"Get me that bottle of whiskey you keep in the medicine chest, Almeda!" he cried.

"What is it?" we all asked, terrified from the look on his face if nothing else, as Almeda ran for the whiskey.

"Alkali's had a bad fall. Becky, you've got to ride for Doc Shoemaker. Get him here as fast as you can. Corrie, can you get our bed ready for him in the bunkhouse."

"Of course."

Almeda ran into the room with the bottle and handed it to Christopher.

"He's unconscious," he told her. "I'm hoping I can rouse him with this!"

Christopher turned to leave, then stopped and turned back again.

"Bring up some blankets," he said. "We'll make a stretcher to carry him down with."

He ran out and was gone.

None of us said a word. Almeda went scurrying around for blankets. Becky and I ran out to the barn—Becky for the horses and I for the bunkhouse. I heard her gallop off a minute later while I was getting our stuff off the bed and a new blanket thrown over the top of it. Then I ran outside and met Almeda hurrying up toward the mine. I took half her armful of blankets, and we ran up together.

We found Pa and Christopher and Tad huddled around Mr. Jones, Pa kneeling down and holding a wet cloth on Mr. Jones' forehead while Christopher was trying to dribble bits of the whiskey into his mouth.

"What happened?" said Almeda as we rushed up.

"He was trying to climb up around that boulder there," answered Pa with a toss of his head. "I'm not sure what he was thinking, but the rocks gave way and started to slide under him. He toppled over and rolled down here to the bottom."

The blood had drained from Mr. Jones' head, and his face had become so pale it was pure white. His features always had such a weathered look—I'd never seen him like this. If I didn't know better I'd have thought he was dead, lying there so still and with his eyes closed.

"Did . . . he strike his head?" I asked.

"I don't think so," said Christopher. "Nowhere that I can find, at least."

"Why is he unconscious?"

"He's old, that's why, Corrie," said Pa. "Old folks aren't meant to be climbing around rocks or falling down either."

There was frustration in his voice, and it was clear Pa blamed himself for not paying closer attention.

"Do you think anything's broken, Drummond?" asked Almeda. Before Pa could answer, a groan sounded from Mr. Jones.

As miserable as it sounded, we were glad at least to know he was alive!

He didn't open his eyes, and I don't think he was even conscious yet, but after another groan or two, his lips started twitching, and his tongue seemed to be looking for more of the whiskey it had felt.

"Open up your mouth, Alkali," said Pa.

His lips seemed to part a crack. Christopher tipped the bottle toward it. Though most of the amber liquid went off down his chin, his tongue and lips started moving a little faster to retrieve what they could of the precious brew.

Meanwhile, Almeda was spreading the blankets out beside him, folded double-thick. I helped her, and we put down three blankets in all.

Pa and Christopher now stood, Pa at Mr. Jones' shoulders and Christopher at his feet, and lifted him just enough to ease him over onto the blankets. Then we laid the fourth blanket out over the top of him.

"If we all five grab at a piece of the blankets, we oughta be able to lift him and get him comfortably down to the bunkhouse," said Pa. "Tad, you and me'll get the two corners up here at his head. Christopher, you get the other end—you can manage both corners. Almeda and Corrie, you hold on there in the middle, by his waist, on both sides."

We all did just as Pa had said, took our positions, and laid hold of the blanket edges.

"Okay, let's lift him up—gentle as we can," said Pa.

With all five of us, Mr. Jones was lighter than I'd have thought. Working our way gradually down off the rocky slope, with Pa and Tad leading the way, we inched our way down onto the level ground and then toward the house, almost like we were carrying a funeral casket. All we heard was another groan or two, but Mr. Jones must have still been unconscious because he hardly moved a muscle.

In five minutes we had him on top of our bed.

Pa pulled his boots off—what a smell it was when he got them off, too! Our helping Mr. Jones with his wash hadn't seemed to do much for his socks!

Christopher unbuttoned his shirt to look for any injuries we hadn't seen, but there didn't seem to be any.

We all gathered around, and as Pa began to pray we all inched closer to poor Mr. Jones.

"*Father,*" he said, "*we'd like to all ask you to take care of your son here, our good brother and friend Alkali Jones. Bring him back to us, Lord, and help us to be able to do what we need to get him back on his feet again.*"

"*Amen,*" said Christopher. "*Restore him to health, Lord.*"

"*Amen again,*" added Almeda. "*Bless him, Father. Keep him in your care.*"

We all fell silent. It was a somber moment, and we all felt it.

"Well, let's let him rest," said Pa. "I'll sit here with him a spell, till the doc comes."

"You've been trying to get him to give up that cabin of his all summer, Drum," said Christopher. "Corrie, let's you and me take what we'll need over to the main house. I think Alkali has just moved in."

CHAPTER 34

WAITING

By the time Doc Shoemaker arrived, Mr. Jones was showing some signs of life, but mostly just groaning and licking his lips for more whiskey.

The doc spent thirty or forty minutes with him doing all the things doctors do, listening to his heart and feeling his pulse and looking into his eyes and poking around everywhere to see if anything was broken. Nothing was, though the doc said he had enough bruises to keep him sore for a month.

By the time Doc Shoemaker left, Mr. Jones had woken up, still groaning but awake enough to talk and answer a few questions and have a good glassful of the whiskey before he rolled over, with more groans, and went back to sleep.

I saw Pa and the doctor come out of the bunkhouse. They talked for several minutes. Then Doc Shoemaker got in his buggy and went back to town. Pa came into the house where the rest of us were waiting.

"What'd he say, Pa?" I asked, hardly giving him a chance to get the door closed.

"Is he going to be all right, Drummond?" asked Almeda almost as quickly.

Pa sat down and sighed.

"Yeah, he's gonna be all right . . . for now," he said. "Doc said he couldn't find a thing wrong to be concerned about, except . . ."

"Except what?" asked Christopher.

"Except just that he's so weak. He asked me if he'd been eating.

159

Course he's been eating, I told him. We been feeding him ourselves. 'Then it don't figure why he's so weak,' the doc said. He said he seemed like he was too worn out to keep breathing. All Alkali said when he woke up was asking where he was. I told him he was in Corrie and Christopher's bunkhouse and that's where he was staying for a spell, and at least he didn't argue none this time. I think he finally realized he wasn't in very good shape. Doc said we oughta make sure someone's with him most of the time."

"Why, Pa?" asked Tad, "if he's all right."

" 'Cause he's old, son."

"But if he's okay—"

"He's old and he's weak, Tad," said Pa sharply. "Ain't no more reason than that."

Tad was quiet. Pa saw that he'd taken out his frustration by speaking too harshly.

"I'm sorry, son," he said. "I had no call to be rude to you. I'm just worried about Alkali, that's all."

"Forget it, Pa," smiled Tad. "I know you didn't mean nothing by it."

"It's just that sometimes things happen when folks get old, things you don't expect. That's why you gotta be watching, you gotta be ready in case they need you."

Again it was silent. We all understood well enough what Pa was getting at.

"Pa," said Tad.

"Yeah, son?"

"Is Mr. Jones gonna die?"

"Someday, Tad."

"I mean soon."

Pa let out a long breath.

"I don't know, son . . . I don't know. He may. Only the Lord knows when a man's time is."

"But you said he was weak."

"Yeah, that's right, I reckon he is. But we'll do all we can for him, and we'll hope that tired, old body of his has a few more years in it."

We would pray too, of course.

We all took turns sitting beside Mr. Jones' bed the rest of that day and all night. Pa took some blankets out and slept the night on the floor.

Mr. Jones seemed better by the next morning. He woke up and was able to drink some soup, but he didn't talk about getting up. He slept most of that second day, too—at least he seemed to be sleeping. Maybe he was just lying there with his eyes closed.

I read to him some from the New Testament that afternoon when I was pretty sure he was awake, and he said he liked it. Pa stayed there with him through the second night, too.

Doc Shoemaker came out on the third day to check on him. He said Mr. Jones seemed better, but he didn't look too happy when he said it, and I didn't know if I liked the sound of his voice. He said he'd check on him in another few days.

After three or four more days, we didn't have to stay with Mr. Jones all the time. He wasn't groaning anymore, and he remained awake through most of the day. But I knew Pa was still worried. I don't think an hour would go by that Pa didn't go into the bunkhouse and check on him and see if there was anything he wanted.

"He ain't eating, Almeda," I heard him whisper to her one morning in the kitchen.

I saw her nod her head, but the rest of their conversation was too low for me to hear. I knew they were both concerned but didn't know what to do.

CHAPTER 35

LOSING AN OLD FRIEND

It was the next evening after that when Tad came running into the house. He'd been out with Mr. Jones for a while.

"Pa, Pa," he said as he came in. "Mr. Jones said to get you."

Pa jumped up and headed for the door. "Is he . . . all right?"

"I don't know, Pa. His voice was real soft—I could hardly hear him. He just said to get you."

Pa went running out.

All the rest of us looked around at each other. I know what we were all thinking, but nobody said anything. All at once we were all on our feet and hurrying after Pa.

"You stay here, Ruth," said Almeda, pausing and stooping down.

"But I want to go, too."

"You have to stay here and pray, Ruth. Pray for God to be real close to Mr. Jones right now. Can you do that?"

Ruth nodded.

We all ran across the ground to the barn, but there was a feeling of having to stay quiet, too. Nobody said anything.

My heart was pounding, and it wasn't from the run. I was afraid. I knew I shouldn't be and that there wasn't anything to fear, but I couldn't help it.

Christopher hung back, not being one of the immediate family. Almeda opened the door and crept inside with Tad, Becky, Zack, and me right behind her. Then I felt Christopher's hand on my shoulder, stopping me.

"I'll run for Nick," he whispered.

I nodded, then went inside. The atmosphere in the small bunk-house room was hushed. The air felt momentous.

Pa was already at the bedside, kneeling down, and Mr. Jones was speaking to him in a voice so soft you could barely hear it.

" . . . been as good a friend as a feller coulda had."

"And I'm gonna keep right on being your friend, you ol' rascal," said Pa, trying to sound gruff, like there wasn't anything wrong.

"Ye know it's my time, Drum," croaked Mr. Jones. "Don't ye try t' preten—"

His voice broke off and he started coughing, real deep, down in his lungs.

"It ain't no such thing, Alkali. Why, we're gonna have you up and outta here in no time."

Poor Pa. He was trying so hard to be brave, but one look at his face said that he was fighting back the tears.

Suddenly Mr. Jones saw the rest of us inching toward the bed.

His eyes lit up, and I saw his eyes try to smile.

"Why there's the rest of 'em . . . come t' pay yer last respects t' the ol' coot, eh—hee—"

But he couldn't finish his laugh without starting to cough again.

Almeda came forward, knelt down beside Pa, and gently took Alkali's old rough hand in hers.

"Alkali Jones," she said, and I'd never heard her voice sound so tender. "Maybe you are an old coot. If you are, you're sure an old coot that this family loves as much as any other man we've ever known." She bent down and kissed him gently on the forehead.

"Hee, ye hear that, Drum? Yer wife called me an ol' coot, hee. . . . That's a fine woman ye let snag ye, Drum, though at first I thought it'd be the death o' ye sure. . . ."

Weak as he was, Mr. Jones never lost his sense of humor.

"Alkali Jones, are you saying you didn't think I'd be good for this partner of yours?" said Almeda, now doing her part to try to keep the spirit of the conversation light.

Mr. Jones didn't say anything, just smiled, gave her a wink with the twinkle that, though fading now, had always been in his eye. Then he looked at us four kids—Tad and Zack, Becky and me.

"I ever tell you young rascals about the time . . . I found me a nugget as big as . . . big as my fist, it was. . . . Had t' wrestle me a dad-blamed bear fer it, though . . . hee, hee, hee. . . . The big grizzly was usin' my stream . . . usin' it t' catch his supper an' was sittin' right on top—"

He closed his eyes and took a breath. He was so weak and tired he couldn't even finish his story. A year before, we'd have all been laughing and kidding him by this time.

Nobody was laughing now.

"You need to rest, Alkali," said Pa. "You can finish that story tomorrow. It's been a long day. We need to get you settled down for the night."

"Yer right about that, Drum, hee, hee—"

More coughing.

" . . . an' a longer night . . . than *yer* talking 'bout. . . ."

The door creaked open behind us. We turned to see Uncle Nick walk in, followed by Christopher.

"Nick, ye ol' rascal," whispered Mr. Jones as Uncle Nick approached.

"Heard you wasn't feeling too well, Alkali," said Uncle Nick. "What's the matter, ain't these folks feeding you?"

"Tarnation, they's shovin' more food at me than a body can well eat in a month. Ain't the food, Nick . . . that's . . . that's why I wanted t' see the two o' ye . . . gotta tell ye—"

He stopped again, closed his eyes, and breathed in and out a few times like he was exhausted. His face was so white.

"Gotta tell us what, Alkali? You find a new strike upstream?"

His eyes opened a slit, and his lips smiled. "Hee, hee . . . that's a good one, Nick . . . a new strike, hee, hee. But ye all gotta promise me ye won't give up on the new mine. I tell ye there's gold there. This ol' nose o' mine kin smell it. Ye gotta promise ye'll keep at it till ye fin' it."

"We . . . we promise, Alkali," said Pa.

But Mr. Jones wasn't satisfied. He looked feebly around at the others, waiting to hear the words from them, too.

Everyone nodded, and a few other words of promise were mumbled.

"So that's what you had to tell me, eh, Alkali?" said Uncle Nick.

"No, it . . . it ain't that. . . . Gotta tell ye that the good Lord's given me . . . given me the best dang frien's in the world . . . taken right good care o' me . . . all o' ye . . . made this ol' coot feel like he was somebody worth . . . like he was somebody that—"

He broke off and never finished the sentence, breathing heavily but with shallow breaths, like the strain of filling up his lungs was finally too much for him.

He lay there for several minutes with his eyes closed, hardly a sign of life in him. Every one of the eight of us stood there stock-still. I'd never felt so much love coming out of a group of people for one man as in those quiet, solemn moments as we stood around the bedside with our eyes fixed on the fading earthly form of the old miner Alkali Jones.

CHAPTER 36

SAYING GOODBYE

After a minute or two, Mr. Jones opened his eyes again.

"Eh—there's the young preacher-lad," he breathed softly, seeing Christopher now standing behind me for the first time as we all crowded around the bed. "Corrie, lass," he said, "ye done mighty fine fer a man. . . . Ye make yer Pa proud . . . hee, hee—he told me so hisself. He thinks . . . thinks the world o' ye, he does—that's just what he told me . . . and you, Rev'rend," he said, lifting his eyebrows up toward Christopher, "I reckon it's about . . . about time fer you t' be doin' yer work, eh . . . hee, hee—"

Again he started coughing.

"Would you like me to pray with you, Mr. Jones?" Christopher asked.

"Aye, that I would, young feller," scratched Mr. Jones' tired voice, "though I don't . . . don't figure I oughta . . . let you do all the prayin' yerself. Don't ye reckon, seein's . . . I'm about t' meet him myself that I . . . oughta talk t' him myself?"

"That's a good idea, Mr. Jones," said Christopher. "Shall I begin?"

Mr. Jones coughed lightly again, nodded, and closed his eyes.

Again the door opened, and Aunt Katie stole quietly in, though Mr. Jones didn't see her. He had his eyes closed, waiting for Christopher to pray.

Christopher began to pray.

"Our Father," he said, *"we come to you in this holy moment, committing into your care the life of our friend and brother and the son*

166

*whom you love, Alkali Jones. We thank you, Father, for the privilege
of knowing him, and we thank you that he is one of your family. We
ask that you would restore him to health. Restore him, Lord, to perfect
health and vitality of life and limb . . . and especially spirit. Thank
you for his life and for the great joy he has brought to every one of us."*

Christopher stopped.

"Hee, hee . . . that's mighty fine, young feller . . . hee, hee . . .
you and ol' Rutledge, ye was always both mighty fine . . . at the
prayin' . . . though I don't reckon I'm gonna help ye git yer prayer
answered. . . . I ain't feelin' much o' that there vitality. . . ."

He closed his eyes. His breathing was so soft.

Christopher did not respond to Mr. Jones' misunderstanding
of his words, but I knew what he meant well enough.

"Would you like to pray now yourself, Mr. Jones?" encouraged
Christopher gently.

A faint nod came from the bed, though he didn't open his eyes.

He waited another few seconds, then began.

"Well, Lord," breathed Mr. Jones in the faintest whisper, *"I
reckon it's about time . . . fer ye t' see if there's anything worth keepin'
in this ol' soul o' mine. Ye been mighty . . . mighty good t' an ol' varmint like me. Ye gave me frien's . . . that loved me more'n a feller deserves . . . an' that I loved more'n I ever told 'em—"*

A stifled sob broke from Almeda's lips. She clutched her mouth
and turned away for a moment, eyes filling with tears. When she
glanced back, she took the miner's two hands tenderly in hers once
more.

I was crying by now too. We all were. Pa's face was wet, and I
know he wasn't ashamed.

I blinked a few times and closed my eyes again while Mr. Jones
struggled to get the words of his prayer out, though his voice was
fading so soft I could barely make them out.

*"Like I was sayin', Lord, ye . . . ye been good t' this ol' codger. . . .
I'm mighty obliged that ye kep' lovin' me all them years when I wasn't
payin' as much attention as I shouda . . . an' I wanna tell ye thank ye
again, that ye seen fit them months back t' hear me when I . . . when I
prayed an' told ye I wanted t' be in yer family, Lord. You was mighty
good t' let me in . . . and now I'm . . . now—"*

Suddenly he stopped.

His eyes, which had been closed, shot open wide.

I saw from the white grip of his fingers that his two hands had clutched the two of Pa's and Almeda's that they still held with a grasp tighter than would have seemed possible.

Almost at the same instant, he seemed trying to sit up in the bed, though all he could do was barely lift his head off the pillow.

There was almost a glow on his face and such a light in his eyes that I was sure he had seen something across the room. Unconsciously I turned to follow the direction of his gaze. As I did, I noticed that Pa and some of the others had turned as well.

Mr. Jones was struggling to talk, but mostly his lips were moving rapidly and silently. It seemed like we were only hearing a small portion of what was passing through his brain.

"He's . . . there he . . . Drum," he said, and for the first time his voice was almost strong again. Though he was fumbling for words, those that did come out were loud and vigorous. "Drum, he's . . . he's comin' . . . he's tellin' me t' git up . . . t' take his hand . . . t' follow . . . he's takin' me t' see . . . so bright an'—"

The next sound to come from Mr. Jones' lips is one I'll never forget as long as I live.

Suddenly the words and strength were gone, and nothing was left but a long, slow sigh as the last air of life gradually eased out of his lungs.

I turned back toward the bed.

Mr. Jones' eyes were closed and his head had sunk back into the pillow. The glow on his face was gone. Pa and Almeda still had hold of the two hands, lifeless now.

We all knew he had seen Jesus and was now on his way with him to meet his Father.

Pa and Uncle Nick wept.

Almeda stooped down and again kissed one of the aged, bearded cheeks. "Bless the dear, dear man!" she whispered, then raised herself back up, gazing upon him with eyes of love, tears falling down her cheeks.

"Godspeed, friend and brother," said Christopher. "We will miss you . . . but we will all see you again—and soon."

The room was silent a moment.

"Goodbye, Alkali," whispered Pa.

CHAPTER 37

A HAPPY CELEBRATION

The funeral of Alkali Jones was a big event in Miracle Springs. Whether or not it was true that he had made the strike that began the town didn't seem to matter anymore. The legend of it had grown through the years to the point that, even if it wasn't true, it might as well have been. Mr. Jones had been here longer than just about anybody and so was a legend himself, even if more than half his stories were mere tales.

It wasn't by any means the first funeral Rev. Rutledge had been called on to perform as minister of Miracle Springs, but it may have been the most widely attended.

Everybody for miles around came. The church couldn't begin to hold all the people. So we all stood outside in the small cemetery near the church, next to the mound of fresh earth taken from the new grave that Pa and Uncle Nick and some of Mr. Jones' other close friends had dug.

It was a funeral to remember!

We were sad to lose a friend, of course, but the service seemed more a celebration than a time of mourning, like a farewell before a long trip.

Rev. Rutledge's words were more happy than they were sad, and they set the tone for the rest of the day. He told as much as he knew about Alkali Jones' life, which wasn't really too much.

"I think perhaps some of the sadness we cannot help feel on a day such as this," he said, "comes not only from the simple fact that we will miss a dear friend, but also from the fact that a piece of our past, our history, our heritage as a community, is now gone. Alkali Jones was here longer, to my knowledge, than any other man or woman among us. We are going to hear from a couple of his oldest friends in a few minutes. But even when they arrived here in Miracle Springs to stake out their first claims shortly after the gold rush, Alkali Jones was already here. In a sense, *he* was our history, because he himself was the main character in the tales he told. Had it not been for him, none of the rest of us might be here now either."

Then he went on to tell about how Mr. Jones had recently given his heart to the Lord.

"So you see, friends and neighbors," he said in conclusion, "this is no occasion for grief, but rather one for rejoicing. Alkali Jones was always a man, if I may say it, just slightly out of step with this world and its ways, a man not altogether at home in this place. I would like to think that several months ago, when he invited the Savior into his heart, preparations began immediately, and that the angels even then began making ready for his arrival.

"He is there now, happy and young again, laughing with joy at the celebration of his own homecoming. He may even be telling some of the younger angels the story of his first big gold strike!"

We could not help smiling at the very picture Rev. Rutledge was painting in our minds. After that it was impossible to be very sad. Although there continued to be tears, I think that for everyone they were tears of happiness and of love.

"Whatever he is telling them," Rev. Rutledge added finally, "it certainly cannot be denied that he has now discovered the greatest treasure of all!"

He stood aside while Uncle Nick said a few words, then Pa.

"You know," Pa said, "as I was listening to Avery here, the most peculiar sensation came over me. I been to some funerals in my life. Most of them aren't all that pleasant, especially when the person that's passed on wasn't of an upstanding sort, because it's hard to pretend that they're playing a harp on a cloud in heaven somewhere when everyone knows they were the sort of person that deserves the other place, and that's likely where they are.

"It's different today with Alkali. I don't know that I ever saw him do a selfish turn to man or beast in my life. He could cuss at his ornery mules. But in his own way, Alkali Jones was a kind-hearted man. I know that's the kind of thing everybody says at funerals. But if you'll all think back on what you knew of Alkali, can anyone here remember a time when he did a selfish thing to any of you?"

Pa waited a moment.

"Neither can I," he said. "So when he prayed a while back and said to God his maker that he wanted to be his son, I think God was downright pleased. There ain't the slightest doubt in my mind that Alkali's with the Lord Jesus today, and so I figure that makes this a pretty exciting day."

Again he stopped for a minute.

"I was fixing to tell you about something I felt a few minutes ago," he went on. "I was standing here listening to the Rev., and all at once I thought I felt Alkali himself standing right next to me. No fooling—I could almost smell him.

"I kinda looked up and around, and I know it was just in my imagination, but I could see his face kind of hanging out in the air here above us. It was like he was right there, looking at us, listening to what we were saying.

"And what do you think was the expression he had? Why he was laughing, of course—what else! Laughing big and loud because he was so happy, and wondering why so many of the women were crying over an old coot like him."

Beside me, Almeda could no longer stifle a sob, though as she cried I knew there was joy mingled in with it.

"Alkali Jones," he concluded, "wherever you are, we love you, dear friend—"

Finally Pa's voice choked. He sniffed once or twice, and his eyes filled with tears.

"—we'll all miss you!" he managed to croak out in a soft voice, then turned and stepped back to Almeda's side.

Rev. Rutledge stepped forward again. He read a scripture, then said a prayer.

We couldn't help it. Joyous though it may have been, everyone was crying again—men along with the women.

Then Pa, Uncle Nick, Sheriff Rafferty, and Patrick Shaw—Mr. Jones' oldest friends—took hold of the ropes on opposite sides of the wood coffin and slowly lowered it down into the ground.

We all turned and slowly made our way out of the cemetery. No one said a word.

There was a hush over the whole town the rest of the day.

CHAPTER 38

HOW TO DISCERN GOD'S WILL

Three Sundays after the funeral, Rev. Rutledge got up to preach with an expression of serious thought on his face.

"I had planned to carry on before this with a topic I spoke of some time ago," he said. "But with the passing of our brother Al-kali, it has not seemed fitting to me until now. I believe, however, that the time has come when it may be helpful to you."

He paused, and then began with a simple question.

"How can you know what is God's will?" Rev. Rutledge asked.

He paused.

"Let me make it even simpler," he said after a moment. "Is it even *possible* for us to really know God's will? If so, how do we discover it?"

Again he waited.

"Several weeks ago," Rev. Rutledge went on, "we spoke together about allowing the Lord to make the decisions in our lives. Now that you have had time to reflect upon this, I would like for us to inquire further into the practical aspects of that question.

"Let us say for the sake of argument that, as you sat here during that previous sermon, you said to yourself, 'All right, preacher, what you say makes some sense. I'll give it a try. I'll let God start making some of my decisions for me.'

"And now you find yourself suddenly facing a situation that has recently come up in your life. It doesn't even matter that I know what it is.

173

"The point is that you are facing a dilemma. You don't know what you ought to do. And perhaps you have determined to try to let God decide for you instead of doing what seems right in your own eyes.

"Your question to me might very well be: *'What do I do now? How do I let God decide? How do I know what he wants me to do? How do I know what his will is? How do I hear God's voice?'*

"If any of you have found such questions in your minds since our last talk together about these things, I hope today's discussion will help you begin listening to your heavenly Father in new and more personal ways."

Rev. Rutledge paused to collect his thoughts before continuing. You could sense an anticipation in the air. Nobody was close to falling asleep. You could tell everyone was eager for what he had to say. After all, what could possibly be more exciting in all the world than actually learning to hear the Creator's voice . . . just like Moses did!

"Let me repeat my question: *How do I hear God's voice?*"

Another brief pause.

"Now, these days God doesn't usually speak loudly and forcefully and audibly like he did to Moses. His voice is much softer. Moses couldn't help hearing God, because God thundered to him from the mountain. For us the situation is completely reversed. We *can* help it. In fact, we won't hear him at all unless *we train ourselves to listen with a different set of senses than most men and women know much about.*

"Hear me well, my friends. I will repeat what I just said: We must *train* ourselves to listen with a different set of senses if we want to hear God's voice speaking to us. Even the words I am using—*hearing* and *listening*—are inaccurate because they imply that what we are listening for is an audible voice that we will hear with our ears.

"We actually need different words to describe the process because God's voice isn't usually audible. *It's a different kind of hearing* that you do with the *heart*, not your *ears*."

The minister paused, took a deep breath, then began again in more of a teaching than a preaching tone.

"I would like to take you through this process I speak of," he said. "For it to work, of course, each of you have to try it for yourselves. But I will do my best to tell you as simply as I can what I have found works for me.

"First, find someplace quiet where you can be alone with your God for a few minutes. Remember, you are his *child*. He is your *Father*. All you have to do, therefore, is ask him what he would have you do. Very simply say to him, *'Father, I ask you to show me what you want me to do in this situation. I seek your will, and I will do what you say. My desire is to do what you want me to, so please tell me what that is.'*

"That is all there is to asking, though certainly not in knowing what to do, which comes later. There doesn't have to be a great deal of fanfare in order to turn something over to the Lord. It is an act of relinquishment that is required, not a long pious prayer. It is very quiet and inward, just between *your* will and *his* will. It is just the act of saying, *'Here, Father, I put this into your hands.'*

"We can say *'Here'* to God anytime." As Rev. Rutledge said this he held out both of his hands toward us.

"If you *want* to do what God wants, your will is in a subordinate position to his. If you are still wrestling with whether or not to follow your will or his—as we all do from time to time—then the spiritual battle is not yet one of hearing the Lord's voice but of relinquishment itself, of deciding which side of the fence you are going to come down on in determining your course of action.

"But once the battle of relinquishment has been fought and you *want* to do God's will, then you can very quietly and deliberately and honestly ask him to speak to you . . . and you can be sure he will.

"I am absolutely convinced that in such circumstances as these, God delights in such an honest and humble prayer as *'Father, show me what you want me to do'* and that he *will* answer such a request.

"In my view, one of the chief impediments to God's speaking to his children is simply this: Our ears are plugged because our *own* wills are still heavily involved in determining our motives and attitudes and priorities."

As I listened to Rev. Rutledge, I thought of what Christopher had said when he and I were talking about Jennie and Tom several weeks earlier. He could be preaching this exact same sermon!

"I do not for a moment say I have conquered this either," Rev. Rutledge continued. "We struggle all our lives with our own wills. It is intrinsic to the humanity of our condition. But we grow capable of hearing from God to the extent that we relinquish our wills and yield them into his. The relinquishment of our own wills removes the wax from our spiritual ears and allows us to hear the still, small voice of God's Spirit."

He paused, cleared his throat, and waited a few minutes. Some people shifted about in their seats.

"Now," he went on, "what comes next? Having asked your Father what to do . . . what then?

"It is now time to wait. You can put the decision out of your mind. *'Be not anxious,'* we are told . . . *'Fret not.'* The time has come to obey such commands.

"The still, small voice of God's speaking direction into your heart and mind is most often a slow process. We are quick-answer people, but God is not always a quick-answer God.

"It may take a while. You may not feel you know what you are supposed to do concerning what you have prayed about for six months, perhaps more. If you have relinquished the matter into his hands and your own will is not vying to gain a hearing, then the Lord *will* speak in due time.

"When I speak of *waiting*, however, I do not mean passive waiting—merely letting time pass while you do nothing. I speak rather of *active* waiting. It is the attitude a servant adopts when he is *waiting on* his master. It is an attitude of vigilant readiness, all senses alert and awake and awaiting the master's summons. We wait, but with our eyes wide and our faces turned toward our Father.

"We wait, and what happens next?

"Too often, we simply grow impatient. We grow weary of the waiting. Doesn't the Lord know how desperate we are for an answer? we say. Does he not realize the urgency?

"How many of you have felt such things?"

Rev. Rutledge paused with a smile. "I see by your nods that you know what I am speaking about. I, too, have grown impatient with the Lord more times than I like to remember.

"And then what happens?

"Then we make one of two mistakes. Either we decide to just

go ahead on our own, or we try to convince ourselves that we *have* heard the Lord and likewise just forge ahead.

"Yet if our own impatience is behind the so-called 'leading,' what have we *really* heard? Only our own desires. You have heard me say it many times, and I will remind you of it again—God's purposes cannot be rushed. Human impatience is yet another blockage to divine leading."

He drew in a breath, then continued.

"But let us move forward and talk about what it is like when the season of patient and prayerful waiting has borne its fruit and at last the Lord does begin to truly speak his leading into your heart. What, you may be asking yourself, does God's leading actually *feel* like?

"There have been very few signs and wonders in my life, no visions or audible messages from on high. But I *have* witnessed the Lord's leading over and over. He has been speaking direction to me for the ten or fifteen years in which I have come to be open to it, although in very quiet and almost invisible ways.

"Thus I am absolutely convinced that the prayer, *'Lord, show me what to do,'* when prayed humbly and honestly and without one's own will in the way, will result in some kind of direction from him.

"So, how *do* you hear it, feel it?" Rev. Rutledge asked.

"Usually it is a sense that grows steadily stronger and stronger that such-and-such a course of action is the right one. God speaks through your brain, through your thoughts, and he also speaks to your heart, indicating a very quiet sense of peace, of 'rightness'— or, if he is directing you differently, of 'wrongness'—about the thing you feel inclined to pursue.

"I call it a *sense* that grows steadily stronger. Think of it, perhaps, as a divine *pressure* on your inward being that either says, *'This is right'* or that makes you feel *uncomfortable.* As long as your wishes in the matter are not influencing this pressure, then these quiet and subtle feelings are ones you can learn to trust as coming in response to your prayers.

"As these feelings and thoughts begin to come, and you begin to think they *may* be in answer to your prayer, you can add the following to your conversations with him: *'Lord, it seems you may be indicating that you want me to do such-and-such or not to do such-*

and-such. I ask you to confirm whether this is truly your voice. If not, tell me otherwise.'

"Then again, you can rest, and wait for him to answer this new prayer. Either the sense of leading, the divine pressure or discomfort, will grow stronger, or it will diminish."

He paused and chuckled good-naturedly.

"I understand how vague this all may sound to you this morning," he went on. "It would be much easier if the Lord sent telegrams with direct and specific messages to us. But that is not his way, because it would not be best for us. It would not teach us to trust him, to be patient, and it would not enable us to learn his ways through the long, slow, silent, invisible obediences of life. And it would not help us learn to listen.

"This process of learning to attune ourselves to God's still, small voice is foundational to the walk of faith. This is what Jesus was doing constantly, what he did when he arose a great while before day to be alone with his Father in the hills.

"It *is* a vague and subtle process. There are no lists anyone can write down that will automatically tell everyone in every set of circumstances 'how to know God's will.' God did not intend there to be.

"Jesus said we are to follow his example. He said he did not do anything except what his Father told him to do. He did not specify how exactly we are to do that same thing. Clearly, though, he gave us all the information we are supposed to have.

"Therefore, we have to learn to hear the still, small voice *without* benefit of lists and telegrams. That is the process of growth. That is the walk of faith. That is the reality of John 15—*abiding* in the vine so that the life, that is the will, of the Father more and more flows into us and through us."

CHAPTER 39

CHRISTOPHER'S QUANDARY

All the way home from church, Christopher was real quiet. It was hard not to think it had something to do with me, even though my brain told me it surely didn't.

As soon as we got home he saddled up his horse.

"I'm going for a ride, Corrie," he said somberly.

"Christopher, what is it?" I asked.

"Avery's sermon really got into me," he said. "I've never heard another man preach quite like he has recently."

"But, Christopher, I've heard you say almost the same things."

"Perhaps. But hearing them from someone else always makes it slightly different. Something has come over Avery that is powerful. I don't know about anyone else, but I was sitting there riveted to his every word. It is just how I wanted my preaching to effect people—convict them deeply so they would be able to live their faith practically. Now his preaching is doing just that to me!"

"What does that have to do with going for a ride?"

"I have to be alone, Corrie. I have to do what Avery said. There are some things I have been struggling with. I have to ask what God wants me to do. I have to know what his will is. I can't just listen to a sermon like that and then not apply it where I most need the Lord's direction in my own life."

He wheeled the mare around and rode off.

Christopher was gone two hours. When he walked into the bunkhouse, I could tell he was temporarily at peace, but his red eyes showed that whatever he was going through was a struggle that went deep.

"Can't you tell me what it is?" I asked.

"Not yet, Corrie," he replied. "I'm sorry, I just can't."

An awkward silence followed. He sat down. I fixed a pot of coffee and began heating up some cold stew I had saved him from dinner. Gradually we began to talk and found ourselves discussing the sermon we had heard that morning.

"Do you really think," I asked, "that people are as inexperienced as he said at asking for and then listening to God's voice?"

"Yes," replied Christopher thoughtfully, "I suppose I do. I'm not sure I could think of a single individual whom I knew in my church back in Richmond who ran his or her life that way. I'm not saying there were none, only that I didn't know of them—they didn't make that aspect of their walk with God known to me."

"It would seem that asking God what he wants and then waiting for him to tell you would be the most normal part of being a Christian."

"It was for Jesus. But it's not nearly so natural for us."

"Why?" I asked. "Is it because we aren't trained to hear God's voice like Rev. Rutledge said this morning?"

"We don't train *ourselves* in it. Usually our own wills are so involved that we place ourselves in a position where it will be very difficult to hear when the Lord does speak. When one's own will remains strong, prayers may go up, but a thick brick wall remains that can prevent the still, small voice from penetrating. That is why so many pray, yet hear little from God. It takes an abandonment of what *I want* to enable one to detect what *God wants*."

"How do you abandon what you want? It seems like a contradiction."

"Just as Jesus did. His prayer in the garden represents the climax of the biblical account and the Gospel story—'Father, not my will but your will be done.' What happened on the cross the next day, in a sense, was only the natural working out of that prayer. Theologians may disagree with me, but I believe the victory was won in the garden even more significantly than on the cross. Jesus' own will was utterly abandoned, laid down, relinquished. Thus was Satan defeated. And therein was our Lord's very practical example given to us."

"How is that an example to us? We won't face what Jesus did."

"Not many will be called upon to die on a cross, that is true. But we are *all* called to the garden with Jesus."

"You mean to give up our own wills?"

"Exactly! To lay down what we want in favor of what God may want. When we do as he did, and pray the prayer he prayed, and mean it—then is Satan defeated in our lives too. The enemy cannot touch us when our wills are abandoned into the Father's."

Christopher sighed. "But I'm no better off than my former parishioners," he said. "I certainly didn't hear much from God this afternoon. And I don't *know* whether or not my own will in the matter has been relinquished."

"But you heard what Rev. Rutledge said, that God's answers take time. What did you expect, an instant answer?"

Christopher laughed.

"I suppose I fell right into the trap he warned about," he said. "Good old impatience . . . though I have already been praying about the question for some time."

It was quiet for a while. I could tell Christopher was thinking. A moment later a little smile came to his lips.

"What?" I said.

"I was just thinking about how you and I met," replied Christopher, now smiling in earnest, "how we came to love each other."

"What could that possibly have to do with all this?" I laughed.

"Everything!" Christopher replied. "Don't you see—it's wonderful how it all ties in. God led us together, right?"

I nodded.

"But not by miracles and trumpets—"

"It was sort of a miracle," I said.

"You're right," Christopher laughed, "but it happened more through quiet ways that worked themselves out in our daily lives. It's just like Avery was saying—you have to wait patiently for the still, small voice to speak."

"I'm still not sure quite how it all ties in."

"I believe in miracles," said Christopher. "But I believe that God's normal mode of working in most lives is quiet and almost invisible, that the most important spiritual growth occurs not through observing or even participating in signs and wonders, but through the quiet and invisible obediences of a life lived in ongoing, moment-by-moment relinquishment of the will. We grow as we make Jesus' garden prayer the undergirding perspective of our entire being, *'Father . . .* your *will be done.'* Therein do the roots go down that will produce a life of maturity and wisdom and fruitfulness in the kingdom. Therein are sons and daughters fashioned into the likeness of Christ."

I tried to take in the magnitude of Christopher's words. Sometimes he could say such beautiful things about how God worked!

"So you see," he went on, "you and I were both going about the work we had been given to do until the day came when I suddenly found you lying beside the road unconscious. Neither of us could have known that our lives would be changed forever by that moment. We were not aware that God was making his will known right then. But I believe God was able to work so profoundly through that moment because we had both previously given direction for our lives to him. That is what enabled him to do it."

"Now," I said, "what does all that have to do with this morning's sermon?"

Again Christopher laughed.

"You are *not* going to let me off until you find out what it is that I have been praying about, are you?"

"All is fair in love and war, as they say."

"This isn't war."

"But isn't all fair in love and theology too? Haven't I heard you say that?"

"I've never said such a thing!" laughed Christopher.

"Well, it *sounds* like something you would say," I rejoined.

We joked a little more, but then the conversation grew serious once again.

"Do you think very many of the people who were there this morning will do what Rev. Rutledge suggested?" I asked.

"I don't know. It may be more than we think. I have been very impressed with the general spiritual maturity in Miracle Springs. I can tell that Avery Rutledge has been steadily adding meat to the spiritual diet of his flock, probably for years."

"Rev. Rutledge is a remarkable man," I said. "Everyone for miles has grown to love and respect him as much as anyone in the community."

"But about what you asked—there are only two people in that congregation for whom we are responsible, and that is us. Why don't we make sure we apply what he said and don't just analyze it? Why don't we each take something to the Lord that we are wondering about and ask him what he would have us do? Then as time goes on we can share with each other how it feels when we think God is answering. Maybe we can learn more about listening to his voice from each other."

"Good idea. But I thought that's what you were already doing this afternoon."

"I was. But believe me, I have plenty of things I can ask the Lord about!"

We fell silent for five or ten minutes and both just talked silently to the Lord. I asked him what he wanted me to do and say to Jennie. Did he want me to speak to her about marriage, about trying to love Tom and be patient with him . . . or did God want me just to be a friend but not offer any counsel or advice?

"Not only is hearing God's still, small voice vague, quiet, invisible, and subtle, exactly as Avery pointed out," Christopher said reflectively after a while, "it is a very *personal* process. Every man or woman has to learn the particulars of how God's voice speaks to him or her on his own. Someone else can only point in general directions and say how it feels *to him*. But everyone has to learn to detect that voice for himself. It will have different subtle nuances for each. What did you ask him about? if you feel comfortable telling me."

I told him about my concern for Jennie.

He gave a little laugh. "I guess Jennie and Tom are important to us," he said. "I asked him about Tom. I just don't know how to get on any footing with him. Are we supposed to say anything, do anything? Or should I just let events take their course? I don't know. That's where I need some guidance, too.

"I suppose that is another reason why there are no lists of instructions—God desires to speak to each question in a unique way. Circumstances vary, and personalities vary. It's wonderful, isn't it! You have to learn to hear his voice because it's going to have a slightly different sound in *your* ears than anyone else's. That's how personal is God's love for you, that he will speak to you and me as he speaks to no one else in all the universe."

"But what if God doesn't speak?" I said. "There have been lots of times I have prayed and never did feel like I received an answer."

"We have to remember that there are times when God *won't* speak. If his will is clear, then we're wasting our breath asking him to show us more specifically what he wants us to do. Sometimes it is obedience that is required, rather than prayer for additional leading."

Christopher paused reflectively.

"I remember a young woman in my church in Virginia," he said. "She wanted to do something she knew was wrong. The Bible made that clear. Yet she kept praying that God would let her do what she wanted to do."

"What happened?"

"Eventually she convinced herself that God was speaking to her in confirmation that he was leading her."

"She went ahead?"

Christopher nodded.

"And you don't think she heard from God?"

"What she did was contrary to Scripture. God does not contradict himself."

"How do you know if it is really God's voice you heard or your own desires interfering with the process? Seems like it would be easy to fool yourself."

"You have to confirm what you think you've heard with all the other ways God speaks. Is it consistent with advice and counsel you have received from wise people? Does it make good common sense? Is it a *sound* decision? Does it seem to fit with circumstances or go contrary to other things God has been doing in your life? And especially—is it consistent with Scripture?

"God never contradicts himself, as I said before. So if he has spoken, he will gradually confirm what he has said in all these other ways. If there is conflict anywhere, it may well be that it is not God's voice you heard at all. God's true voice may be faint and indistinct at first, but it will steadily grow more clear through our lives as we practice and as we obey what he tells us to do."

As if talk of obedience had stirred him to some action, Christopher got to his feet, then reached down to grab my hand and pull me up, too. He draped an arm around my shoulder as we went out through the bunkhouse door. I circled my arm around his waist, and by silent agreement, we started walking up the trail that led to the mine.

We didn't say anything for a long time. We were both caught up in our own thoughts and our silent prayers. I must admit I was still worrying a little about whatever it was that was bothering Christopher. But I was also praying silently about turning that worry over to the Lord. And I was enjoying the walk, just being out under the bright blue sky and looking around at our familiar land and being close to the man I loved.

Finally, as we were nearing the mine, Christopher spoke.

"I am very grateful for Avery's talk this morning. Sometimes we know bits of information, but they are like a map to a gold mine that three or four partners have torn in pieces to insure its safety. Their pieces can get each of them close but they need the whole map to fit together correctly to see the entire picture. I feel like Avery's teaching us that simple prayer and then his counsel to wait has perhaps been one of the missing pieces of my own map."

I didn't answer, just walked along beside him, wondering if maybe I had found a piece of my own map as well.

No matter what, I thought, *I have a lot to think about.*

CHAPTER 40

LOOKING AHEAD ON THE SHOULDERS OF THE PAST

For weeks after the funeral I couldn't get out of my head Rev. Rutledge's words about Mr. Jones sort of representing the history of our Miracle Springs community.

It was the same feeling I sometimes used to get when I'd feel an article starting to bubble up from down inside of me. Right off I knew this was something I wanted to write about.

I'd been writing in my journals, of course, all along. Even marriage and talking to Christopher all the time couldn't stop that, but it had cut down the *amount* I wrote by at least half. For one thing, I didn't have so much time by myself anymore. Besides, much of the energy and thought I used to put into my journal writing now went into face-to-face dialogue with Christopher.

I hadn't written a newspaper article in longer than I could remember. But the minute I started writing about Mr. Jones I knew I wanted to send it to Mr. Kemble. I didn't even care if he paid me for it. I felt it was an important story, important not just for Miracle Springs but for all of California.

I'll have to admit I was nervous as I sent the finished story in to Mr. Kemble. I hadn't heard much from him since I had decided not to write about Mammy Pleasant's boardinghouse. He had accepted my regrets graciously enough—after all, I had gotten him his dinner!—but I knew he thought my refusal was silly. What if he decided never to publish my work again?

I needn't have worried. Mr. Kemble was delighted with the

story and paid me twelve dollars for it. When we opened the September 17 issue of the *Alta* to read it, Christopher dove right into the article. I was more concerned to see if they had gotten my new name right.

I was proud in a whole new way as I read the words: "Colorful History Fades with Passing of Old Forty-Niner," by *Corrie Hollister Braxton.*

Here is the article I wrote:

I have been a Californian now for more than fifteen years, exactly half of my still-young life. When I first came here in 1852, it seemed as if the gold rush and all the excitement and wonder of that time was already past. Yet now, to look back, I realize that I was right in the middle of it and hardly knew it.

Time is like that. Things look different to your eyes as time goes by.

California was still young then, still wild, still populated mostly by men who still had that look of gold fever in their eyes. What women and children happened to be in the West were here, as was I, almost by accident. The men, however, had come for only one thing—to strike it rich!

Some of them did. Most didn't. But nearly all of them stayed, for gradually they, and those who came after them, discovered that there was more on the shores of the Pacific than gold. There was a land to grow with, a good land, a land where homes could be built and families could be happy.

Through the years people continued to come, but fewer and fewer were coming for the gold.

And now that almost twenty years has passed since that first nugget gleamed up from out of the water at Sutter's Mill, California looks different. It feels different. A colorful and historic era is slowly fading into what we call "history." Do what we will, we are powerless to halt time's wheels slowly turning across the events of our lives.

And as we pause to glance backward, it is not the shiny lure of gold we first see, but rather stains of red.

This nation has recently endured the strife of a great war whose bitter bloodshed further separates us from the memories of the first half of this century. Glancing forward again, those wheels grind steadily onward toward the century's final decades.

I stood some weeks ago beside the new grave of an old prospector by the name of Alkali Jones. It seems unlikely that was his given name, for what mother would call a little baby Alkali? But it was the only name any of us knew him by. We used it with affection, for he was greatly beloved by all.

Alkali Jones was a forty-niner of the original breed— tough, hardworking, a loner, adventurous, and with more tall tales than any ten ordinary people. He came west before there was even thought of statehood. He was here in the little town of Miracle Springs before any of the rest of us arrived. No one knew Miracle Springs without Alkali Jones.

But from this day forward we will have to know our town without him, for he has left us for a greater adventure still. His era is passing. He has now gone to join the rest of our memories in the quiet places of our hearts, where we go to reminisce with fondness about days gone.

How many other places in the mountains and foothills of California have lost their own beloved Alkali Jones in recent years? How many more will lose them in the not-too-distant future?

These are the men to whose legacy we owe our statehood and all the promise of its future.

With the passing of Alkali Jones and a thousand like him, the era of the gold rush is slowly receding into the distance. For as it always does, death symbolizes both an end and a beginning.

A new era continues to dawn over this land at the Pacific border of our continent. It is an era that will see families and churches and industry and commerce and farming all replace gold as that which holds communities together. Many of these changes are already upon us. California is growing into a maturity of its own alongside its older sister-states. Even now, thousands of workers are straining their backs to link the Pacific with the Atlantic by rail. New times are coming, and it will not be long before a new century dawns.

All this passed through my brain in a second or two as I stood solemnly by that old forty-niner's grave. When I turned to walk away, I knew I was leaving something precious behind, and yet realized at the same time that much more yet lay ahead.

Alkali Jones, we will miss you. You were a dear friend. We thank you for what you gave us—a history to be proud of. Upon your shoulders we now stand, that we might look forward to the new eras ahead.

CHAPTER 41

STRANGER IN MIRACLE SPRINGS

Marcus Weber was the first person in Miracle Springs to spot the stranger. He was just coming from the General Store back to the Mine and Freight when he glanced up to see a filthy rider on a tired-looking horse clopping slowly up the street.

After reaching the opposite side he paused and turned back, following the rider with his eyes as the man dismounted in front of the saloon, spat furiously into the dust, tied his horse to a rail, and walked inside.

The silent observer shook his wise old graying black head back and forth a few times. "That there be a bad-looking man," he muttered to himself.

Had Marcus only known how bad, and what exactly was the stranger's business in Miracle Springs, he would not have let the incident pass so uneventfully. The faithful old man would have given his life for any one of the Hollister clan, who had employed him since his first days working for the Parrish Mine and Freight Company in the early 1850s.

But Marcus did not know. He simply mopped his copper-colored brow with a big blue bandana and continued on his way back to work.

In the Gold Nugget, meanwhile, not so thriving an establishment as during the height of the gold rush, yet still making enough of the old miners drunk with sufficient regularity to stay in business, the stranger at the bar was already downing his second glass of whiskey and inquiring as to the whereabouts of certain of the town's well-known inhabitants. Thinking nothing unusual about the request, the bartender obliged him with the information. Only later did he recall those fiercely glinting eyes and wonder if he had done the right thing to tell the stranger where Drummond Hollister lived.

Thirty minutes later, the man was on his way out of town along the dirt road the bartender had so helpfully and unknowingly pointed out. As he made his way into the foothills, the rider grew ever more vigilant. That his errand was a deadly one could be seen by the way his right hand wandered from the rifle strapped to the saddle behind him to the pistol tucked into a holster at his side.

Ascending the final ridge about which the bartender had told him, the stranger finally dismounted to proceed on foot. He would survey the area first and learn what he could of the lay of the land.

He led his horse off the road and tied it to a tree out of sight. He drew out his pistol and held it in readiness in case he encountered someone unexpectedly. Then with stealthy step, keeping off the road, he proceeded cautiously over the ridge.

CHAPTER 42

THE HUNTING TRIP

Fall came right on schedule.

The green of the leaves began to evaporate into hints of yellow and red, then turn deeper golds and more brilliant reds and fiery oranges. Gradually a nip crept into the air in the evening and morning, though for a while the days remained nearly as warm as the summer.

I knew what was coming when Pa started looking up into the mountains with a faraway gaze, and then when he and Zack started cleaning and oiling their rifles and checking the sights. Then came target practice at cans and fenceposts and trees, and I knew it wouldn't be long. This was one of the times of the year Pa loved most.

I came upon Zack alone in the barn once, practicing his quick-draw with his new pistol. I'd heard shots off in the distance that were different from rifle shots, and I knew them to be from Zack, too. He had always been more fond of guns than I was comfortable with. But he was a man now, and there was nothing I could do about it.

One evening during the first week of November, Pa announced at supper that the time had come.

"Time to be heading up into the hills to get started on our winter's meat," he said.

Zack and Tad were nearly out of their seats and on their way to saddle up their horses the next instant!

"Hold on!" laughed Pa. "We still got a few preparations to

192

make. I figure two days from tomorrow morning, we'll head out."

Christopher was the only one around the table who didn't know what was going on, and he listened to Pa with raised eyebrows.

"Besides, we've gotta get Christopher instructed with his rifle before then," Pa added in answer to his look of question.

"What—I don't own a rifle," he said.

"You will before we leave. I'm buying you a new one myself."

Tad and Zack gave out exclamations of their approval.

"What need do I have of a rifle?" asked Christopher.

"If you're going to go hunting with us," rejoined Pa, "then you've got to know how to use one. We're going to come back with a couple of deer, maybe a fat bear getting ready to settle down for a long sleep—meat enough to smoke and dry to last us into the winter at least. When the first snows come, we'll go out again to get more to freeze."

The very next day Pa and Christopher went into town together to pick out a new gun. Christopher was uncomfortable, I could tell, but he went along with it for Pa's sake. I knew as well that despite his nervousness he was looking forward to a hunting trip up into the Sierras with the men.

"We'll make a Westerner yet out of this husband of yours, Corrie," said Pa that evening around the table. "I'll teach him to shoot, to track, to know where the game is, and to read the weather."

"It sounds like you plan to turn him into another John Fremont!" I said with a laugh.

"Nah, I just want him to know where to go out and get himself a couple deer every year."

We all laughed.

"I had to shoot an occasional fox for Mrs. Timms," said Christopher, "and took her rifle out to get her a deer or rabbit when I could, but it seems like half the times I missed and the critter got away."

"I tell you, Christopher," Pa went on, "things and critters are different out here. Back in New York and Virginia bear and deer have been hiding from men for a hundred years. It's easier to find the game here."

Christopher loved being part of this group of men. He'd never before had the opportunity to enjoy this sort of thing. But he was strangely quiet for a while after Pa's comment about turning him into a Westerner. I didn't know why.

When we were alone I asked him about it.

"Why did you get so quiet?" I asked at length.

Christopher sighed and shrugged without answering.

"Pa didn't mean anything by what he said."

"I know that," Christopher replied. "But maybe I'm not cut out to be a Westerner."

"I . . . I'm not sure I understand what you mean."

"Corrie," said Christopher firmly. "I really don't want to say anything until I have some sense of the Lord's mind on the matter."

"You mean—does this have to do with what you've been thinking about that you haven't wanted to tell me?"

He nodded.

"Christopher, I really don't understand this. If we're going to base our marriage on communication, then it seems—"

"All right," he interrupted. "If you really have to know, I'll tell you. I've been praying about whether we might be supposed to leave Miracle Springs."

I looked at Christopher with my eyes wide open in disbelief. I was stunned. I couldn't believe what I'd heard, and I wasn't sure I wanted to hear any more. I certainly didn't ask any more questions.

Pretty soon Christopher went for a walk by himself. It was cloudy and silent between us the rest of that day and the next. Now I wished I hadn't pushed Christopher so hard to tell me, because knowing what he was thinking was worse than not knowing had been!

We didn't talk about it anymore before the hunting trip.

Three days later they set off, all the men of our little community: Pa and Uncle Nick, Christopher, Zack, Tad, and Uncle Nick's oldest son, Erich, leaving Almeda, Becky, Ruth, and me at our house and Aunt Katie and her youngsters at hers.

To tell the truth, we were looking forward to the few days they would be gone, thinking of all the baking and sewing and cleaning we would be able to get done without men underfoot. I planned to go through our little bunkhouse from top to bottom! Katie was planning to come down to join us making enough soap to last the winter.

So we told them all goodbye with more anticipation than sadness, and we watched them ride off with a sense of satisfaction and
pride. I was thinking how *right* it all looked—our men riding off
together to provide for our family.

The only thing that didn't look right as they rode off eastward,
waving to us as they went, was the six-shooter Zack had in the holster on the belt he had strapped around his hip. I'd only seen him
with it that once in the barn, and he had never mentioned it, probably because he knew well enough that Almeda and I would dis-
approve. I don't know if Almeda even knew he had it, unless Pa
had told her.

But it didn't look right sitting there on Zack's hip, to the eyes
of his sister at least. What could wearing a gun do but invite trouble? I imagined he was good with it. Zack was the kind of guy who
was good at anything if he worked at it long enough. But being
good with a gun only made matters worse. I didn't like it. But
again, there was nothing I could do, so I just waved back and put
the gun out of my mind.

Not an hour after they'd disappeared through the trees, Almeda
and Becky were scrubbing away in the kitchen of the big house,
and I was already starting to perspire from a thorough sweeping
of our bunkhouse from one end to the other.

By afternoon, every available line was filled with wash hung out
to dry.

CHAPTER 43

A FEARSOME VISITOR

It was two days later when the knock came at the door.

I was closest and went to answer it. I thought something was odd because we'd heard no one ride up.

"I'm lookin' for Hollister," said the man standing there on the porch. He was a stranger, and the instant I laid eyes on him I felt myself shiver. He hadn't shaved in probably a week, and his clothes were dirty and smelly. My eyes went straight to the gun on his hip, probably because of the memory of Zack's being so fresh. But the gun I now saw wasn't new like Zack's. It looked like it had been used many times. His face was dark and weathered and rough, and a big scar down his cheekbone onto the top of his neck made his appearance all the scarier. What teeth he had, which was only about half of them, were yellow, and his eyes were full of suspicion and hate.

"He . . . he's not here," I said hesitantly, trying to keep from shuddering again.

"Where is he?" said the man gruffly.

"Mr. Hollister is away for a short time," said Almeda, walking up from behind. I knew her well enough to tell from her voice that she was more than just a little concerned.

"Him and me's got business."

"Anything I can help you with?"

"My business is with Hollister. What about the young'un?"

"You mean. . . ?" Almeda hesitated.

"Hollister's boy," snapped the man.

196

"Which one—Zack or Tad?"

"Zack . . . Zack Hollister."

"He's gone too," replied Almeda. Her voice was starting to tremble, but she was doing her best to stand there firm and keep her composure.

The man seemed to think for a moment, then turned and walked away without a word.

Almeda shut the door. When she turned back to face me, her face was ashen white. Both of us knew it was the man Pa and Zack had been worried about.

"That was not a good man, Corrie," she said. Her voice had a slight quiver to it. She hesitated a moment, then went carefully to the window and looked out. As soon as the man was gone, Almeda grabbed her coat and headed for the door.

"I'm going for Sheriff Rafferty," she said.

"Wouldn't it be better if I went," I suggested.

"He would be less likely to harm me, Corrie," she said. "There are a few times when gray hair and a few wrinkles are an advantage, and this is one of those times. I would never forgive myself if something happened to you. You and Becky stay here with Ruth."

She opened the door and stepped out.

"Bolt the door behind me," she said, pausing and glancing back, then turned and continued on to the barn.

I went inside, bolted the door like she'd said, and sat down with Becky. We were both afraid. We'd heard enough about Demming's threats to know this was serious.

All was silent for about five minutes, then we heard Almeda's horse canter off. Again silence fell.

Five more minutes passed.

Suddenly a knock sounded on the door. I nearly leapt out of my skin. Becky and Ruth both turned to me, their faces white.

I stood up and slowly walked forward. Again the knock sounded.

"Corrie . . . Corrie, it's me," came Almeda's voice.

Relieved beyond words, I dashed the rest of the way toward the door, unbolted it, and the next moment was pulling Almeda inside. Her face, however, contained the exact opposite of the joy I felt.

"He's out there," she said softly.

"What—watching you?"

"He stopped me and told me to get back inside," she said, closing the door behind her and slumping into a chair as if she had been drained of energy.

"Where?" said Becky.

"Right out there," Almeda said pointing, "just a hundred or so yards toward the road. He had a gun pointed at me. He said if any of us tried to leave, he wouldn't hesitate to use it. He kept the horse."

CHAPTER 44

PRISONERS IN OUR OWN HOUSE

The four of us sat for several minutes in silence.

"What does the man want?" asked Ruth at length.

"I'm afraid he wants your father and brother, Ruth," said Almeda. The fear was evident in her voice.

There were times in the past when I had seen Almeda ready to take on any six men, with guns or without them. Somehow it was different this time. I think she knew just how dangerous this situation was and that the man meant what he'd said.

She was worried for Pa and Zack and for us three girls. Had she been alone, I wouldn't doubt she'd already be loading up a rifle to take the man on. But now there were others to think of. We knew well enough that Demming had vowed to kill Pa and Zack, and we were pretty sure he wouldn't mind if any others got hurt in the meantime.

"We have to get word to the sheriff," I said.

"That man is standing guard up on the hill right now," said Almeda. He can see the house and the barn and road. We can't make a move in any direction without him knowing it."

We were silent a while, thinking.

"You mean . . . we're prisoners in our own house?" said Becky at length.

"I'm afraid so."

"What about Aunt Katie?" I said. "We ought to warn her."

"You're right," sighed Almeda, "though I don't know how."

199

She paused.

"The one we *really* need to warn," she added, "is your father."

"That's right. If he and the others come back," I said, suddenly realizing the danger, "and don't know he's here . . . he might . . ."

I did not finish what I was about to say. Almeda knew well enough what I was thinking. That was obviously Demming's plan.

"We can't let Pa and Zack ride straight into his trap," said Becky, now seeing the full implications of the situation.

Almeda nodded.

"We have to warn them," insisted Becky.

"But how?" I asked.

"We have to get word to them or signal them somehow," said Almeda, "*before* they just ride in unsuspectingly."

We were quiet all the rest of the day. We couldn't stop our hearts pounding, but there wasn't much to be said. We tried to keep busying ourselves with cleaning, but all the fun had been taken out of it. Before dark I went out to feed and water the animals, but I was afraid to go back out to sleep in the bunkhouse by myself.

That evening, as dusk began to fall, Becky and Almeda and I began talking seriously about what, if anything, we ought to do.

As we talked, it began to come to me what was the only thing we could do to help . . . and I knew I had to be the one to do it.

"I have an idea," I said.

Almeda looked at me with a curious and worried expression. She knew well enough some of the hairbrained things I had done in my life!

"It's the only way," I said, answering her raised eyebrows even before explaining what was on my mind.

"We're listening," she said slowly.

"I'll sneak out of the house in the middle of the night," I said finally. "I'll get to the woods without him seeing me, then I'll go find Pa and Christopher and the others."

"Corrie, I won't hear of it," objected Almeda.

"It's the only way to warn them," I repeated.

Almeda thought for a minute.

"Will you be able to find them?"

"Pa and the boys usually make camp up on Panther Flats on

the Bear River," I answered. "It's not that far."

"Can you find it in the dark?"

"I'll ride slow. I know my way. Besides, there's a moon out—there'll be some light."

It was clear it was already decided, even though Almeda continued to be anxious about the plan. She saw too that we *had* to alert Pa before he came back and that there just wasn't any way to do it without somebody getting away from the house.

I was the only volunteer.

CHAPTER 45

NIGHT ESCAPE

Almeda woke Becky and me in the middle of the night. She held a small candle so I could see to dress, but we whispered and kept away from the windows.

The house only had the one door, which faced the road where Demming had been watching all day.

He *had* to sleep sometime and might well be asleep right then, yet I couldn't risk going out that way and having him see or hear me. The three-quarter moon would make my ride easier once I got away, although it would make it easier for him to spot me in the meantime. Somehow I had to sneak to the barn, saddle one of the few remaining horses, and get away without him hearing or suspecting anything was amiss.

Working together, Becky and I carefully opened one of the windows at the back of the house. The casing made a little scraping noise, but we managed to get it open wide enough.

I climbed up and put one leg through.

"You be careful, Corrie," whispered Becky.

"I will."

"Don't take any chances," said Almeda. "If there is danger, or if he sees or comes after you, come straight back to the house—do you hear me?"

I nodded.

"If he hears you in the barn, don't try to make a run for it. There is no telling what he might do. I'm afraid he might try to shoot you."

"I'll watch myself," I said.

"I will cover you as best I can out the front window with the rifle. If I see him, I'll start shooting over his head, and you run back here."

I finished climbing out, and a moment later was standing on the ground outside at the back of the house.

We whispered goodbye. I walked slowly around to the side of the house, then crept very slowly toward the barn. There were enough shadows that I managed to reach it unseen.

I stopped and took several breaths. I was going slow but was breathing heavily. The night was tense. I knew that any sound might bring me face to face with that awful scarred cheek and those evil eyes!

Slowly I worked my way along the outside wall of the barn in the darkness and eventually found the door and latch. I was just about to attempt to open it when the impossibility of what I was trying to do hit me. There was no conceivable way to open the door, saddle a horse, and get a big animal like that away from here in the dead of night . . . without a sound. This had been a stupid plan. He would hear me for sure!

I thought for a moment. Then a new idea struck me.

I let loose of the latch and continued on against the wall to the far side of the barn. I crept away from the building and, again following the shadows, made my way as quickly as I could to the old barn, breathing a little more easily, knowing that I was now a good distance from Demming. Once safely at the back of the old building and out of sight from the road, and after climbing a couple fences and keeping away from any animals who might make noises and give me away, I was able to run the short distance across the pasture and over the small creek.

Presently I was at the edge of the woods.

From there I worked my way up the hill from tree to tree, still being careful as I planted my feet not to break any dried twigs. I came eventually to the area of the old mine, and after ten or fifteen slow and careful minutes was approaching Uncle Nick's and Aunt Katie's place through the shadows of the nearby pines.

Aunt Katie knew about Demming by now, and that he was watching us all. We had seen her try to come down earlier in the day, and he had intercepted her with a warning just as he had Almeda, telling her to get back in her house and stay put and that he'd be watching.

I crept to Aunt Katie's window and knocked on it just loudly enough to wake her. She came to the window with a look of fear on her face.

"Corrie!" she exclaimed as she opened it.

"Shh!" I said quickly. "Demming doesn't know I'm here. I got away. I need a horse."

"What are you—?"

"I'm going to try to find Pa and Uncle Nick and Christopher and the boys," I said. "I've got to get away without him seeing me."

Aunt Katie was already dressing and a minute or two later was outside with me. We walked to their stables. A couple of the horses started fidgeting about restlessly, but Aunt Katie spoke to them in low tones to quiet them. Together we managed to get a saddle on one of the mares I knew reasonably.

"Do you need anything?" Katie asked.

"Just to get out of earshot without the horse whinnying."

"Then, talk to her—and here," she added, pulling several lumps of sugar from her pocket. "These should help."

I took the sugar and held one lump up immediately to the big inquisitive fleshy lips. The mare took it, and as she was enjoying her treat, I took the reins from Katie and led my companion off eastward toward the woods and the foothills beyond them.

"Good luck, Corrie," said Aunt Katie behind me. "God be with you."

CHAPTER 46

INTO THE HILLS

Leaving Aunt Katie, I continued on foot for twenty or thirty minutes into steadily more wooded terrain, being overly careful about noise probably longer than I needed to. My supply of sugar was quickly depleted.

Once I felt it safe, I mounted and walked the mare another half an hour. In the faint moonglow I couldn't gallop safely anyway. I figured it was somewhere between four-thirty or five by now. It would be light in another hour or so, and I would walk carefully until that time, hoping by then to be well into the foothills.

I was generally familiar enough with all the country within an hour of home. I also had a pretty good idea of where the men were. I headed first toward Chalk Bluff to Red Hill Springs, then southeast down into the Bear River valley.

I descended into the valley just about the time light began to illuminate the sky, a little after five-thirty, by my guess. By six it was light enough for me to increase my speed. I reached the river and began making my way eastward along its northern bank and within two hours was entering the clearing called Panther Flats.

There was no sign of anyone!

Neither was there sign they had pitched camp here at all.

Had I been mistaken, or had they changed their plans? How would I find them now!

I had to stop and think. I'd heard Pa mention Sawtooth Ridge a time or two. Its southern flank was almost straight east of me by four or five more miles, across the river and a little bit south.

205

· If I could work my way southeast, then south a bit through Blue Canyon, I'd come up at the southern end of Sawtooth Ridge. Then I could work my way along the top of the ridge and hopefully, if they were anywhere in that vicinity, they would spot my approach.

Now that I remembered, along with the Bear River region, I'd heard Pa mention the good hunting between Blue Canyon and Sawtooth, too, along Fulda Creek. If I didn't run into them from the ridge, I'd circle back down north and to the north of Blue Canyon. If I still hadn't located them, from there I'd go straight back over to the Bear and follow it west back to Panther Flats from the opposite direction as before.

I mounted back up, forded the Bear River, and made for the southern flank of Sawtooth Ridge.

The way had grown mountainous so I couldn't safely run the mare at full speed, but I gave her the feel of my heels a time or two and let her know with the leather that we had important business and couldn't take our time. She increased her pace without objection.

I rode the rest of the way through the Dutch Flat region, crossed Canyon Creek, entered into the very southern tip of Blue Canyon, and at last began the steady climb up the southern slope of Sawtooth Ridge.

When I reached the small summit above Humbug Bar, I stopped for a rest.

It was chilly. Summer was most definitely past. The ridge was only about a thousand feet in elevation, but I knew snow would be lying in the shadows and hollows in another month or two. It wouldn't be long in coming now. Even though it was a month too early, I imagined that I could almost smell the snow in the air.

I glanced around.

The sky was partially clear, but a thick black series of clouds hung over the mountains farther to the east, mountains whose very tops were already white from unseasonably early snows.

Soon I was on my way again, reaching the ridge trail along the Sawtooth and working my way, galloping when I felt I could risk it, northward past Helester Point, then eastward across Willmont Saddle. I pushed the mare hard for the next two hours.

All day as I rode, I couldn't help thinking about what Christopher had said about our moving from Miracle Springs. I almost felt guilty for thinking about it, because I was worried for everyone's safety, too, and my own future seemed a small thing in comparison. But I couldn't help it. I loved it here, and I didn't *want* to move.

Even as I rode, I was so aware of how beautiful these mountains were. Ever since we'd come from New York, this had been "home." I would miss it so badly if I had to live somewhere else. I didn't think I could bear it!

And I have to admit I had some negative thoughts about Christopher, too. I tried to fight them, but like the others I couldn't help it. It was hard not to be angry with him even for thinking about such a thing as moving.

I paused in my ride to rest again, trying to think about now rather than the future.

It was probably close to noon by now.

I dismounted and sat down to eat some of the dried meat I had brought and an apple. But first I took a long drink from my canteen.

"Help me find them, Lord," I said softly.

Till then the thought of *not* finding them hadn't even occurred to me. Suddenly it dawned on me that we could be miles apart! This was an enormous country! What did I think—that I was just going to ride out and run into them?

What if they had seen tracks leading south? They might be halfway to Grass Valley by now or tracking along the American River miles and miles from here.

Worse, what if they were already headed home another way and walked unsuspectingly straight into Demming's trap!

I began to be afraid.

Suddenly in the midst of my thoughts a scripture verse came into my mind.

Trust in the Lord with all thine heart, I could hear Rev. Rutledge say as if he had spoken the words yesterday. In fact I probably hadn't heard him preach on that passage in years. *And lean not unto thine own understanding. In all thy ways acknowledge him, and he shall direct thy paths.*

I paused.

He shall direct thy paths, came the words again. *He shall direct thy paths!*

"Lord," I prayed again, *"I do acknowledge you in all my ways and for everything in life—for life itself. Thank you for reminding me. I ask you to direct my paths, Lord, and lead me to Pa and Christopher and the others. Lead me, Lord . . . guide me to them."*

A while longer I sat, then remounted. An inner sense told me to keep riding in the same direction as I had been going.

I turned the mare's nose again, and we continued northeast along Sawtooth Ridge.

CHAPTER 47

A SHOT AND WHAT
FOLLOWED

It was nearly sunset of a long and tiring day. I had probably covered fifteen or twenty miles altogether, and most of it over hilly and rocky terrain. I was sleepy and exhausted and already starting to think of making camp for the night, when suddenly I heard a shot in the distance.

It was not so close that the sound made me start. But instantly I reined in the mare and listened intently. I was sure it had been gunfire. I judged the distance to be a mile or two.

After about ten seconds, another shot sounded.

I lashed at the rump of the mare and made for the spot the sound had come from. It didn't occur to me the danger I could put myself in. What if it was a stranger who didn't take kindly to someone riding in and disturbing his game? Or what if I had not heard the sound of hunters at all but of a gunfight and now was riding right into the middle of it?

At the time, however, I didn't think of such things. I only knew there were people out there somewhere, and I had to find out who they were!

I rode hard. No other sound met my ears except the clomping of the mare's hoofed feet over rocks and dirt and dried grass and brush.

At an angled incline, I rode down the slope of the Sawtooth, now up a steep short rise, across its top, where I looked this way and that, then down the other side toward Burnett Canyon, across

209

a creek, up a short uneven hill, and toward a wide meadow that spread out at the bottom of the canyon.

Gradually I slowed. I was just about to despair again, thinking I must have mistaken the direction of the gunfire, when I heard a welcome cry.

"Corrie!" came a shout.

I reined in and turned, glancing frantically about.

There was Tad running toward me from a wooded area at the edge of the meadow!

I turned toward him several paces, then leapt down and ran into his arms.

"Tad . . . I didn't think I'd ever find you!"

"What are you doing here?" he exclaimed.

"Where's Pa?" I said, suddenly remembering the urgency of what had brought me out into the mountains.

"Back there," answered Tad, tossing his head back in the direction from which he had come. "And how *did* you find us?"

"Jump up behind me," I said, "and I'll tell you as we go."

I remounted, then made room for Tad's foot in the stirrup. A few seconds later he was sitting on the mare's back, behind my saddle, and holding on around my waist. I gave him the reins, and he urged the tired horse forward at an easy canter.

"However you found us, you were lucky," said Tad.

"Why's that?"

"Because this morning we were making due south from here."

"What brought you back?"

"Pa got onto a bear, and we tracked it back up this way all day."

"Was that the shot I just heard?"

"I think so. I was out on the eastern flank, so I'm just making my way back in the direction of the others to see if they got the brute."

Ten minutes later we were riding into the little camp they had made about an hour before. Christopher, Uncle Nick, and twelve-year-old Erich were the only ones there.

I jumped down and was crying in Christopher's arms the next instant, with questions coming at me from all three at once. Before I had the chance to answer them, however, Pa came tramping into the little clearing, holding his rifle.

"Got him!" he exclaimed. "He's back about seventy or eighty yards. It's gonna take every one of us to move—"

He stopped, suddenly seeing me in their midst.

"Corrie!" he cried, "what in tarnation are *you* doing here?"

The next moment Zack came bounding in.

"Great shot, Pa! That bear didn't have a—"

Now it was his turn to notice me. Gradually the hubbub died down.

"I snuck out in the middle of the night," I said. "I had to try to find you before you came back."

"Why—what in tarnation for?" exclaimed Pa.

"It started with a knock on the door," I said, "yesterday morning."

"Who was it?" Already Pa's expression had grown serious.

"He didn't give his name, Pa," I said. Then I described him. I saw Zack's face begin to lose its color. "He just asked for you," I said, "then Zack."

I went on to explain the rest of what had happened, including how the man had stopped Almeda and threatened her.

Everyone listened intently until I was through with what I had come to tell them.

CHAPTER 48

A DIFFERENCE

After I was done, the silence gathered itself for a few seconds like a giant thundercloud. It didn't take long for the storm to break.

"Why, that miserable no-good scum," shouted Pa, "I'll kill him!"

He was mounting his horse the next instant, his face red, and fury in his eyes. I'd never in my life seen him with such an expression.

Christopher jumped up and grabbed Pa's arm from where it was clutching the saddle.

"Drum, don't!" he cried. "It's not the best way."

"Don't try to stop me, Braxton!"

Pa shook loose Christopher's grip, then swung his leg up over the horse's back and onto the saddle.

"Drum . . . no!" said Christopher, and his voice was one of command. As he spoke, he quickly reached up and yanked the reins from out of Pa's hands. Then he stood calmly right in front of the horse and blocked his way.

"Confound you, Braxton!" shouted Pa, and it was obvious he was fighting-mad. "I failed my family once on account of that man, and I don't aim to do it again. Now get outta my way before I knock you down!"

Christopher stood his ground.

Pa grabbed for the reins, then lashed at his gelding. It immediately lurched forward, sending Christopher sprawling to his back in the dirt. I was terrified and ran to him.

212

Pa wheeled and headed for the edge of the clearing. But from where he still lay on the ground, Christopher called after him.

"When you ran off before," he cried, "it was only to make yourself a thief. If you go after this man now, Drum Hollister, you won't be helping your family at all! You'll be making Almeda the wife of a murderer!"

Christopher's words sounded as a thunderclap to punctuate the storm that had erupted over the tiny clearing.

Pa reined in the horse and stopped.

The air hung heavy and silent, as if echoing the word over and over in all of our ears—*murderer . . . murderer . . . murderer!*

Pa turned his mount's head and walked slowly back as Christopher climbed to his feet.

We all stood spellbound. I was terrified, yet unable to move so much as a muscle.

Pa dismounted and walked slowly forward, then stood in front of Christopher. Both men were breathing heavily.

"In my younger years I'd have horsewhipped you for saying a thing like that," said Pa. His voice was soft. The anger had drained from him.

"I'm sorry, Drum," said Christopher, returning Pa's gaze with an intensity of love. "But you're too good a man for this. You're a man of God. You can't do what other men might do."

Still Pa stood, looking him straight in the eye.

"Besides which," Christopher added, "I love you too much to let you do what was in your mind a minute ago. I'd sooner shoot you out of love with the rifle you gave me than let you shoot another man out of anger and hate."

Still Pa stood.

"You'd shoot me to protect a man like Harris?" he said finally, not sure if he'd heard Christopher aright.

"No," replied Christopher. "But I would do it to protect *you* from shooting him. The harm you were about to do was to *yourself.*"

Gradually Pa saw his meaning and slowly nodded.

"When we tell the Lord he can have his way with us," Christopher repeated, "we can't do what other men might do. We've relinquished that right."

214

A moment or two more they stood, my father and my husband—father-in-law and son-in-law.

Pa nodded again, this time more decisively.

"You're right," he said, then stepped back, glanced away, and let out a sigh. "I'm much obliged to you for stopping me. What you did took guts."

He gave Christopher his hand.

"I understand a little how you feel," said Christopher, shaking it. "Part of me is fighting mad that he threatened Corrie, too. But we've prayed for that man, Drum. We can't just go rushing off now and try to shoot him or lynch him. We prayed for his good. There's an obligation on us. We have to do what God would have us do, not what we might do if left to ourselves."

"What do you figure that is?" asked Pa, letting out a sigh and stooping down. He took a seat on the ground. All thought of retrieving the bear he had just shot was now far from his mind.

"I don't know," replied Christopher, sitting down next to him. "We're going to have to talk about it, I imagine, and then ask him."

I sat down beside Christopher. Gradually Uncle Nick and Erich, Tad and Zack sat down too. It was quiet again for a moment.

"I'm sorry I knocked you over," said Pa to Christopher. "You okay?"

"Nothing a little liniment from the hands of my wife won't fix," laughed Christopher. "I've been knocked around worse by unruly horses."

"Well, you got my apologies anyhow."

"Think nothing of it, Drum."

They were silent a minute, then Pa's mind came back to the present.

"Well," he said, looking around at the others, "if we still have any thoughts about saving that bear meat, we'd better get back and bleed him and cool him before he stiffens up any more than he has already."

They all rose and followed Pa through the woods.

CHAPTER 49

A COSTLY PRAYER AND A PROMISE OF PROTECTION

I built a small fire while in the twilight the men went to slit the bear's throat and stomach to bleed him and keep him from bloating. They hoisted it up by his feet with ropes slung over a stout tree branch to cool it down and drain out the last of the blood. Then after about fifteen minutes, they hauled him back to camp, where the hulking brown and blood-smeared carcass now lay covered with sheets and blankets at the edge of the small clearing.

If I could smell it, which I could, certainly so could animals for miles around. Somehow I had the feeling they would be able to detect what I yet couldn't, that death was now mingled with its odor, and I suspected we might have unfriendly visitors before morning.

Now the men were back, and the fire was blazing. A night nip was in the air too. I was so glad I'd found them!

We had been talking quietly while the moon rose and the darkness completed its descent.

Zack and Pa were for setting out immediately in the direction of home. The rest of us were of mixed opinions. Everybody had their ideas and suggestions, but none of us knew what was the best thing to do. There was the night to think of, and the footing between here and Miracle Springs was not the best for horses even in the middle of the day. But we were afraid for Almeda and Katie and Becky and the children. It gave us all the shivers just to think of them being watched by that horrible man, and all of us so far away and unable to do anything.

215

What if he wanted food and took it into his head to go down to the house and get what he wanted from Almeda? What if he forced himself upon her? He'd seen me when I'd answered the door—what if he discovered I was gone and got mad and took it out on the others?

There were so many what-ifs, and none of them were good! The longer we sat there talking, the more I could see Pa getting agitated again.

"I'm for saddling up and heading down the mountain," said Uncle Nick after a lengthy pause. "I don't like the thought of that varmint hanging around there watching my family."

Suddenly we all knew the decision had been made. It wasn't even a matter of whether it was the right or wrong thing to do. We *had* to go, and now.

"The sky's clear enough," said Zack. "The horses'll make it fine if we don't push them."

"We gotta go back tonight," agreed Pa, "or at least get close enough and then stop for a couple hours' sleep."

Sleep! I was *so* tired . . . I could barely stay awake now as it was! How could I possibly ride all night?

"What about the bear, Pa?" asked Tad.

Pa thought a minute.

"The meat hardly seems important alongside what's at stake now."

"How long would it take us to cut it and pack it up and load it onto the pack horses?" asked Christopher.

"Half-hour, an hour maybe," suggested Uncle Nick, "to skin and quarter it and salt and wrap him up good."

"Yeah," sighed Pa, "I reckon we might as well take the brute with us. That's what we came for. What the horses can't carry we'll leave for the mountain lions. We'll smoke and dry the meat as soon as we get home. Or as soon as. . . ."

He didn't finish. A few nods went around. The men all rose to their feet, took out their knives, and began the gruesome work. I wanted no part of the awful, messy process! I rose and went in the other direction and began saddling up the horses, one at a time.

About forty minutes later, the chunks of what used to be a bear were caked with salt and wrapped up tight to keep the flies out and roped onto the backs of the pack horses. All the other horses were saddled and the gear loaded. The horses were moving around uneasily, unsettled by the excitement and the bear smell.

The men came and sat down around the dying fire again for one round of coffee to empty the pot we'd made an hour earlier.

We were quiet a few seconds. By now it was dark. The fire flickered low.

Then Christopher spoke.

"There is one more thing we need to pray for before we go," he said. "It will not take long, and the situation is dangerous. "

"We're listening, Christopher," said Pa.

"We have to pray for protection," said Christopher.

He let his words sink in just a moment, then went on.

"Even though we're so far away, we can pray for our Father to surround Almeda and Katie and Becky and Ruth and Nick's little ones with his care. We can pray for his hand to shield them from harm. We can pray, as the Bible says, for him to build a hedge of spiritual protection around those two homes that no evil can penetrate. We can even pray for God to send angels to stand guard around them and watch over and protect them."

"Do you really believe in angels?" asked Tad, as if the thought had never occurred to him.

"You bet I do, Tad," replied Christopher. "And I believe God wants us to ask him to send angels to help us. You've heard of guardian angels?"

"You mean those angel-women with wings you see in picture books? Sure, but I always figured they were just for little kids and babies in cradles."

"We're all babies in cradles, Tad," smiled Christopher. "This whole world is our cradle. It's just that the older we get, the less we realize it. No, guardian angels are for *all* men and women. That's their job, to guard and protect us. We only need to ask, and God will send them about their work. When we pray these things—asking God for protection, asking him to build a hedge around us to keep out the devil and send his angels to guard us—we can know that he hears and will answer our requests. The Old Testament tells of a time when the Israelites looked out over the battlefield and saw the warrior angels fighting for them."

We all took in Christopher's words.

"How do you know so much about these kinds of things?" asked Tad.

Christopher laughed lightly. "I spent a good many years studying them. It was my profession, remember. I was *supposed* to know about spiritual things to help the people in my churches. Of course, knowing them and experiencing them by practice are two different things. I don't know about God's protection because I studied about it, but because I've learned how to pray for protection in my own life."

He paused.

"But I don't think your Pa wants to hear about that right now," he added. "I'll tell you all about it later, Tad, if you want. Right now we need to pray and then get on our way."

"Go on ahead, Christopher," said Pa. "What you just said is new to me, and I'm curious to know more. But you're right about us needing to get a move on. So for the time being *you* pray, and we're all in agreement with you."

Christopher nodded. He and Pa were back to the way it had long been between them, trusting each other completely. It warmed my heart to see it after the dispute that had erupted earlier.

"Our Father," Christopher prayed, *"we ask for your protection. Encircle our dear loved ones round about with a hedge as is said you did for your servant Job. Undergird them with your one hand and cover them over with your other. Send your guardian angels to stand round those two homes as mighty invisible warriors for truth, repelling any advance against them by the enemy. Keep the man Harris at a good distance, and let no harm come to them."*

Christopher paused, but only momentarily.

"And now, Lord," he went on, *"we pray for your protection for ourselves as well. Guide our way as we return. Send your angels to go before us. Watch over us, make straight our paths, protect our animals from misstep."*

Again he paused.

"There is yet one more thing we need to pray for," he said. *"We mustn't forget the Lord's injunction—we are commanded to pray for our enemies."*

The silence which followed was deep. Now that lives were in

danger, what we had done months earlier took on a whole new meaning. It hadn't been easy for Pa to pray for that man back then. Now it was *really* hard. Yet every one among us knew well enough that Christopher was right. If we couldn't obey the Lord's commands in the crucible of trial, then I don't suppose it meant very much that we did them when everything was pleasant.

There was barely flame left in the fire. We all stared into it, mesmerized by the small flickers struggling to keep going. It was Pa's voice that broke the silence.

"Well, Lord," he said, *"I don't claim that it's an easy thing to do, but I'm gonna summon what little willpower I've got to pray again for Jesse Harris. I don't especially like doing it. But if you told us to, then I figure there's gotta be a good reason. So I pray for him, and I pray that you'd do whatever you've got a mind to do with him. In the meantime, show us what we're supposed to do about him, because right now I can't see how I can pray for good to come to him on the one hand and go down out of here and try to keep him from killing me and my son on the other. If you've got some way to do both, I reckon you'll have to show me. That's about it, Lord . . . amen."*

I hadn't even realized it, but sometime during Pa's prayer we had all taken hands, and now we sat in a circle around the fire with our hands in one another's—me and Christopher, Pa, Tad, Uncle Nick, Erich, Zack, and back to me.

A few quiet amens followed from the rest of us.

"There is one of the Psalms," said Christopher, "which is a beautiful promise from God about the many ways in which he will protect his people. I memorized it long ago and say it whenever I am facing any kind of anxious circumstance—both as a prayer offered to God and as a reminder of his promise. I would like to say it now, as our way of committing what follows into his hands. Join in with me as you can. Most of it will be familiar to you."

Then Christopher began, and we sat there, the six of us hand in hand, staring into what was now merely a pile of glowing embers, quietly saying aloud together the words of the ninety-first Psalm.

"He that dwelleth in the secret place of the most High shall abide under the shadow of the Almighty," Christopher began. *"I will say of the Lord, He is my refuge and my fortress: my God. In him will I trust."*

I joined in with him as best I could, and soon the others were voicing out the familiar promises.

"*Surely he shall deliver thee from the snare of the fowler, and from the noisome pestilence. He shall cover thee with his feathers, and under his wings shalt thou trust: his truth shall be thy shield and buckler. Thou shalt not be afraid for the terror by night; nor for the arrow that flieth by day; nor for the evil that walketh in darkness; nor for the destruction that wasteth at noonday.*

"*A thousand shall fall at thy side, and ten thousand at thy right hand; but it shall not come nigh thee. Only with thine eyes shalt thou behold and see the reward of the wicked. Because thou hast made the Lord, which is my refuge, even the most High, thy habitation; There shall no evil befall thee, neither shall any plague come nigh thy dwelling. For he shall give his angels charge over thee, to keep thee in all thy ways. They shall bear thee up in their hands, lest thou dash thy foot against a stone. Thou shalt tread upon the lion and adder: the young lion and the dragon shalt thou trample under feet.*"

Christopher paused.

"The psalm ends," he said, "as from the mouth of God himself, speaking out his personal promise to those who give their lives into his care. As we say these words, try to remember that our Father is actually saying this *to us* right now at this fearful time."

He took a breath, then continued.

"*Because he hath set his love upon me, therefore will I deliver him: I will set him on high, because he hath known my name. He shall call upon me, and I will answer him: I will be with him in trouble; I will deliver him, and honour him. With long life will I satisfy him, and shew him my salvation.*"

"Amen," said Pa, after a brief silence.

"*And now, Lord, we commit our way to you,*" added Christopher.

We released hands and stood. Uncle Nick kicked at the fire with his boot. The boys joined him, and soon we were left with only smoke ascending in the glow of the moon.

We turned and walked to the waiting horses, then mounted up. Pa took the lead, and the rest of us followed him back in the general direction from which we had come.

CHAPTER 50

OUT OF THE MOUNTAINS

The going all night was slow.

I became so sleepy on and off that I could hardly prevent my eyes from closing. Yet somehow you manage to do what needs to be done, and somehow I managed to stay in the saddle.

Every time we'd stop for water or a rest, I would lay down and sleep for five or ten minutes. That made starting up again all the more difficult, but it helped me get through the night.

We stopped around three or four in the Bear River valley. Everyone was exhausted by then, and Pa said we needed to get some sleep. I had hardly rolled out my blanket and plopped down before I was out like a lump of rock. The men took the heavy sides of bear meat off the pack horses and hung it high up in some trees away from camp, but I didn't hear or see them do it. I didn't hear or think a thing until suddenly I woke up several hours later.

It was light. A cloud cover had drifted in. I found myself squinting about in a cold, gray, damp, dreary dawn. The others were stirring. Pa was standing over a small fire, holding a cup. I smelled coffee. Beside me, Christopher was still asleep, breathing deeply.

Pa saw I was awake.

"Time to be at it, Corrie Belle," he said. "Like some coffee?"

"Yes, thank you, Pa," I said, sitting up.

He brought me a cup of the steaming black brew he had made. I sipped at it. It was strong and bitter, but I knew I needed *something* to wake me up and get me through this day, so I gradually drank down the whole cup. By then everyone else was either up or

221

close to it and also getting down what quantities of Pa's coffee they could.

I don't know if Pa had slept at all that night, because by the time the rest of us were up, the horses were saddled and the bear was already loaded back onto the pack animals.

No one mentioned breakfast. Obviously we were all hungry by this time, but there were more important things on our minds, and we were anxious to be off.

As we rode, every once in a while Pa and Uncle Nick would draw close together and talk for a bit, sometimes with Zack and Tad, or sometimes the two boys would ride side by side talking intently. I knew they were all talking about what to do once we got back to Miracle Springs.

They obviously had some kind of plan, but I didn't know what it was.

After crossing the Bear, Pa increased the pace, and we rode hard the rest of the early morning. We arrived at the top of the foothill ridge above our place sometime around nine-thirty or ten.

Pa reined in. We all did likewise and stood in a group, waiting for what he would tell us to do.

Pa dismounted.

"I think we oughta walk from here," he said. "We can't risk the horses getting jittery or making too much noise."

"Let's leave the horses here, Pa," suggested Zack. "Tad and I'll come back for them later."

"It's a mite far yet," said Uncle Nick. "A mountain lion comes along and gets a whiff of that bear, he could kill every one of the horses."

The others nodded.

"All right," said Pa, "we'll walk them on down as close as we dare, then tie them up. The closer we get, the less likely there'll be any varmints prowling about. But it's a chance we have to take. The families are more important than the horses."

We each took the reins of our mounts and began slowly down the final incline through the forest. No one uttered a peep. The only sounds were the hooves over the ground and occasional snorts.

Finally, Pa became nervous about the tramping noises through the dry underbrush on the ground.

"This'll have to be as far as they go," he said. "We'll have to go the rest of the way ourselves and hope they're all right."

We tied our horses to trees and branches. Then the men got their rifles, cocked them, and made sure they were loaded.

All except Christopher.

He and I looked at each other in silence. He had never been in a situation like this before. I think for the first time the difference struck him between the tame East and the wild West. I knew he was praying that none of the weapons would have to be used.

CHAPTER 51

DEVISING A RISKY PLAN

We reached Uncle Nick and Aunt Katie's place safely, set as it was so far from our house and the road.

"Oh, Nick!" exclaimed Aunt Katie when we walked in, then she ran, throwing her arms around him, and then gave Erich a hug.

"Almeda and the others all right?" asked Pa.

"I think so," she answered. "He hasn't bothered us. He's just kept us from going anywhere. He's just sitting there waiting for you."

"Where is he, Katie?" Uncle Nick asked.

"On the top of that little hill across the creek from your place, Drum—you know, that clearing where the children used to play?"

Pa nodded.

"From there he can see the road in both directions, your house, and up the hill this way.

"Why didn't you send one of the kids through the woods to Little Wolf's for help?" Uncle Nick asked.

"That awful man said he was watching both houses, and if we tried anything he'd shoot first and ask questions later. I was afraid, Nick. What if he'd have seen them?"

Uncle Nick nodded, then glanced back at Pa.

Pa and Uncle Nick looked at each other, obviously thinking.

"Yeah, that's right," sighed Pa. "He'd have a clear shot at us however we came."

"How we gonna get the drop on him there, Drum?" said Uncle Nick. "We'd have to circle back south halfway to town to sneak up on him from the other side."

"I'm thinking more that we need to make some provision for Almeda and Becky and Ruth," said Pa. "If we circle around like you say, that leaves him between us and them. He spots us, he could make for the house and hole up there with them inside as hostages. Somehow, I gotta get to the house while he's still where he is."

"If you make for the house, Drum, he'll spot you."

"And shoot you!" added Katie. "I know that's what he's thinking. You can see it in his eyes. We've all been so scared!"

"Don't blame you," said Uncle Nick. "We both rode with him, remember. We know what kind of vermin he is."

"How about if we circle around south, like Uncle Nick said," offered Zack, now adding his suggestions to the plan, "while you, Pa, go up behind the mine and circle down through the woods and try to get to the old barn."

"That's the direction I went to get away," I said.

"Then you could make for the house," Zack went on. "If he spotted you or tried to shoot, we'd fire in the air or distract him some way."

Pa thought for a moment.

"What you say makes sense, son. Yeah, it does—'cause I gotta get to the house before we do anything foolish that sets him off shooting."

"What about the sheriff?" asked Aunt Katie. "Almeda tried to ride into town, but—"

"Corrie told us," said Pa. "Yeah, we also gotta find some way to get Rafferty out here. It looks like he's got one more prisoner to take in for his jail before he thinks any more about giving up the law for the life of a rancher."

"I could ride into town," said Christopher. "If it comes to a shoot-out, I won't do you any good anyway."

"Good, thanks—that's it," said Pa, his face lighting up as he suddenly saw the pieces of a workable plan fit together. "The three of you—Nick, Zack, and Christopher—you circle through the foothills from here, work your way below Little Wolf's and south. When you get to the road, Christopher—we can't risk a horse, he'd hear it—you make for town on foot—"

"I'll sprint the whole way."

226

"Right. You get Rafferty, tell him what's going on out here. Nick, you and Zack then work your way back up behind Harris."

"What about me, Pa?" asked Tad.

"You're coming with me around the north end," replied Pa. "I may need you to cover me or get a message back to Zack and Nick."

"And me, Pa?" I said.

"What are you asking me for?"

I glanced at Christopher.

"Aren't you staying here with Katie?" he said, incredulous that there was even any question about it. I don't suppose he yet knew everything about me and my propensity for jumping into the middle of things!

"I want to go, too. I want to help."

"Then go with your father," said Christopher. "But stay behind him. I don't want you in any danger."

"What are we gonna do supposing you get to the house without being spotted, Drum?" asked Uncle Nick. "You want me and Zack to take him from behind?"

"No. If I get to the house and you have him covered, then our immediate danger's past. He's not going to hurt any of the women then. So we wait for Rafferty. You'll be watching for him, and when he comes up the road from town you can tell him how things stand. Let him handle it from there. He can arrest Harris, and we'll be done with it."

Everyone looked around.

"You all know what to do?" asked Pa.

Nods followed.

"Then, let's go."

CHAPTER 52

A DASH FOR THE HOUSE

It was probably thirty or forty minutes later when Pa, Tad, and I reached the edge of the woods across the little creek from our pasture. We could see the stables and the old barn less than a hundred yards away. Beyond it stood the house.

All was quiet.

We'd heard not so much as a peep from any direction as we slowly and carefully worked our way above the old mine, then down between it and the new mine to where we presently stood. Where Uncle Nick and Zack and Christopher were we hadn't an idea, but we hoped they were in position south of Demming—or Harris—by now, with Christopher running into town.

Pa looked over the situation.

"I think I see him there," said Pa, squinting into the distance. "You make anything out, Tad, there off behind the roof of the barn, on that rise where Katie said?"

"Can't be sure, Pa—I might see him."

"Hmm . . . I think—if we get down low and stay behind the old barn, we may be able to keep out of his line of sight."

Pa worked his way twenty or thirty yards west along the creek until he was in position. We followed.

"Yeah, look," he said, "he can't see us here. Come on!"

Tad and I followed, crouching down, sloshing across the little creek, hurrying across the pasture, climbing over the fences of the stables, and in another minute we were standing safely behind the far wall of the old barn, puffing from the run.

Pa crept to the corner of the barn and glanced around.

Now the house was only about seventy-five yards away. But there was no more cover. All the ground between here and there was wide open.

I was scared.

What if the gunman not only saw Pa making a dash for it—what if he shot him in the process?

"Why don't we wait here, Pa?" I said. "We're close enough that if something happens you could make a move then. Why don't we just wait till the sheriff comes?"

"I've gotta know if they're all right inside there," replied Pa in a tone which I knew meant he'd already made his mind up.

"You two stay here," he said, then suddenly broke away from where we stood hiding and ran out across the open area toward the house. He didn't exactly dash across the ground very fast, wearing heavy, water-soaked boots and carrying his rifle.

He hadn't covered half the distance when suddenly a shot sounded.

I screamed in terror and looked out from behind Tad's side.

Pa was still running. I saw an explosion from the hill opposite the road, followed half a second later by another sharp rifle report.

Pa stopped. He put his gun to his shoulder and returned the fire with two quick shots. He took off running again. Two more shots came, accompanied by shouts of Pa's name.

But the next instant, Pa reached the back of the house and was safe. Tad and I breathed gigantic sighs of relief. All was quiet again.

CHAPTER 53

CLIMAX

Tad and I stood waiting from our point of safety behind the old barn, poking our eyes out from behind the edge of the building to see whatever might be going on.

Everything was quiet for a long time. I wondered where Zack and Uncle Nick were.

What happened next will be vivid in my brain as long as I live. Though it all took place in less than two or three minutes, everything slowed down, as if the incredible drama were taking days before my eyes instead of only a few hundred seconds.

From our vantage point we saw the same man who had appeared at the door of the house three days earlier start down the hill toward the house. He had his rifle in his right hand and wore a second gun at his side.

I don't know if he realized the rest of us were around. If he did, he showed no fear. He came down to our road just on the other side of the Miracle Springs Creek, crossed the wooden bridge, then came straight on toward the house.

"Hollister!" he called out. "Yeah—that's right. I found out yer real name. And I know yer in there. I'm callin' you out!"

He waited a few seconds, but there was no reply.

"You hear me, Hollister?" he cried. "I aim to git what's comin' to me. Now, either you give me my share of the loot from back in New York here and now, or else come out and we'll settle it like men. You hear me, Hollister—I'm callin' you out once and fer all. Ain't no more place you kin hide like the yeller coward you are!"

Again he waited, then tossed his rifle to the ground.

"Look, Hollister, I throwed my rifle down. I got nothing in my hands. I'm comin' just like you see me. Now, you gonna come out and face me like a man, or do I have to come in after you?"

This time there was a long wait. The man swore and yelled a couple more times, but the threat of coming in where Almeda, Becky, and Ruth were was enough.

Finally the door of the house opened.

Tad and I heard the steps of boots on the porch, but we couldn't see the front of the house. We ran around the old barn to the other side. Just as we got there and poked our heads out, we saw Pa walking slowly away from the house. He had no weapon at all—no rifle or pistol!

He walked off the porch and slowly continued toward the man he had not seen since they rode together as outlaws some twenty-five years earlier.

"There's no money, Harris," said Pa quietly.

"Don't lie to me, Hollister—or Drum, or whatever your real name is!"

"Nick and I ran without a penny."

"You're lying! I don't believe you!"

"That's why Nick and I came here, to get away from the law and hoping to make a strike." Pa's voice was calm and controlled. I could tell, even from this distance, that something had come over him in the time since he had left us and ran for the house.

"I don't believe you for a second! Where's the loot?" cried Harris, swearing.

"Judd had it all along."

"Judd! Why that double-crossing—what makes you think he had it?"

"Confessed on his deathbed. Told his son everything, including where he'd stashed the money. Young Judd didn't want any part of it. He went straight to the sheriff, told him about it. They recovered the money, and that was that."

The man seemed to be thinking about what Pa said. Every word I knew was true because I'd told it all to Pa myself, and I had heard it straight from the sheriff's mouth in our old town of Bridgeville.

"I don't know whether to believe you or not, Hollister," the man said after a minute. "But it don't mind much now, 'cause you and me's still got us a score to settle. Go back inside and git yer gun—that is, unless you want to do it with fists."

All of a sudden I remembered the last of what I'd heard from the sheriff in Bridgeville—*the two the sheriff figured had done most all the killing, Jesse Harris and Big Hank McFee . . . a couple of nasty coots, those two are.*

I remembered being relieved at the time. Now the words from out of my memory sent a chill of fear down my spine. *The two who done most all the killing*—and there was Pa facing one of them right now . . . without a gun!

"There's better ways of settling things than with fists or guns, Jesse," said Pa. Still he stood calmly and spoke in a voice that seemed to contain no fear.

"What kinda ways?" taunted Harris, adding a curse.

"The way real men do, Jesse," said Pa, "by giving God control of their anger and their desire for revenge."

"God?" cried Harris. "You done gone and got religion, Hollister? Ha, ha, ha!" Again he swore, ridiculing Pa.

"It's the only way to know peace in your heart, Jesse. Only God can take away that bitterness that's eating away inside you."

"Bah! You're a fool if you believe that! Only one thing's gonna take it away and that's putting a bullet in your head and watching you die in a pool of your own blood. Now, you gonna come and fight me like a man or not?"

Tad and I now saw Uncle Nick behind them, inching forward from about the same place Harris had been watching the house. He'd come up behind and followed Harris toward the house.

Then suddenly I saw Zack to our left, under cover of the barn.

"How'd Zack get over there without being seen?" I whispered.

"On his belly, next to the creek bed," replied Tad. "We used to do it all the time."

"No, I'm not gonna fight you, Jesse," said Pa calmly. "Not like you mean. I'm going to do what a *true* man would do, Jesse—what a friend would do."

"Yeah . . . what's that?"

232

"I'm going to pray for you, Jesse."

"Yer a blame fool, Hollister." The curses that followed this time were horrible to listen to.

"I mean what I say, Jesse. I'm going to pray for you right now, right here. I'm going to pray that you would lay down the bitterness that's in your heart, and turn to God, and accept the love he has for you, and tell him you want to be his son."

Uncle Nick had stopped. Zack now stepped out from behind the barn, into the open and began walking toward them.

My heart leapt to my throat! What was Zack thinking! He was going to get himself killed, too!

"I don't want no such fool thing!" shrieked Harris. "And if you utter so much as a word that sounds like yer prayin', I promise you, Hollister, you're a dead man, 'cause they'll be the last words you ever speak!"

If Pa hesitated, it was not for more than an instant. Calmly he bowed his head and closed his eyes.

"Father," he began to pray in a firm and commanding voice. *"In the name of your son Jesus Christ, I now pray for your love to show itself to—"*

Pa never saw Harris go swiftly for his gun.

A scream sounded from the house where a terrified Almeda watched at the window.

Gunfire exploded.

There was only one shot. As its echo died down, Harris slumped to the ground.

Uncle Nick came running forward, as did Tad and I. Almeda dashed from the house to Pa.

The only one who stood unmoving in the few seconds that followed was Zack. He was still holding the smoking pistol that had saved the life of his father.

For the first time I couldn't fault him for buying that gun or for practicing his draw! None of us had any idea he was so fast.

Whether it was a coincidence of timing, or whether they had been watching from somewhere, Sheriff Rafferty now galloped up the road with Christopher holding on for dear life behind him.

The sheriff jumped down from his horse as Zack walked up, holstering his gun.

"That's mighty fine shooting, son," he said.

Zack shrugged. It was obvious he felt no pleasure in what he had done.

"Ain't what guns are for," he said. "But sometimes I reckon it's gotta be done."

The sheriff stooped down to where Jesse Harris lay on the ground.

"He's been wounded pretty bad in the shoulder," he said. "Losing some blood, but he's alive. You got someplace we can put him, ma'am?" he said to Almeda as he stood.

Almeda nodded.

"Well, then, let's get him inside—then somebody oughta go for the doc."

It was Pa and Zack who now bent down, got hold of the upper half and feet of the man who had come here to kill them both, and carried his unconscious form into the house he had held hostage for the last three days.

CHAPTER 54

THE PRAYER OF MATTHEW 5:44

Jesse Harris lay unconscious in our house for a week, in the bed and room that used to be mine and more recently had belonged to the very young man who had shot him.

Doc Shoemaker dug out Zack's bullet, dressed the wound and bandaged the shoulder, and afterward came and went every day.

"He lost a fair amount of blood, all right," he declared on the fourth day, "but it's not so serious a wound that he should be unconscious all this time. Something is strange here."

"What, Doc?" asked Pa.

"I don't know, Drum," sighed Dr. Shoemaker. "I don't know—he oughta either be dead or waking up by now."

Zack especially was worried. Having actually shot a man who now struggled between life and death was an experience unlike anything he'd ever been through. Now he was pulling for Harris to live, even though it had been his gun that put him there.

The whole atmosphere around the place gradually changed. At first there had been such fear, then relief when it was over and everyone was all right. But now it grew quieter and quieter as we saw that everyone *wasn't* all right.

Realizing a man might be dying right under our own roof had a very sobering effect on all of us. Without anyone saying anything, gradually we began to think of him differently.

He was a human being, a fellow creature of God's making. The longer he lay there unconscious, the more we all began to think of him less as a hateful outlaw and more as a person. Soon we found ourselves praying desperately that he would live.

It seems such an unlikely thing to say, but what I think was happening was that in some miraculous way we were starting to care about that man. Whether it had something to do with the fact that we had prayed for him or whether it was because he was now so close to death, I don't know. But it was clear that our feelings toward him had changed within just a few days.

Pa and Zack, I think, spent more time in the sickroom, sitting at his side, than any of the rest of us. Anyone except Becky, that is. She was as devoted to him as if she were his personal servant, checking on him, keeping the room clean and warm, trying to get what liquid she could between his lips even though he was unconscious. I found myself thinking what a good nurse she would make.

Zack was real quiet all week. Sometimes he'd come out with his eyes red, and I knew he'd been crying. It was a hard thing to face what he'd done, and I knew he was trying his best to come to terms with it.

Christopher didn't say much. I knew he was wondering what God might be doing in all this. I told him every word Pa had said to Harris, and he was moved by what Pa had done.

As he listened, Christopher just kept shaking his head and saying softly, "God is really going to use your father's faith. I don't know how, but he is really going to use it in some powerful way. It's one thing to talk about loving your enemies, but I've never seen it *done* so powerfully."

He looked at me with an expression almost of disbelief.

"He actually did that?" he asked again. "Bowed his head and started to pray immediately after that threat?"

I nodded.

"He's a man of God, Corrie. He got angry, but then he turned that anger straight around back on itself and transformed it into the greatest kind of love in the world—love that is willing to give its life for a brother. It is an honor to call him my father-in-law."

That same evening, the sixth day after the shooting, we had the chance to see what Christopher meant even more.

A half an hour or so after supper was over, I suddenly realized that Pa wasn't at the table with the rest of us. Everyone had been coming and going, and I hadn't noticed when he'd slipped away.

I looked around and saw the edge of his back through the door into my old room where Mr. Harris lay.

I got up, went to the door, and looked in. Pa was just sitting there at the bedside, one of his hands stretched out and laid on top of the other's lifeless arm.

I stood watching the silent exchange a moment, knowing full well what was going on. I was moved. I felt tears coming to my eyes.

"What are you doing, Pa?" I asked finally, walking into the room.

Pa glanced toward me unembarrassed, with a gentle, humble, almost tired sort of smile, but good-tired.

"Praying for him, Corrie," he sighed. "Praying like we did before, that God would do his best for him."

He paused briefly.

"And," he added, "praying that if God decides to take him, that somewhere deep down inside the man, the Lord'll be talking to him, maybe like he did to the thief on the cross that repented right at the last."

"Mind if I join you?" I said.

"I'd be pleased if you did, Corrie Belle. Pull up a chair."

I did. I'd only been seated a minute when slowly the others began to wander into the room too. Christopher had seen me come in and had followed, then came Almeda, and within two or three minutes everyone of the household was standing or sitting in a circle around the bed, hands stretched out and laid on Jesse Harris's arms and head and legs, all of us murmuring our own prayers.

It was Pa who first prayed aloud.

"*Lord,*" he said, "*I pray you'll forgive my attitudes against this man that weren't what they should have been. I'm still learning what it means to do like you say—trying to learn, I should say, and sometimes it ain't easy. But I thank you for what Corrie's man, Christopher, told me about praying for people. Hasn't been easy to do with this here fellow that's laying here in our home. But I have been praying for him, and I pray for him again right now. I ask you, Lord, that you'd be inside him and you'd put the strength inside him to pull out of this. I'm asking for his life, Lord. I'm asking you to save his life and bring him*

*back. I don't know what we'll do then, but I know you do. All I'm
asking is that you'd heal him and fix him up."*

"*Amen,*" came Almeda's soft voice.

"*Help the man to wake up,*" prayed Ruth simply.

I prayed, then Becky prayed, and Tad. Christopher remained
silent. He knew this was time for others to take the lead.

Zack was the last to pray. His eyes were full of tears as he did.

"*Oh, God,*" he said, and his voice was so soft I could hardly hear
it, "*I'm asking the same thing as Pa prayed—that you'd bring Jesse
Harris back, and make his body strong again. I can't help feeling horrible for what I did. I don't know if it was right or wrong, I just didn't
know what else to do when I found myself standing there and realized
he was about to kill Pa. But I never meant to kill him, Lord. And now,
seeing him there, seeing his face sleeping so peaceful, I . . . I can almost
feel myself loving him, maybe a little.*"

His voice caught. He looked away a moment.

"*No matter what he's done, I can't think that he's so bad that you
couldn't do something with him if he had another chance. As much as
I thought I hated him when he was trying to kill me in the Nevada
territory, looking at him now, I know how you must love him no matter
what he's done. So save him, Jesus. Save him, and heal him, and give
us a chance to see if we can love him instead of hate him. Amen.*"

Long before Zack was through, every one of the rest of us were
crying too.

CHAPTER 55

STRAIGHTFORWARD CHALLENGE

Jesse Harris woke up the next morning.

It was Becky who first heard him groan. She went running in and saw him opening his eyes.

"Mr. Harris," she exclaimed, "you're awake. Could you drink some water?"

He nodded faintly.

By the time she had returned, he was dimly trying to take in his surroundings. She handed him the glass and helped him to get a few sips down.

"Who're you?" he asked.

"Becky . . . Becky Hollister."

Hearing the name of his enemy seemed to bring him a little further awake.

"Where am I?"

"In our house, Mr. Harris. We've been taking care of you—and praying for you."

"Prayin'—I don't need no prayin'!"

Already his old orneriness was starting to return.

He twisted a little in the bed, winced in pain, then lay still. By that time, Almeda had come in, then Tad and I. We were the only ones in the house at the time. He glanced around, obviously recognizing both Almeda and me. Then his eyes came to rest on Tad.

"You ain't the Hollister kid—leastways, I don't think . . ."

He paused as if trying to remember something from a long time ago.

"You must mean my brother, Zack," said Tad. "No, I'm Tad Hollister."

"What is this—a whole blame house full of Hollisters? Where is Hollister anyway—I wanna see him."

Again his face grimaced from the hurt in his shoulder, and he closed his eyes and relaxed a bit against the pillow, breathing deeply. He was obviously weak, and his face was pale.

"Do you think you could eat something, Mr. Harris?" asked Almeda gently. "A biscuit, a cup of soup . . . some coffee perhaps?"

He only nodded, then coughed a couple of times, still with his eyes closed. Obviously the coughing was difficult and painful. He wiped at his mouth with the back of his hand.

Almeda turned and went back to the kitchen. About a minute later we heard the door of the house open and Pa's boots coming across the floor. He was followed into the room by Christopher, who had run to fetch him the moment Mr. Harris awakened.

Pa came into the room, then slowly approached the bed. The rest of us made room for him. He walked up and sat down at the bedside.

Gradually Mr. Harris's eyes opened again. He saw Pa sitting beside him.

"What is this, Hollister?" he said in a soft, raspy voice. "What'm I doing here?"

"This is my home, Jesse," Pa replied as if he was talking tenderly to a child. "You were hurt. We've been taking care of you."

"How was I hurt?"

"You were shot, Jesse."

"Shot! Who in tarnation shot me? I don't remember nothing 'cept you standing there like a blame fool that wouldn't fight me."

"I didn't shoot you."

"Then, who?"

"My son."

"The Zack kid? I never saw him."

"He was behind you, Jesse—waiting to see what you were going to do."

This information silenced Mr. Harris for a minute.

Almeda returned with a cup half full of coffee and a buttered

240

biscuit. She and Pa tried to help him sit up in the bed against several pillows. He didn't seem to like anyone touching and fussing with him, but he accepted their help with only a few gruff expressions and grunts.

"Why wouldn't you fight me, Hollister?" he said after a minute. "I never took you fer one to go yeller."

"Because to fight a man like *you* mean, Jesse," replied Pa, "you've got to hate him. I *don't* hate you, Jesse. I love you."

"Confound you, Hollister! Don't say things like that—you sound like a blasted woman!"

"It's true, Jesse. I *do* love you. It isn't because I've gone soft and yellow, but because I've discovered the true meaning of manhood. That's why I prayed for you instead of fighting you."

"Yer a fool like I said before, Hollister, if you believe that kind of woman-talk!"

"It's *life*, Jesse—for men as well as women."

"Bah, yer a coward! You wouldn't fight me like a man!"

"What do you think takes more courage, Jesse," asked Pa, "to fight back when a man who's your enemy is trying to kill you or to bow your head and ask your heavenly Father to do good to him?"

"That's moonshine!"

"I've done both, Jesse, and I can tell you which one takes more guts. You talk about manhood and cowardice—I done lots of fighting in my life, Jesse, which I ain't proud of now. I finally see it's the *coward* who tries to settle things with fists and guns."

Pa paused a moment, then looked Mr. Harris straight in the eye.

"It's you that's the coward, Jesse Harris," he said. "You're afraid to look yourself full in the face."

"What the devil do you mean? I ain't never been called a coward! You think 'cause I'm layin' here in this bed you kin git away with that?"

"You'll take on anybody in the world. You'd fight me and a hundred men like me. But there's one man you're afraid of, Jesse Harris, and that makes you a coward when it comes to the truest kind of manhood of all."

"I ain't afraid of nobody, I tell you!"

"You're afraid to look at *yourself*," Pa repeated, "and at what you've allowed yourself to become."

"Blast you, Hollister! I won't listen to yer insults!"

"I'm sorry the truth makes you uncomfortable, Jesse."

"Confound this shoulder!" he cried, struggling as if to get out of the bed. "By heaven—if I weren't laid up like this, I'd beat the tar out of you right where you stand! Get out . . . get out of here, you hear me? If I could git up I'd throw you out myself!"

"No need for that, Jesse," replied Pa calmly, turning. "I'm gonna leave peaceful."

As he went, he motioned for the rest of us to follow, which we did, leaving the invalid alone with his smoldering thoughts.

CHAPTER 56

STRAIGHTFORWARD
WITNESS

It was early that same afternoon when Mr. Harris sent word
through Almeda that he wanted to see Pa.

Pa asked Christopher and Zack to go with him. The three of
them went into the sickroom and closed the door. The rest of us
waited in the sitting room, wondering what was going on, talking
softly amongst ourselves, and praying. Aunt Katie and Uncle Nick
had come down and were with us with their three rowdy
young'uns. Ruth and the cousins had been sent outside.

Christopher told me afterward what happened.

"Hollister," Mr. Harris said in a tone that didn't have the anger
in it from before. "I can see you are tryin' to help keep me alive,
and I'll try to watch my tongue."

"Don't mention it, Jesse."

Pa introduced Christopher to Mr. Harris as the two younger
men took chairs on the other side of the bed from Pa.

Mr. Harris and Zack nodded to one another.

"Been a while, young Hollister."

Zack nodded.

"Never expected to see you again like this. That's the second
time you outsmarted me."

"I'm sorry I had to shoot you, Mr. Harris—that's what Pa says
your name is."

"Well, I reckon a feller's gotta stick up fer his own. I don't
reckon I can fault you fer sticking up fer yer own pa. I reckon I

oughta thank you fer not killing me. But layin' here like this, I think I'd have been better off if you'd done it."

"I was aiming for your arm, just so you'd drop the gun," said Zack. "I didn't mean to lay you up so bad as this."

Mr. Harris stared down into the bed in front of him for a minute.

"I gotta tell you, Hollister," he said at length, "I ain't feeling none too good. All the while I been laying here—asleep, I reckon, though I ain't sure if it was altogether like normal kind of sleeping—as I laid here I was having dreams that weren't like anything I ever had afore. I saw the faces of men I killed and other things I don't even know what they was."

His voice was agitated and fearful.

"I tried to holler out," he said, "tried to make myself wake up, but I couldn't do it. I saw things that'd make any man tremble, things that would—"

He stopped, then glanced up first at Pa, then over to Zack and Christopher, his eyes wide.

"You gotta tell me straight, Hollister," he said, turning back toward Pa with a wild fear in his eyes. "Am I dyin'? Is that why my brain's goin' loco?"

"I don't know, Jesse," answered Pa calmly. "I hope not, 'cause we've all been praying mighty hard for you. But if it's your time, then none of us can stop the Lord from doing what he has to do."

Again it was silent.

"You believe in heaven and hell, Hollister, now you got religion?" Mr. Harris asked.

"Yep, I do, Jesse."

"I reckon we all know where a no-good varmint like me is headed, eh?"

"It don't have to be that way, Jesse."

"I done some pretty bad things, Hollister. Durned if I ain't just exactly what the preachers call a sinner waiting fer the flames of hell. I heard them fellers plenty of times when they'd come into some saloon, trying to scare us out—bunch of women, I always thought. Leastwise, I don't reckon there's time left fer me to do much about it."

Pa glanced over at Christopher with a look of question. He

didn't know what to say in reply and silently beckoned Christopher to jump into the conversation.

"There is always time, Mr. Harris," said Christopher.

"Time fer what? What kin I do?"

"The single most important thing in life."

"Don't talk in riddles, young feller! What in tarnation do you mean by the most important thing?" he asked, coughing again.

Pa handed him a towel. He coughed into it again a time or two.

"Believe in the Lord Jesus Christ."

"Ain't no time for that" he returned spitefully. "My life's near over. For all I know, it *is* over."

"It takes no time to *believe*, Mr. Harris."

A long silence followed, during which Mr. Harris calmed.

"What'm I supposed to believe about him, then?" asked Mr. Harris at length.

"We must believe *in* him, not *about* him," said Christopher. "We must take what he has done and bring it into our hearts—each of us for ourselves. He is mankind's Savior and Lord, but we have to make him our *own* Savior and our *own* Lord."

Both men fell silent. Mr. Harris seemed to be thinking. How much of what Christopher had said he could grasp, Christopher couldn't tell.

"It all sounds like nonsense to me—I can hardly make out what'n the heck yer talking about."

"It's never too late to tell God you're sorry for what you've done, that you're finally ready to do things his way," said Pa, now resuming the conversation with Harris.

"Being sorry don't much make up fer the wrong a body's done."

"I reckon you're right, Jesse," said Pa, "leastways the way we look at it. But God's got a different way of figuring things. And when a man's sorry enough for what he's been to repent of it, then God has a way of setting it all right no matter when that time is."

"Even if a man's dying?"

"If dyin's what it takes to wake a man up, then sometimes that's what God's gotta do—though he'd rather people woke up before then, so he could show his love to them while they're still here. That's why we're here in the first place, you know, Jesse."

"Why?"

"So God can show us how much he loves us."

"There you go again, talking about love. Whoever loved a mean, no-good killer like me? Ain't nobody ever loved *me*. Not even my own daddy loved me."

"The God who made you loves you. You're his child—how could he do anything but love you? And because *he* loves you, so do we."

This time the silence that followed was lengthy.

"I gotta tell you, Hollister," said Mr. Harris after a while, "what you did out there—whenever it was—it ain't somethin' I kin git outta my mind. It weren't natural, Hollister. Why . . . blamed if you wasn't gonna let me kill you! Dad-burned, Hollister—how could you do that? You wasn't gonna lift a finger against me! Why . . . it was almost—but whoever heard of such a thing? It was almost like you. . . ."

He stopped and glanced down, his voice choking. Christopher told me later that Mr. Harris was starting to cry. He and Zack looked down at the floor, not wanting to embarrass the poor man.

Only Pa kept looking straight into his face.

"Like what, Jesse?" Pa said.

"Like . . . like you were putting me ahead of yerself . . . like you were willing to die *yerself* rather than hurtin' a hair of *my* head."

"I ain't saying I wasn't scared, Jesse," said Pa. "I was. I didn't know what you'd do. But you're right—I was willing for you to put a slug in me if it came to that, 'cause I *wasn't* going to hurt you."

"But . . . but *why*, Hollister?" stammered Mr. Harris.

"I told you before, Jesse—because I been *praying* for you ever since we heard that you were coming here, looking for us. Zack and I and Christopher here, we've been praying for you, praying for your *good*. As we prayed, we couldn't help growing by and by to *love* you just a little, Jesse. That's why."

In the silence that followed, Mr. Harris's tired, worn, pale cheeks began to glisten from the tears trickling down them, right down into the big scar above his neck.

That fearsome outlaw lay listening like a little child to words too incredible to believe. Yet because of what he had witnessed, he *did* believe them. What he would have scoffed at in a sermon, he could not help believing—because he had seen it lived out in a man's life before his very eyes.

"But that's not the best of it, Jesse," Pa began again with a child-like enthusiasm. "*Our* love isn't anything compared to the love *God* has for you. In fact—do you want to know something that'll really surprise you, Jesse? There is somebody that wasn't just *willing* to die, but who *did* die just for you."

Mr. Harris glanced up, puzzled. He obviously had no idea who Pa meant.

"Why don't you tell him about it, Christopher," said Pa, glancing across the bed.

"You're doing great, Drum," replied Christopher. "I don't know when I've ever heard the gospel make so much sense. I want to hear what *you* have to say."

Pa took a breath, then continued.

"You know who I mean, don't you, Jesse?" he asked.

Mr. Harris shook his head.

"Don't reckon I do, Hollister."

"It was Jesus, the Son of God. He died for you Jesse—just for you."

"Well, I heard about that, of course—but how do you mean, just for me?"

"He died for me, too, and for all of us. But that don't take nothing away from his dying for every one of us like we were the only ones. When *he* died, it was different than if I'd died."

"How you figure that?"

" 'Cause you see, Jesse, he was the Son of God. He didn't have to die."

"Why did he, then?"

" 'Cause he loved us. When he died, his dying took care of all the sin of the world—and that means yours and mine, Christopher's here, Zack's . . . everybody's. Took care of it all ahead of time. That's what I was talking about before, about how God's got a way to make things right when a man makes up his mind to repent. That's how he does it—Jesus' blood washes all that sin away."

"I heard those words before—never thought much about 'em."

"That's why you can tell God you're sorry, and repent of the man you've been, and tell him you want to be his son. Tell him you're ready to do things his way. Don't matter if you're gonna die tomorrow or if you got fifty years left—the blood washes away the sin all just the same. That's what Jesus died for, so that we could become God's children."

CHAPTER 57

JOHN 2:3

A long silence.

Mr. Harris glanced over toward Zack.

"You believe all this stuff, young Hollister?"

"Yep, I do, Mr. Harris," said Zack. "Everything my pa's telling you's true—every word."

"What about ol' Nick?" asked Mr. Harris, looking at Pa again. "He was always a pretty tough feller—he go in for all this religious way of looking at things?"

Christopher was already on his way to the door. He opened it a crack and motioned for Uncle Nick to join them.

Uncle Nick approached the bed, then gave Mr. Harris his hand. The sick man shook it feebly.

"How's it going, Belle? Been a long time."

"Jesse," said Uncle Nick.

"Drum's been telling me some of the durndest things I ever heard, and I asked him if you go along with it all."

Pa briefly recounted the conversation.

"I reckon I'd say I do," said Uncle Nick when he was done. "I was a little slower than Drum to see some of it. Reckon my pride got a mite more in the way than his did. But yeah, Jesse—what he's telling you's the truth. If you wanna make things right and you wanna get rid of the wrong you done, then you gotta let God do it. Ain't no other way. You can't get rid of the sin yourself. Nobody can. That's why we gotta give it to God. Every one of the four of us here's done it—and we're all here to tell you that God keeps his word. And we're all better men for it."

Pa and Zack and Christopher all nodded as Nick spoke. Another long silence.

"Blamed if it don't sound too good to be true," said Mr. Harris, shaking his head slowly. "But I reckon there ain't nothing else left but for me to try it, seeing as how I've made a worse mess of my life than most folks. I gotta tell you, it ain't been no way to live."

No one said anything. Jesse Harris lay in the bed with his thoughts. The four men around the bed waited for the Spirit of God to carry out the final persuasion and take conviction to the needful corners of his being. They wouldn't say or do anything to force the heart's door open ahead of its time.

"So tell me," said Mr. Harris after five or ten minutes, "what do I gotta do fer God to make what I done all right, like you say he can?"

Both Pa and Uncle Nick glanced over at Christopher. Pa gave a little nod.

"All you have to do, Mr. Harris," Christopher said, "is tell God that you're sorry for what you have done and the kind of man you were. Tell him that you repent of it, and ask him to forgive you. It's as simple as that. Ask him to take away your sin. The Bible calls it being born again. It's not something you can do for yourself. But he can do it for you, and all you have to do is ask him to."

"Well, I reckon I ain't got nothing to lose but my pride—what do I say?"

"Would you like me to help you tell him?"

"I reckon I would."

"All right. Then, I'll say some words, and you repeat them—but say them to God, do you understand?"

"Don't sound too hard."

"Dear God," began Christopher, "I want to tell you that I'm sorry for the life I've lived. . . ."

Mr. Harris closed his eyes where he lay in the bed.

"Dear God," he repeated, *"I reckon I'm sorry—"*his voice broke momentarily, *"fer the kind of life I lived."*

"I repent of it, and I ask you to forgive me."

"I repent, God, and I ask you to forgive me."

"Forgive me both for the things I have done and for the sin itself which lies in my heart."

"Forgive me fer the things I done and fer the sin in my heart."

"I ask you to wash me clean by Jesus' blood. . . ."

"I ask you to wash me clean by Jesus' blood."

" . . . and to make me be born again."

" . . . and to make me be born again."

"Most of all, God, I thank you that you love me."

"I thank you that you love me, God, though I got a hard time believin' ye do, but I will 'cause these four men here say it's so."

"Help me to live from now on like you want me to."

"Help me to live like you want me to."

"I am ready to make Jesus *my* Savior."

"I am ready to make Jesus my Savior."

"I am ready to make Jesus *my* Lord."

"I am ready to make Jesus my Lord."

"Help me to learn to think of myself as your son, God. . . ."

"Help me to learn to think of myself as yer son—"

Here his voice choked.

" . . . and to think of you as my Father and Jesus as my elder brother," said Christopher.

"And to think of you as my Father and Jesus as my elder brother."

"Help me to do what you want me to do."

"Help me to do what you want me to do."

"Amen."

"Amen."

The four men around the bed were all smiling. In the midst of them, still weak but looking noticeably less pale, a thin sheepish, childlike smile now breaking upon his lips, lay Jesse Harris.

It was the first full smile his face had felt in years.

CHAPTER 58

A SURPRISE OFFER

Two days later, Sheriff Rafferty and Mr. Harding, the mayor of Miracle Springs, came out to pay a visit to Pa.

When I saw them ride up, I figured it had to do with Mr. Harris, who had continued to improve and who was now eating and drinking as if he only had two or three days to make up for the whole week he'd been unconscious!

Pa had said that the sheriff would have to be brought into the situation and that if Mr. Harris recovered he would probably have to go to jail since there were still warrants out on him. I shuddered to think that he had actually killed people, but I knew it was true, and becoming a Christian didn't remove the consequences of his past. We didn't know what would happen. In the meantime, he continued to recover in my old bed.

As it turned out, though, the visit of the two men wasn't about Mr. Harris, at all—at least not directly.

They came up to the house and asked if they could talk to Pa in private. Almeda and Becky and I happened to all be in the kitchen at the time, getting some things ready for lunch. So Pa took them outside, and they walked off toward the pasture and talked as they went.

"I ain't as young as I used to be, Drum," Mr. Rafferty said. "I'm fifty-six. And I got a nice little spread started down in the valley west of here."

"I know, I know," laughed Pa. "You been talking about retiring for six months."

251

"I think it's time I settle down and enjoy what I worked for. There's more people coming in every year, and I reckon it's time for a younger fella to take over this job."

Pa nodded. If anybody could understand, he could. I'm sure he'd felt much the same way when he decided not to run for the legislature anymore.

"I hear what you're saying, Simon," he said. "Things change when a man gets older. Happens to all of us. You got anybody in mind to replace you?" he asked, looking at both men questioningly.

"That's what we came out to talk to *you* about," said the sheriff.

"Hmm . . . I don't know who'd be good," said Pa. "You been talking it around town—no takers?"

"Nobody in *town*," said Mr. Harding, though Pa did not seem to notice his emphasis.

"What about Duncan, the feller that lives in Almeda's place," said Pa, still oblivious as to what the men were driving at. "He's pretty handy with a gun."

"The respect of folks is what's needed even more. I can't remember the last time I had to pull my gun on someone. This is California, Drum, not Texas or Kansas. But, I think Duncan's got his mind set on doing some farming and raising beef of his own."

"After what happened out here last week, it may be that a gun's more necessary than you think," laughed Pa.

The sheriff and the mayor glanced at each other. They had clearly been thinking exactly the same thing, despite Sheriff Rafferty's words to the contrary.

"Duncan was just out looking at the old Perkins place yesterday," added Mr. Harding. "No, I doubt he's our man."

"Well, I'll keep my eyes and ears open," said Pa.

The two men just stood there. Finally Pa realized they had something else on their mind.

"We was wanting to know what you'd think of us asking Zack," said Mr. Rafferty finally.

"*My* Zack!" exclaimed Pa. "He's nothing but a kid!"

"He's only two months or so shy of twenty-nine, Drum. What were you doing at twenty-nine?"

"Yeah—hmm . . . I reckon I see your point there."

"Zack's got the respect of folks, *and* he's showed clear enough that he's plenty handy with a gun," said Mr. Harding.

"Well," sighed Pa, "I don't like it. But at the same time I don't reckon I got much right to object. Zack's a man, like you say—gotta be his decision."

"You want to talk to him first?"

"Yeah, give me a day. Why don't the two of you come out again tomorrow."

They shook hands and the sheriff and mayor returned to Miracle Springs.

Later, we all listened as Pa gathered us together to recount his conversation with the two men. He paused for a long several moments.

"So then," he said finally, "they asked me what I thought about them offering the job . . . to Zack."

Exclamations and shouts and not a few concerned looks spread around the table.

"As sheriff!" exclaimed Tad excitedly.

"Why not?" said Zack with a big grin. That he could not be more pleased at the prospect was just as obvious as that he was trying his hardest not to show it.

"You think you could do it, son?"

"Sure, Pa—why not?"

Pa thought for a moment, then began to nod his head slowly back and forth.

"Yeah, I reckon you could at that, Zack, my boy," he said.

"It could be dangerous, Drummond," said Almeda with concern in her voice.

"I don't reckon it's no more dangerous than the Pony Express or the Paiutes that were after him that time . . . or—" he added in a low voice so he wouldn't be heard in the bedroom, "when Jesse was trying to kill him out there in the desert. Not to mention what just happened last week. I reckon Zack's pretty well able to take care of himself. He's been up against the worst," he added, nodding toward the bedroom.

More discussion followed, but mostly among everybody but Zack.

"What do you think, son?" asked Pa at length.

"I'd like to do it, Pa," replied Zack. "Can't say I wouldn't. But

I'll have to find out if it's what I'm *supposed* to do before I say one way or the other."

"Well, however the Lord leads you, it's your decision," said Pa, "and we'll all back you up."

CHAPTER 59

TWO DECISIONS

There was a spirit of jubilation about the place for a couple of days. It was one of those times when life seemed especially good and everyone was happy. Mr. Harris was very weak but able to get up on his feet and had begun to take meals with us.

As yet there had arisen no unpleasant discussion of his future, and Sheriff Rafferty did not seem inclined to press the point. I think he might have been hoping Mr. Harris would just ride away so that he could ignore the past warrants.

If Zack became sheriff, what would *he* do?

In any case, there was a happy feeling about. If only I had known what was coming I might have felt differently.

Two or three days after the announcement about Zack and the sheriff's job, Christopher turned silent again.

I didn't notice it too much the first evening. Christopher was reading, and I figured he was just preoccupied. But the next morning when I woke up, he was gone, and I didn't see him all morning. He was quiet at lunch, disappeared again all afternoon, and hardly said a word the whole night.

I knew something was wrong, but I was afraid to say anything. I was afraid I already knew what it was.

We had not talked any more about the possibility of moving from Miracle Springs. In all the excitement over Mr. Harris, I guess there was part of me that hoped Christopher had forgotten all about it—even though I knew better. Now I just waited, scared and nervous, for Christopher to tell me what I had guessed.

The following afternoon I saw Christopher and Zack off walking together. I did not know it at the time, but they were discussing and praying together about their two respective decisions over the future. In the past, both would have turned to Pa. But each felt, on this occasion, that the decision was something they had to make between themselves and the Lord. But both felt keenly the need for a friend close to the same age to talk the factors over with.

Finally that evening, after we were alone in the bunkhouse, Christopher unburdened himself and told me what it was that had been plaguing him.

"This is not easy, Corrie," he began, then let out a great sigh. "I have been struggling and struggling over it, hoping that I was not hearing the Lord correctly, begging him for any other answer."

I sat listening in dread, not saying anything, willing him not to say what I feared was coming.

"Believe me, this is not what I *want*," he went on. "But I feel it to be what the Lord is saying, and so I cannot ignore it."

A long silence came. Finally I couldn't stand it another second.

"But what *is* it, Christopher? Is it about . . . about leaving. . . ?"

Slowly he nodded.

"You heard what your father was saying a while back—about the mine, about the future. He is absolutely right; there is no future for me here. Financially we are a drain on your family. We simply cannot stay indefinitely as things presently are."

Now he was pacing about the small room in obvious turmoil.

"Don't you see, Corrie?" he said, "We've got to think about your father and Almeda and what is best for them. And I have to think about what I'm going to do with the rest of my life—and what is best for us."

He stopped pacing and looked at me with pain in his eyes.

"I feel the Lord saying it is time for a change. I have been asking him what he wants us to do, pleading with him for clarity, for a sense of direction—for months. You know how I've been struggling over this."

"Yes . . . yes, of course. We talked about it way back at the beginning of the summer. And then . . . you wouldn't talk to me. . . ."

"I'm sorry it has been so hard on you, Corrie. But I *couldn't* talk with you about it. And when I tried, it came out all wrong."

"But that's what I don't understand!" I said. "I thought we promised to talk with each other about everything."

"This is different, Corrie. I just . . . I didn't want to hurt you. I didn't *want* to tell you what I have been feeling we are supposed to do."

Christopher stopped momentarily from pacing about the room, then sighed.

"Do you remember when we prayed that night in San Francisco?" he asked.

"Yes, of course."

"We asked God to show us what to do."

I nodded.

"Well . . ." he said, turning now toward the darkened window as if looking out. "I think he *has* been showing me," he went on with his back to me, ". . . and that's what I haven't been able to talk to you about."

"But *why*, Christopher?" I said yet again.

"Because—" he said, then blurted it out. "—because I believe the Lord wants us to return to the East."

The words fell like a thunderbolt out of the sky onto my ears. Now he turned and faced me.

"I *like* it here, Corrie," he said, almost in a pleading tone. "But I have sought the Lord's will, and I'm feeling like he might want me to work in a church again, and I really believe this is the right decision."

I was devastated. It felt like my whole world was crumbling around me. Even though I knew there was a chance we might have to leave Miracle Springs, I had never in my wildest dreams imagined we might have to go so *far!*

Part of me felt angry, too, and that made the tears start to flow. "So I don't have any say in it at all!" I blurted. "You weren't even going to talk to or pray with me about it?"

By now I was sobbing. Christopher looked stricken. He came over and sat down beside me and took me in his arms. I cried even harder from being angry with him and yet needing him all the more.

"Oh, Corrie, I'm so sorry," he kept murmuring over and over. We sat together like that for probably fifteen or twenty minutes.

"Can you tell me *why*, Christopher?" I finally said. "Why do we have to go East? What will you do there that you can't do here?"

He sighed.

"I don't know if I can tell you. I'm not sure I know myself. I just . . . it seems to me that this is what the Lord is saying."

Again it was quiet for a long time. Again I was the first one to break it.

"I made you a promise, Christopher," I finally said, sniffing and wiping at my eyes, "that I would love you and go with you whatever came to us and wherever the Lord sent us. I meant it, and I do love you so much. But leaving my family will be the hardest thing I have ever done."

"I wish it hadn't come to this, Corrie. I love it here, and being with your family."

Again we sat for some time in silence.

"I'm sorry," I said softly, "if it sounded like I wasn't trusting you to do what is best. I love you more than I love any one place. My home is with you, wherever the Lord leads you."

"That means more to me than you can know, Corrie."

"I do love you, Christopher—so very much."

"And I love you, Corrie."

CHAPTER 60

ANOTHER LONG AND PRAYERFUL RIDE

The first snows came early to the lower regions of the Sierras that year.

One morning in the first week of December we suddenly found ourselves blanketed in white. We'd felt the chill in the air the previous day, and the wind whipping up should have let us know something was coming. But the sky had been clear, and no one guessed such a big storm would move in so quickly.

Then, just as quickly, the storm was gone. The weather warmed right back up, and within days the snow was gone, too.

I knew what it would be like up in the higher elevations—bright and fragrant, the ground wet, snow still lying deep in the shadows and woodsy places. It was one of those rare times when, if you got high enough, everything would be white and bright and glistening, yet when the sun beat down, the air would be warm enough to ride in without a coat.

I knew I needed a long ride by myself, and this was the perfect opportunity for it!

Being married meant I'd had a lot less time alone, for myself. But marrying Christopher hadn't changed who I was and what I was like inside. There were times when I had to retreat back into the quiet places that had before been reserved only for the Lord and me.

Now Christopher shared my heart. In a sense, three people lived inside of me: myself, Christopher, and the Lord. Yet some-

260

times I still found that I had to go down there and talk something over with the Lord that I couldn't even let Christopher in on.

I would tell him when it was all over, of course—we were committed to talking to one another about everything. But there are certain inner battles you must initially fight alone . . . and this was one of those for me.

Once I realized that, I understood a little better why Christopher hadn't been able to talk to me when he was first wrestling with the question of whether we needed to leave. At the same time, I really wished he'd been able to talk to me sooner. I suppose we still had a lot to learn about communicating with each other.

The main part of my struggle now was: *I didn't want to go to the East.*

There is just no other way to say it.

Try as I had ever since Christopher had told me of his decision, and as much as I had prayed, I could not come anywhere near being happy about it. I still didn't want to go.

For years I had done what *I'd* wanted. Of course, I had tried to do what God wanted. But all my life since coming to California and since Ma had died, I'd really been answerable to no one else.

Now all of a sudden here was someone else telling me what we were going to do—something I didn't *want* to do. Of course I trusted Christopher, and I loved him more than I could have imagined loving anyone. But that didn't change the fact that I didn't want to go. It was hard to be told what to do, even by the man I loved and trusted more than anyone in this world.

I rode out from home in late morning. The sun was climbing in the sky to the south as it always did this time of year. It was a wonderful day for a ride, and I couldn't have enjoyed myself more—except for that nagging knowledge that I might have to say goodbye to it all. How could I ever do that?

I headed up toward one of my favorite places of all, Fall Creek Mountain, even though I doubted I had time to make it that far. That area would probably still be covered with snow anyway. But I still set out eastward, climbing steadily through the foothills, winding through still-snowy pine woods and then out into open pastureland where most of the snow was by now melted away.

As I rode, my thoughts were first occupied with what had been on my mind for the past several weeks. I had expected difficulties and hardships. What marriage doesn't have them?

But I hadn't expected them so soon!

We'd only been married eight months, and this was really hard. I didn't want to go to the East. I wanted to think that maybe Christopher wasn't hearing accurately from the Lord. But how could I think my perspectives would be any clearer when my own wishes in the matter were so strong?

Gradually as I made my way northward over Chalk Bluff, I began to think back over my past.

Already the snow was deepening beneath my horse's feet. I decided to see if I could get to the top of Remington Bluff, and if so that was as far as I would go. I could see it not too far away—the slope leading up to the top looked pretty white. I struck out toward it.

I made the crest of the bluff about forty minutes later. It was still warm up there, and open as it was, half or so of the snow on top was melted off. There was enough clear ground for me to dismount.

My feet got cold through my boots, but I walked about, gazing out over the foothills below me, reflecting on all that I'd experienced since arriving in California over these same Sierra Nevada mountains—finding Pa after Ma's death, meeting Almeda, finding the new gold mine, beginning to write and then writing for the paper, all the dangers we'd experienced. Then getting involved in politics, going East for two years, meeting Christopher, falling in love, writing letters back and forth, and finally getting married earlier this year.

"Oh, God," I sighed, *"you really have given me a wonderful life, and I am very thankful for it all."*

I had been from the East Coast to the West and back again in both directions. Now it appeared I was about to embark on that cross-country journey yet again.

I thought what a huge country it was and how long was the journey, with so many unexpected things that could arise along the way.

Suddenly it struck me how similar that was to one's spiritual life. You could never tell where he was going to lead you or what

he was going to show you next. It was an adventure no less un-
predictable and as exciting as a journey across this great land.

But if the Lord was the one leading the journey, just like Cap-
tain Dixon had led the wagon train that we'd been part of back in
1852, then how could I be anxious? Wherever it led, it had to be
good!

*"I'm sorry for doubting you, Lord," I prayed. "I'm sorry for won-
dering whether you have been speaking to Christopher or not. I'm sorry
for not trusting you both more than I have. I know I have much to learn
about being a wife, about trusting someone else instead of making my
own mind up about what you want me to do. Help me learn that, Lord.
Deepen trust in my heart for both the leaders in my life—you and my
dear husband, Christopher."*

I walked about a little more. My feet were almost frozen, but
the rest of my body was warm, and it was so quiet and beautiful
and peaceful that I wasn't ready to leave.

I remembered all I had learned the year before about how the
Lord had shown me that he had given me Christopher as a home
for my heart. I had been so happy then. Was I going to so quickly
forget?

No, I couldn't do that. The Lord was still good. And he would
do his best for me—as hard as it might sometimes seem.

Christopher was my home now—not Miracle Springs.

*"Thank you for reminding me of that, Lord," I said quietly. "I will
be content wherever you take us. I will be content because I am yours
and Christopher's. As Rev. Rutledge said several months ago, I give my
anxiety over this to you, Lord. Here—"* I said, gesturing with my
hands as I remembered him doing in the middle of his sermon—
*"I place my anxiety and worry and concern and even the doubts I've
had into your hands. I give them all to you, Father. I don't want to
carry these concerns any more. I trust you, as much like a child as I
know how to be, to do what you want with them. I want you to make
this decision for us. I relinquish my own will and desire. Help me to
learn more and more how to lay down my own will for yours."*

I sighed, breathing deeply of the warm mountain air.

It felt so clean, and I felt alive and happy. It felt good to let go
of something that had been so troubling me. I knew it was in God's

hands now, and so I could be thankful for it. I *would* be thankful for it!

My feet were too cold to continue! I turned and ran back to my horse, spraying up snow with my boots. I mounted and led her back the way we had come, through the tracks her hooves had made earlier.

Whatever the future held, wherever the Lord took us, I would be content.

He and Christopher both lived in my heart. We all three loved one another. How could I not be content with such an arrangement?

I rode down out of the mountains, feeling the exuberance of the warm breeze on my cheeks mingled with the lingering hint of a wintry aroma left by the storm. Gradually my feet began to feel life in them again!

"Thank you, Lord," I whispered. *"I do love you, and I am thankful for the life you have given me."*

ABOUT THE AUTHOR

MICHAEL PHILLIPS is one of the premier fiction authors publishing in the Christian marketplace. He has authored more than fifty books, with total sales exceeding 4 million copies. He is also well known as the editor of the popular George MacDonald Classics series.

Phillips owns and operates a Christian bookstore on the West Coast. He and his wife, Judy, live with their three sons, Patrick, Gregory, and Robin, in Eureka, California.

If you liked *The Braxtons of Miracle Springs,* you may also enjoy these other books and series by Michael Phillips:

THE JOURNALS OF CORRIE BELLE HOLLISTER (Bethany House Publishers)

My Father's World (with Judith Pella)
Daughter of Grace (with Judith Pella)
On the Trail of the Truth
A Place in the Sun
Sea to Shining Sea
Into the Long Dark Night
Land of the Brave and the Free
A Home for the Heart
Grayfox

Good Things to Remember:
333 Wise Maxims You Don't Want to Forget

The practical wisdom and spiritual perspectives that Michael Phillips' readers have come to associate with his uniquely insightful fiction are available now in this thought-provoking collection of maxims and quotable quotes from Phillips and other sources. Get to know Michael Phillips, the man behind the bestselling books.

Tales from Scotland and Russia (Bethany House Publishers)

Adventuresome, dramatic, and mysterious stories from the romantic worlds of nineteenth-century Scotland and Russia. Coauthored with Judith Pella, these books are packed with abiding spiritual truths and memorable relationships. If you haven't yet discovered the worlds of adventure and intrigue opened up by these series, a wonderful treat awaits you!

Scotland:
Heather Hills of Stonewycke
Flight From Stonewycke
The Lady of Stonewycke
Stranger at Stonewycke
Shadows Over Stonewycke
Treasure of Stonewycke

Jamie MacLeod, Highland Lass
Robbie Taggart, Highland Sailor

Russia:
The Crown and the Crucible
A House Divided
Travail and Triumph

The Secret of the Rose (Tyndale House Publishers)

This is the newest series from the pen of Michael Phillips, set in Germany before World War II—a page-turner with spiritual content and rich relationships you won't soon forget!

The Eleventh Hour
A Rose Remembered
Escape to Freedom
Dawn of Liberty

Nonfiction by Michael Phillips
A God to Call Father (Tyndale House Publishers)

THE WORKS OF GEORGE MACDONALD (Bethany House Publishers—selected, compiled, and edited by Michael Phillips)

Twenty-eight books in all, both fiction *and* nonfiction, that will delight and edify both adult and young readers. Please consult your bookstore or write for a full list of availability. Especially recommended titles include:

Fiction by George MacDonald Edited for Today's Reader:
The Fisherman's Lady
The Baronet's Song
The Curate's Awakening
The Highlander's Last Song
The Laird's Inheritance

Nonfiction From the Writings of George MacDonald:
Discovering the Character of God
Knowing the Heart of God
George MacDonald, Scotland's Beloved Storyteller
(a biography of MacDonald by Michael Phillips)